Praise for the A:

────── *The Question of the Absentee Father* ──────

"Fans coast to coa: quirky hero remai lous La La Land."

"The reader has th and a respectful tre

—*Publishers Weekly*

────── *The Question of the Felonious Friend* ──────

"The investigation is entertaining, but the cleverness of this book is its treatment of the personality disorder, which manages to be funny and at the same time accurate and respectful."

—*Ellery Queen Mystery Magazine*

"Samuel Hoen g takes on a real puzzler in Copperman and Cohen's winning third Asperger's mystery."

—*Publishers Weekly*

"The ways of the neurotypical continue to perplex this unusual protagonist, much to the delight of readers of all cognitive stripes."

—*Kirkus Reviews*

────── *The Question of the Unfamiliar Husband* ──────

"Captivating."

—*Publishers Weekly* (starred review)

"Samuel is a fascinating character … His second adventure will captivate readers."

—*Library Journal*

─────── *The Question of the Missing Head* ───────

A Mystery Scene Best Book of 2014

"[A] delightful and clever mystery."

—*Publishers Weekly*

"Delightfully fresh and witty, this story about a detective who has Asperger's syndrome illuminates the condition for the reader and is also a perfect traditional mystery, told with humor and originality. You'll be forgiven for being reminded of Detective Monk, but this is a detective whose deductive methods fit right alongside Sherlock, Columbo, and, yes, Monk. Pure heaven."

—*Mystery Scene*

"In this well-crafted story, the Asperger's element…provides a unique point of view on crime-solving, as well as offering a sensitive look at a too-often-misunderstood condition."

—*Booklist*

"Copperman/Cohen succeeds in providing a glimpse not only of the challenges experienced by those with Asperger's, but also of their unique gifts."

—*Ellery Queen's Mystery Magazine*, four stars

"Cleverly written and humorous."

—*CrimeSpree Magazine*

THE QUESTION OF THE
ABSENTEE
FATHER

THE QUESTION OF THE
ABSENTEE FATHER

AN ASPERGER'S MYSTERY

E.J. COPPERMAN

JEFF COHEN

MIDNIGHT INK
WOODBURY, MINNESOTA
MIDNIGHT INK

First Edition
First Printing, 2017

Book format by Cassie Kanzenbach
Cover design by Ellen Lawson
Cover illustrations by James Steinberg / Gerald & Cullen Rapp
Editing by Nicole Nugent

Midnight Ink, an imprint of Llewellyn Worldwide Ltd.

Library of Congress Cataloging-in-Publication Data
Names: Copperman, E. J., author. | Cohen, Jeffrey, author.
Title: The question of the absentee father : an Asperger's mystery / E.J.
   Copperman, Jeff Cohen.
Description: First edition. | Woodbury, Minnesota : Midnight Ink, [2017] |
   Series: An asperger's mystery ; #4 | Description based on print version
   record and CIP data provided by publisher; resource not viewed.
Identifiers: LCCN 2017012763 (print) | LCCN 2017022006 (ebook) | ISBN
   9780738753058 () | ISBN 9780738750798 (softcover)
Subjects: LCSH: Asperger's syndrome—Patients—Fiction. | Missing
   persons—Investigation—Fiction.
Classification: LCC PS3603.O358 (ebook) | LCC PS3603.O358 Q43 2017 (print) |
   DDC 813/.6—dc23
LC record available at https://lccn.loc.gov/2017012763

Midnight Ink
Llewellyn Worldwide Ltd.
2143 Wooddale Drive
Woodbury, MN 55125-2989
www.midnightinkbooks.com

Printed in the United States of America

To the good people of the Rutgers Cancer Institute of New Jersey,
who have kept at least one of us alive.

ACKNOWLEDGMENTS

It's always difficult to split up the work when collaborating, especially when Cohen insists he does almost all the writing (no you don't, Jeff!), but it's not the authors who are the unsung heroes here. They're sung plenty.

Those whose names don't appear on the cover do their jobs beautifully and deserve some credit for that. So thanks to the wonderful Terri Bischoff, who literally (and we mean that *literally*) made it possible for you to meet Samuel & Co. It's always a joy to send the manuscript off to Terri because we know she enjoys seeing what the gang is up to this time. And occasionally she lets us write a book where nobody gets killed.

Nicole Nugent, who oversees the editing of the book (by overseeing, we mean she does the editing of the book), turns what we write into something you can read without wondering what those two maniacs might be talking about. You're invaluable, Nicole, and we appreciate it.

Of course we are crazy about our agent, Josh Getzler, and all at HSG Agency, who see to it that we can afford to keep doing this for a living. Your enthusiasm and your sincere care for the work take you beyond the realm of "agent" and into the area of "friend," and we can't say enough about that.

Thanks to Cassie Kanzenbach, who did the book format, to Ellen Lawson for the cover design (we are hopeless with cover ideas and always knocked out by the final artwork) and to James Steinberg/ Gerald & Cullen Rapp for the illustrations on the cover. Thanks so much for making the books look good enough to interest a browser in a store. If they pick it up because it looks so good, that's on you and we are very grateful.

Reviewers who have been kind to us: You make a dreary day brighter. Reviewers who think we could do better: We can't possibly say you're wrong, and hope to improve with each try.

To all readers, everywhere, who have ever read one of our books: You are the reason we do this. It ain't easy to sit in a room and make something up out of thin air. The idea that there are those who actually get some enjoyment out of the final product is what keeps us going. You have our eternal thanks.

—E.J. Copperman and Jeff Cohen

July 2017

ONE

A LETTER ARRIVED IN the daily mail.

It is not my custom to retrieve the mail from the box at the front door of the home I share with my mother because I work in my office at Questions Answered every day and am usually not home when the mail arrives. Mother most often brings it into the house, but it had been raining hard in the afternoon when the postal carrier had visited our home and Mother had not wanted to open the front door to get the mail. She does not like the rain to come into the house over the front door threshold.

Knowing this, I had diverted from my usual path upon arriving home that evening. Typically I will walk to the back door and enter through the kitchen when my friend Mike the taxicab driver or (as tonight) my associate Ms. Washburn pulls the car into the driveway to drop me off. I own a driver's license but I do not often drive a vehicle. My experiences in doing so have proven me too nervous a driver to be a reliable or safe one.

It had stopped raining. Ms. Washburn waved to me as she backed her Kia Spectra out of the driveway. I decided to walk up the front steps and retrieve the mail.

Inside the box, which is hung on the front wall of the house a few feet from the door, were two invoices, one from the utility provider and one from the bank holding mother's only credit card. I pay cash for every purchase I make because I prefer not to owe anyone money and because I do not wish to have records made of my financial transactions without my consent or knowledge regarding the use of that information.

There was also a letter, addressed to Mother, the address handwritten in a decipherable but careless scrawl. The envelope clearly held just one or two sheets of paper, given the weight. But considering the rules of style established for mailing items in the United States and most other countries, the envelope was missing a vital element.

It bore no return address.

Surely it was odd that the person who had gone to some lengths to send Mother a letter was taking a great risk in leaving off an address to which it could be returned in case of a Postal Service error or if Mother had chosen to change her place of residence. But whoever the correspondent was, he or she had made the choice consciously—there was no sign of a label having been removed or a stamp having not been pressed sufficiently to be legible. The envelope, other than the stamp and postmark, Mother's name and address, was clean.

This was an interesting curiosity but not a cause for great concern. I opened the front door and walked into the living room. Since the rain had ended I had not been called upon to use my umbrella, so I placed it carefully in the stand Mother had placed near the front door to prevent wet umbrellas dripping on the carpet.

I found her in the kitchen and she seemed briefly startled to see me. "Oh, Samuel! I was expecting you to come in through the back," she said, pointing at the kitchen door despite my understanding what she had meant.

Walking in after hanging my jacket on a hook in the mudroom just to the side of the back door, I explained my reasoning and showed Mother the letter I'd found in the mailbox.

She wiped her hands with a dishtowel. Clearly Mother had been cooking and probably just washed her hands in the sink. I had arrived at 5:55 p.m., as I almost always do, meaning dinner was thirty-five minutes away. I noted the oven was on and something was inside it.

Mother took the letter from my hand. I placed the two invoices in a letter rack Mother keeps on a table next to the far counter. Then I turned back in her direction and was concerned with what I saw.

She had paled considerably and was not breathing in, as if she'd been punched in the stomach. She sat down on a kitchen chair and placed the letter carefully in front of her on the kitchen table.

"Oh my," Mother breathed after she seemed to collect herself.

"What is it?" I walked to her side to evaluate her condition. Mother was starting to get color back into her face and her breathing had become regular. "What is wrong?"

"I was just surprised, that's all," Mother said. "I hadn't been expecting a letter. Would you hand me the letter opener, please?"

That was unusual in its own right. Mother rarely uses the stiletto-styled letter opener she keeps next to the rack on the table. She normally tears an envelope open using the nail on her index finger. There seemed to be something special about this particular piece of mail, but I could not yet determine what it was.

I walked back to the table and retrieved the letter opener, which I handed to Mother. "Thank you, Samuel," she said. I saw her carefully manipulate the blade underneath the back flap on the envelope and then open it slowly as if to best preserve the paper and prevent damage to the contents. I had never seen her take such care in opening mail in my life.

"Do you know the handwriting on the envelope?" I asked. "Who do you think sent that letter?"

"I don't know." She answered quickly, more so than she usually speaks. It was curious. In most people such a tone could indicate the speaker was lying, but this was Mother. She always tells me the truth.

She extracted two pieces of paper, which appeared to be from a lined notebook similar to those students use to take class notes, from the envelope. Mother unfolded the two pages and smoothed them out on the table. Then she took a deep breath and began to read.

I live with my mother because I consider her a good friend and because she understands me when most people do not. But under circumstances like these I consider it her right to be given privacy, so I stepped out of the kitchen and went upstairs to my apartment in the attic. I realized the letter Mother was reading clearly had some kind of significance for her. If I were absorbing that kind of information, I would want to be left alone.

Of course, my instincts about people's behavior are not always reliable. It was equally possible Mother would prefer me to be in the room while she read the letter. Because her response appeared to be emotionally, and not empirically, based, I could not assume my assessment was accurate. I considered calling Ms. Washburn to obtain her perspective but she was undoubtedly still driving. I do not phone people when I know them to be operating a vehicle because the statistics prove conclusively that such distractions lead to a higher incidence of collisions.

I spent the next twenty minutes researching a question Ms. Washburn and I had been endeavoring to answer regarding a kitchen blender, two tomatoes, and an orangutan. The question was not especially difficult, but it required rather arcane information usually found in medical journals and it had been unusually time-consuming.

I knew I would not answer it before dinner, but I could make some headway.

Questions Answered is a business I opened based on Mother's suggestion as a way to best utilize my talents for research. Mother had felt that instead of researching topics to satisfy my own curiosity, I could better monetize my ability and help others by accepting questions from clients. Mother had mentioned something about being a force of help for those with problems. I wasn't sure about that part, but the fees I could charge—and Mother's insistence that I get out of the attic for part of every weekday—were persuasive.

I found an open storefront on Stelton Road in Piscataway, a very short drive and manageable walk (in good weather) from my home. The previous business, San Remo's Pizzeria, had moved out more than a year before so the rental rate was fairly negotiable. Mother had handled the transaction, having been a legal secretary for many years after my father had left the family when I was very young.

The business required little renovation, so I'd been up and running with a desk, a telephone, wireless Internet, and two chairs—one for me and one for my mother when she visited the office—for six months before Ms. Washburn had come in as a potential client and ended up assisting ably on the Question of the Missing Head. It had taken some time and a generous amount of persuasion on my part, but she had eventually agreed to stay on at the business and was now a trusted associate at Questions Answered.

She had also recently kissed me, but that was another issue.

Mother does not climb the stairs to my apartment. She has had knee issues and what doctors have told me was a heart "episode" in the past and does not want to test her legs or her cardiovascular system by climbing two flights of stairs. There was no need to call me to dinner, anyway. People like me whose behavior is consistent with a

5

diagnosis of Asperger's Syndrome are often very good at being punctual. We prefer things to be ordered and predictable. Surprises are not welcome. So doing things at the same time every day is a comforting feature that I try to exercise whenever possible. Dinner, Mother knew, was at 6:30 every evening unless there were special circumstances. Tonight there were no such abnormalities.

I walked downstairs to the kitchen precisely at dinnertime after having obtained one important piece of information—the shirt size of the average orangutan—related to the question at hand. Ms. Washburn would no doubt have put the question out of her mind until the next day's open of business, a talent I sometimes wished I could emulate. But my mind does not shut down at my command; it continues to mull over a question whether I intend to do so or not.

Mother was not in the kitchen when I arrived, which I had not expected. I checked the oven and saw it was still operating, so I took two potholders from the hook on the side cabinet and opened the oven door. Inside was a lasagna, which was clearly for Mother. On a lower shelf were a turkey leg and a baked potato, which were for me. I prefer foods that are separate and not placed together in layers.

I took the two dishes out of the oven and placed them on trivets we keep on the counter next to the stove. I noticed the table was not set, so I took plates and utensils out of the proper cabinets and placed them on the table in the correct configurations. I was finding two drinking glasses in the second cabinet when Mother walked back into the kitchen.

Her eyes had rings of red and were moist. Her hair was not disheveled but two locks were out of place and hanging over her forehead. She appeared to be biting her lips.

I looked at her. "Would you like water or iced tea with dinner?" I asked.

Mother closed her eyes for a moment and inhaled sharply. "Water."

"Fine," I said. I filled the glasses with water from a pitcher kept in the refrigerator and put the pitcher onto the table. I cut a piece of the lasagna for Mother and put it on her plate, doing my best not to look at the cheese, meat, and pasta mingling. Then I served myself and sat down opposite Mother, who was sitting very still.

"How was your day?" I asked, as I always do.

"Samuel." She stopped, reminded herself of something. "I have a question for you."

That was not a response to what I had asked so it took me a moment to process what she had said. "What is your question, Mother?"

"Where is your father living now?"

TWO

I DO NOT KNOW much about my father.

Reuben Hoenig left our family when I was four years old. Mother has told me little about him, but I suppose that is because I have not been interested in learning much. He was not involved in our lives and I have very little independent memory of him, so his absence was not something I felt deeply. It has been said that you can't miss what you never had. My father is one of those things.

On the rare occasions when the subject has been broached, Mother has defended Reuben Hoenig as a good but somewhat fragile man who had been presented with more in life than he was able to successfully manage. My suspicion is that I was the element he found most difficult to incorporate into his life. The divorce rate among parents whose children show behaviors that are classified as on the autism spectrum is quite high. However, a popular urban legend suggesting that 80 percent of couples whose children are considered to be "on the spectrum" divorce is a myth; the number is much lower than that.

I had no opinion about Reuben Hoenig. I simply did not have enough reliable data to form one. Mother is a strong evaluator of personalities. I rely upon her often for assessments of those I meet or people involved in questions I have agreed to answer. But her judgment regarding Reuben Hoenig is not reliable strictly because it is certainly colored by emotion. She loved my father enough to marry him and have a child with him. The idea that she could be completely objective about him even in the context of his leaving is unrealistic.

During the years beginning when he left until the present, I had not asked Mother much about my father other than any relevant medical history I might someday need to know. She has volunteered that he had started in the printing press business and then sold musical instruments to school systems, which in turn would rent them to students who wanted to play in marching bands. That was his profession. I never met my grandparents on the paternal side. Mother informed me that they died before I was born.

It came, therefore, as something of a surprise when Mother suddenly asked about his whereabouts on this particular evening. I ignored the turkey leg in front of me for a moment.

"I have no information regarding my father," I said to Mother. "Are you asking me to research his whereabouts and report them to you?"

Mother appeared to be having some difficulty expressing herself tonight. Every sentence was preceded by a pause during which she appeared to gather her thoughts. "Yes," she said finally. "That is what I'm asking. But that might not be all I'm asking."

That was puzzling. I cut a piece of meat off the turkey leg with my knife and ate it while I thought. "What else might you ask?" I said when I had swallowed.

"That's for later. Right now, I'd like you to find him for me." Mother, I realized, looked distressed. It had taken me a while to recognize the facial expression because it was one I did not see on her very often. The redness around her eyes might have been an indication of recent crying. I could not conceive of a situation that might cause such feelings in my mother.

"Right now?" I asked. I looked at my plate.

"No, Samuel. Not this moment. Go ahead and finish your dinner. But I'd like it to be a high priority for you. Will you promise me that?" Mother had not taken a bite of her lasagna yet. Although I could understand reluctance to do so, she usually enjoyed such things. It was another indication that she was unusually upset.

There was no option. "I promise, Mother. But you know very well that I cannot guarantee results because the question might be beyond my talents. And if I do find enough data to answer the question…"

She finished the sentence for me. "The answer might not be what I want to hear. I know. I just need the information. That's all for now."

"I will add one condition to my promise," I said.

Mother looked up pointedly with an expression of surprise and possibly a little irritation. "What?" she asked.

"You must eat your lasagna," I said.

Mother smiled but it was not her usual warm smile. There was something else in it and I could not accurately say what it might be. We did not converse much more as we ate. Mother seemed preoccupied, and I always prefer to dine without talking because then I don't have to watch someone else eat.

After dinner, I cleaned up the kitchen and went up to my attic apartment. Upon entering, I reached for my cellular phone and called Ms. Washburn.

She listened to my account of the evening and did not ask a question before I had finished. "Was the letter from your father?" she said.

The thought had not occurred to me.

"I suppose it's quite possible," I told her. "There was no return address and she immediately asked for his whereabouts."

"What did the letter say?" Ms. Washburn asked next.

I ignored the idea that a piece of paper might speak because I understood she was using a popular idiom. "I have no idea," I answered. "I did not read it."

"Your mother didn't say?"

"I did not ask her."

Ms. Washburn did not respond for four seconds. "Samuel, I think you need to ask your mother about the situation. Why does she need to find your father after all these years? What did the letter say that prompted all this? Maybe it's too personal to ask her if you can read it. But you need to know what you're getting yourself into because we can't research a question if we don't know what it's about. You know that."

Her argument made sense. "Am I treating this question differently than most?" I asked, both to Ms. Washburn and myself.

Ms. Washburn, of course, heard the question as intended just for her. "It's natural that you would," she answered. "This is not something you're doing because you need the money or because someone asked you a question you found intriguing. This is about someone you care about very much, and about something that directly affects your life."

I searched myself for feelings. There are those who believe that people like me, with what was once called Asperger's Syndrome or another "disorder" on the autism spectrum, have no feelings at all— that we somehow are born without the capacity to have emotions. That is not at all true. We have the same feelings as most people, but we often express them differently. Sometimes I don't express my emotions at all because the people around me have shown me through their behavior that my reactions are outside the norm. There are those who find my displays of emotion, when I exhibit them, disturbing.

Of course, I find most displays of other people's emotions disturbing, but that is seen only as another "symptom." There are times I feel that I am living a conundrum.

When Ms. Washburn kissed me after we answered the Question of the Felonious Friend, for example, I did not have time to process the feelings I had and react appropriately. The act caught me so by surprise that I did not react at all. It was not until later that I had realized I quite enjoyed being kissed by Ms. Washburn, even if the presence of lipstick did make the sensation somewhat uncomfortable.

Mother had often suggested that I had romantic emotions for Ms. Washburn and I had denied it honestly. But the impulsive action on Ms. Washburn's part had me questioning my own thought process.

I had let Ms. Washburn kiss me and then we separated and she took a step back. "Did I scare you?" she'd asked.

As I said previously, I was processing many emotions at once and that is not easy for me. But fear was definitely not one of them. "No," I had said. "I simply wasn't prepared."

Ms. Washburn looked at me for a moment. I could not read her expression. "That's fair," she'd said. "I'll tell you what. If you ever want to try that again, you let me know." Then she had walked out of the office to deliver the documents finalizing her divorce to her attorney.

I had thought a number of times about broaching the subject again, now that I could prepare and control the timing of the event, but so far I had not done so, and Ms. Washburn had not attempted to repeat her action or mentioned it in conversation. I was not sure why I was delaying. It was a question worth considering.

Tonight, that subject was not at the top of my priority list. "I don't see how the question affects my life," I told Ms. Washburn through the phone. "I see how it matters to my mother, but it does not seem like something that will make a significant difference to the way *I* live."

I could almost hear the expression on Ms. Washburn's face, one that combined a knowing amusement with concern for my well-being. "I think you'll find out, Samuel. The key is that you can't turn down your mother, so we need to get to work on finding your father first thing in the morning."

The New York Yankees, the baseball team I follow, was not playing a game this evening because the baseball season had ended. I could play music by the Beatles or work on a painting, although my interest in art was waning. Those of us who have Asperger's Syndrome (I refer to it that way for the sake of simplicity) tend to develop keen interests in certain topics. Mine include criminal justice, the New York Yankees, and the Beatles. Those have been areas of study for me since I was in school. Painting was something that had come and gone. "Special interests" don't always stay with a person for a lifetime.

"I think I might begin tonight," I told Ms. Washburn. "I hope you don't find that insulting." Those who are considered neurotypical have rules regarding what is and is not an offense that I frankly find baffling. But in Ms. Washburn's case I was especially averse to behaving in an insulting manner.

"Not at all." There was a light chuckle in her voice. "If you find out anything interesting you can tell me at the office tomorrow morning, okay?"

"Certainly." I considered bringing up the idea of our kissing again, but since we were in separate towns at the moment it seemed inappropriate to initiate the conversation. "Thank you for your help, Ms. Washburn."

"No problem, Samuel."

"Would you like to know how I'm going to begin trying to answer my mother's question?"

Again, the small laugh. "No, Samuel. Not now. When I mentioned talking to you in the office tomorrow, it was a way of saying that I'm tired and need to end the conversation now. Is that okay?"

I saw no reason she hadn't simply said that. "Of course. I will see you in the morning, Ms. Washburn."

"Good night, Samuel." She disconnected the call.

Ms. Washburn gives excellent advice, and she had suggested first that I discuss with my mother the letter she had received this evening.

If it had indeed come from my father, it would be a very valuable artifact in helping to locate him.

I walked downstairs to the main floor of our house and looked for my mother, first in the living room, where she often watches television at night, and then in the kitchen. She was not in either location. A quick search of the front room and a glance at the open bathroom door indicated she was upstairs.

Normally I am reluctant to enter my mother's bedroom. That seems the ultimate of sanctuaries. Mother tends to stay elsewhere in the house before deciding to read for a while before sleeping. But it was an unusually early hour for that. I did not know what her plans for the evening had been, but it did seem clear she had retreated to that room.

I stood outside the door for twelve seconds before knocking. It was a difficult decision to make; if Mother were sleeping, I'd be an unwanted intrusion. Worse, Mother tends to worry about me, so if I deviate from the typical routine she becomes anxious that there is something causing me distress.

Still, Ms. Washburn had pointed out my lack of data on the letter Mother had received and thought it was best I ask her directly about the whole situation regarding her question. There was no other way to obtain the information. I knocked on the door.

The response came immediately. "Samuel?"

It seemed strange for her to ask. No one else lives in the house. "Yes, Mother," I said without solving that conundrum. "Are you preparing to go to sleep?"

"No. You can come in if you want."

I opened the door gingerly despite her assurance that it was all right to do so. This was something I did very rarely. It had the sensation of a mistake despite there being no risk involved. Mother was

14

still Mother. It was not necessary to be on guard with her. But the letter had opened new issues between the two of us and I was not yet sure how to adapt to them.

Mother was lying on her bed with pillows propped up behind her and her legs under her blanket. But I noticed a bulge in the area of her left knee. This was probably an ice pack. Mother had experienced pain in that knee for some years and frequently used ice to relieve the discomfort. She held a book in her hands, now closed with a bookmark at the page she had been reading.

"Mother, may I ask you about the letter you received tonight?" I asked after walking in.

"That *is* asking about the letter," she pointed out. Mother likes to joke that my habit of taking words literally was inherited, not developed. "But if you want to know about it, that's okay. Will it help you find your father?"

"I can't answer that question until I understand more," I assured her. "Did my father write the letter?"

Mother nodded. "He hasn't written in years, so it caught me by surprise. That's why I reacted the way I did. I'm sorry if that was upsetting for you." Mother knows displays of emotion are difficult for me to process.

"It was not upsetting but it was puzzling," I told her. "Why was my father writing to you at this time?"

Mother looked at me and seemed to make a decision. "Sit down, Samuel. I have a lot to tell you."

"I can listen while standing," I pointed out.

"Maybe so, but looking up at you is a stress on my neck. How about doing me a favor and sitting?" She pointed to a chair to the side of her bed, which I pulled out and sat on. "Thank you."

"You are welcome." That is a statement made in response to the statement of gratitude. It is considered a polite comment, although it is said so often that to my ear it has lost most of its meaning. How would a clerk in a coffee shop know if I am welcome to a corn muffin?

Mother took a deep breath and placed the book, written by an author named Fiorella, on the bed stand next to her. "Samuel," she said, "there is a lot about your father that I haven't told you all these years."

"I assumed that, but I have not asked you anything about him, so you would have had no occasion to inform me. There is very little I have needed to know." I thought briefly of getting a pad and pen to write down anything Mother might want to tell me, but decided it was unlikely there would be much I'd forget.

Mother shook her head. "I didn't tell you a lot because it was easier for me not to say anything," she said. "There were things that were difficult for me and you didn't ask, but it was my responsibility to let you know about the man who brought you into this world."

For a brief moment I thought Mother meant the obstetrician who had delivered me but I quickly realized based on context that she meant my father. People considered neurotypical tend to embellish their conversation with imprecise language they think is emotionally evocative when it is usually just confusing.

In any event, Mother did not provide me with enough time to express that thought. She continued, "Your father is a good man and I don't want you to forget that, Samuel. But he doesn't always see the need to play by the rules and that leads to trouble."

"Mother, you are being imprecise," I said. "Please just tell me what you need to say. You may trust that you are not causing me any serious emotional trauma. I don't really know my father at all, so I have no preconceptions of him. I have no ties to him. Whatever you tell me will be used as useful information if it helps me find him and filed away if it does not. I am not unusually invested in the circumstances of the question."

Mother half smiled. "I know you believe that, but a man has a connection to his father even if they've never met. Nonetheless, your father is not a bad person. He wanted to do the best for us and did what he thought was going to provide that. Do you understand?"

"Has my father been in jail?" The thought had not occurred to me before, but it fit the facts I had been given.

But Mother looked astonished at the suggestion. "No!" she said with great force but without anger. "Your father is not a dishonest man, Samuel. But he was not capable of dealing with a family while trying to make his way in the world. He wanted to provide for us but his work was not enough."

"I have always suspected that he left because having a small child with the characteristics I exhibited was too difficult a task," I said. "I remember how much you had to do to advocate for me even before I was given the classification." I meant the "diagnosis" of Asperger's Syndrome, but Mother understood.

"Your father didn't leave because of you," she said, although I did not find her tone especially convincing. "He left to find a better way to support his family."

"But he never came back," I pointed out. "Surely after twenty-seven years he has discovered a means of income, particularly since our needs are not what they were before I could provide for myself."

Mother, who owns the house in which we live and pays for the groceries and upkeep on our home, certainly knew that my income at Questions Answered could eventually be enough to allow me my own apartment and pay my expenses. In fact, my bank account now could probably fulfill that function. But she knew what I meant about the years of my childhood and adolescence. She nodded.

"I haven't heard from him much after the first year," she said. "He went off to a possible opportunity he'd heard about in Tulsa, Oklahoma, something about working for a company that provided tourists with a real ranching experience. He sent home some money but he wasn't happy with it almost immediately. Said he was going to Seattle, this time to work for a printing company because he had a background in making colors precise on paper, or something. Then I didn't hear from him for five years. I thought he was dead. I called for him, wrote to him in care of General Delivery, but he didn't have a post office box and that was before cell phones. I would have gone out there to look for him, but…" Her voice trailed off.

I finished the sentence for her. "But you had a young son with issues you didn't yet understand and you had no idea of where to look. If I had been old enough and had a computer then, I might have been able to track him down."

Mother nodded. Her eyes did not tear up, but she did not look happy. "It's hardly your fault we didn't have the Internet yet, Samuel, and you were five years old. I don't think it was your responsibility to find your father."

"I do remember the occasional envelope that had money in it," I said. "Was that from him?"

"Yes. It was very infrequent and there was almost never a note, but after he started getting in touch again he would sometimes send money. No explanation, and never a huge amount, but it helped get us through some tough times. I still don't know what he was doing or where the money came from."

The background was illuminating but not particularly helpful in answering Mother's question. "The letter you received tonight, Mother," I said. "What was written in it?"

She did not answer but reached toward her nightstand. She opened the drawer and retrieved the envelope I had seen earlier. Without a word she handed it to me.

I am not well versed in social interaction and there are times when gestures are difficult for me to interpret. This was not one of those times. I took the envelope from Mother and sat back in the chair. I removed the two sheets of paper and, remembering how she had treated them when she first read them, I smoothed them out on my left thigh. Perhaps Mother believed the paper was especially fragile or dry and that it might somehow decompose. In any event I felt it best to mirror her motions.

The letter read as follows:

Vivian—

I am sorry I could not send money this time.

My situation has taken an unusual turn and you might not hear from me again. I want you to understand that I have done the best I could. From what I have heard, Sam has grown up to be a remarkable man. That is a testament to your hard work all these years. You know I wasn't cut out for that.

I hope you are in good health. I find that is the most important thing in life now that I have reached this age.

Suffice it to say you deserved better than me. I hope you found that. In the meantime, if this is our last communication, know that I remain the man who asked you to marry him on that carousel so long ago. Unfortunately, that man couldn't give you the life he wanted you to have.

Say hello to Sam for me.

The rest of the letter was more personal and Mother has not given me permission to share its contents. It was not relevant to the question she had asked.

I looked up after completing my reading. "I would imagine I am the Sam he mentions?" I asked.

Mother laughed. "Yes, Samuel. Your father thought your name was too formal for a little boy."

"He clearly did not understand the little boy in question," I observed.

"He didn't have time. He was gone most of the time on business even then, sales trips for the music company. He tried very hard, but he didn't realize having a family meant more than just paying the bills."

"There is very little information in this letter to help locate my father," I told her. It was best under these circumstances to be certain Mother's expectations were realistic.

"I know," she said. "But he keeps saying we might never hear from him again. That sounds very dire, Samuel. Your father needs your help."

"I doubt I can be of help if his problem is medical, Mother. You have asked me where Reuben Hoenig is and I will do my best to answer your question for you. But I can't promise to fix any of his problems once I do. I intend to provide you with an address, not to travel there for a reunion with a father I don't remember."

Mother looked at me for a moment. "We'll see when that happens, won't we, Samuel?" she said. I did not understand what she meant by that, but the look on her face, which appeared to be hurt, stopped me from asking.

I could not comprehend Mother's apparent pain at my logical attitude toward the question she had asked. I would have to consult with Ms. Washburn in the morning because I could not get an explanation from Mother herself without risking causing more emotional upset unintentionally.

"Mother, I have read the letter you received tonight and I have agreed to answer your question," I said. "Perhaps it is best if we both get some sleep before I begin to work on the answer." I stood up, although I had every intention of commencing my research once I reached my attic apartment. I don't lie to Mother, but in this case I was not telling the whole truth. It is a distinction that took me a long time to comprehend.

"Maybe so," Mother said. There was something in her inflection that I found strangely unconvincing.

Before I reached the door I turned back because a question had suggested itself and I was struggling to find the proper way to ask. Emotional people like my mother can be upset with a turn of phrase even when the intention is clearly not malevolent.

"Mother," I said. "My father has been gone from this house and our lives for many years. It is … confusing to me that you obviously still harbor such deep feelings for him while I truly have none. After all, he has not been your husband in a very long time."

Mother's eyes widened a little and I briefly believed I had offended her, but then I recognized her expression as one of surprise. When I was a teenager and starting with Dr. Mancuso, he had given me drawings and photographs of people's faces with words indicating the emotions their expressions were meant to convey: Sadness, Joy, Anxiety, Anger, and so on. I had practiced my observations mostly on Mother for the bulk of my life and had been studying Ms. Washburn for over a year now. I knew Mother was not angry but I was not prepared for her to be startled by what I had asked.

"Oh no, Samuel," she said. "Reuben has always been my husband, and he is my husband today. We never got divorced."

THREE

"THEY'RE STILL MARRIED?"

Ms. Washburn sat at her desk, which is to my left in the Questions Answered office. The room is large and mostly empty. In the center are the two desks, both wooden but acquired from separate manufacturers because I was not anticipating having an associate in the business before Ms. Washburn arrived with a question and stayed to work with me. Behind us and to the right when one enters are the two pizza ovens left over from when the space housed the San Remo's Pizzeria. They have not been used in some time but are still functional because I find them interesting.

"Yes," I answered her. "Apparently my mother never filed for divorce and my father has not been in touch." I shook my head in wonderment. "There are times I don't understand even what my mother does. The circumstances were clear. My father had left and never returned. If she had gotten a divorce, there might have been monthly alimony and child support payments instead of the occasional envelope of cash. Is there something I'm missing, Ms. Washburn?"

She did not hesitate in her response, and nodded her head affirmatively. "She still loves your father, Samuel. She doesn't want to declare their marriage is over."

"That is not supported by the facts," I argued. "They have not seen each other in twenty-seven years. The legal definition of marriage is upheld only because neither of them ever acted to end it. Financially that could have been a very large mistake on my mother's part."

Ms. Washburn shrugged. "Maybe, but love isn't always about what makes the most sense, Samuel." She looked down at her keyboard for a moment and did not speak again. That was a signal I did not comprehend. I chose not to act.

I looked at my computer screen. I had in fact not done any research intended to locate my father the night before. I had been distracted by my mother's revelations and the lingering feeling that I had somehow caused her some emotional distress, although she denied it. Instead I played *With the Beatles*, a British pressing on vinyl, because it helps me to think. I had taken more time than usual to fall asleep.

Mother had seemed herself this morning, being sure to cook a breakfast she knew I would appreciate and speaking of ordinary things. She did not mention Reuben Hoenig, the letter, or her question at all. She must have felt her message had been delivered.

I did not consider that odd, but I did wonder if she was trying to avoid a painful subject. The traits of my Asperger's Syndrome make it difficult for me to know. But since the morning had been normal and not unpleasant I felt it was best not to question Mother and treated the day as I would any other. Routine is important to me. I was at my desk, after Mother had driven me to the office on Stelton Road, at the usual time.

I began the search for my father's location as I always do. The simplest devices are often the best to launch one's research.

A Google search for the name "Reuben Hoenig" returned only eight results, which is highly unusual. Apparently my father's name is among the rarer ones in the world.

There were only six such listings that referred to a specific individual and identified his location. One was in Austria, one in Finland, one in the Netherlands. There were American Reuben Hoenigs in Houston, Texas; Painesville, Ohio; and Billings, Montana. None was listed in Tulsa, Oklahoma, or Seattle, Washington, the only two cities in which my mother could be certain my father had resided after he left our home in Piscataway, New Jersey.

I would at some point have to ask my mother if she knew of any aliases my father might have used during his life. For some reason, the thought of broaching the subject with Mother again made my stomach feel tight, a sensation I have had during times of anxiety.

I will confess that I had walked into her bedroom that morning when I knew she would not be there and had taken the letter in its envelope from her nightstand. It was a breach of trust that I would normally never commit, but I thought Mother would prefer not to discuss the subject and would want me to have the letter to analyze it for data that might prove helpful in discerning my father's location. I would return it when I went home for lunch at twelve thirty this afternoon.

The Google search had yielded very little, but perhaps that made the task easier. If my father was not living under an assumed name, it would be simple to contact all three of the Reuben Hoenigs in the United States and determine if one of them was the man in question. If none proved to be my father, we could move on to the Europeans in the group and possibly eliminate all six in a short period of time.

Ms. Washburn broke the silence that I had settled into rather comfortably. "Do you think your father loved your mother, Samuel?"

I did not see the relevance of the question. My father's emotional state, particularly in reference to his feelings for my mother more than two decades before, would not help discover his location today. "I could not say," I answered. "I have very few independent memories of my father, and even those might simply be the product of repeated stories my mother has told me."

"What do you remember?" she asked.

It was twenty minutes after the hour and that meant I should begin my exercise program for the day. I stood up and began to walk briskly around the perimeter of the Questions Answered office, raising my arms above my head to increase my heart rate. Ms. Washburn knows I do this routine three times every hour between nine a.m. and five p.m., so she did not react at all. In fact she did not even look up from her computer screen to chart my progress.

"Not very much," I reiterated. "I remember being at a petting zoo and sitting on my father's shoulders. It seemed like I was very high in the air, but from what I know of him my father is not an especially tall man."

I did not see Ms. Washburn but I could hear the smile in her voice. "To a little boy any grownup is a tall person," Ms. Washburn said.

I completed one circuit of the offices. Twelve more to go and then I could purchase a bottle of spring water from the vending machine we keep in a corner next to the pizza ovens.

"It is an issue of perspective," I agreed. "I remember my father urging me to pet a goat and my resistance because it looked very dirty."

Ms. Washburn did not comment on that. "Do you recall anything else? What was he like?"

I had not thought about my father this much since before I started kindergarten so the answers were not definitive or quick to my mind. "He smelled of aftershave lotion," I said. "I do not know which brand."

"That's probably not really important," Ms. Washburn suggested.

"I have seen a few photographs," I continued. "Mother keeps one in her room and I made a point of examining it last night. My father is, or at least was a quarter-century ago, a man with curly brown hair, clean-shaven and well attired. He had no distinguishing marks on his face or neck and none on his hands that I could see. His eyes were dark and I believe brown, but the angle of the photograph and the distance from the camera made it difficult for me to reach a conclusion on that issue." I had completed seven rounds of the office space and my breathing was becoming a bit more labored, although certainly nothing I did not expect. This was the point of aerobic exercise, after all, to increase heart levels and strengthen the system.

"It would help to have a more current photograph," Ms. Washburn mused.

"If we had one, we probably would have found my father's location and the question would be answered," I pointed out.

Ms. Washburn hesitated as I finished the eighth circuit.

"Say what you are thinking, Ms. Washburn," I advised her. "There is no need to worry about my feelings. I am dealing quite rationally with this question."

I stole a glance at her and saw her bite her lips lightly and nod.

"Aren't you the least bit curious?" she asked. "Once we find out where he's living, wouldn't you want to go see him? Ask him about his life? Tell him about yours?"

"You know of my aversion to travel." I much prefer predictable routine to a break in the usual schedule. I do not understand the appeal of surprises. "Besides, I see no point to such a trip. My father has made it clear that his life is not to be shared with my mother and me. I have lived this long without knowing him. I don't understand why it would be relevant now." Nine circuits and now my arms were feeling predictably heavy.

"Because he's your father," Ms. Washburn said softly.

"He has been my father for the past twenty-seven years plus the four when he lived with us," I countered. "Nothing has changed."

My last four trips around the office perimeter were not supplemented with conversation. By that time I am breathing more heavily and concentrating on finishing the task. Ms. Washburn understands that and allows for the adjustment. I completed my exercise, walked directly to the vending machine, and purchased a bottle of spring water. On Tuesday a man named Les would come by, refill the machine, and pay me back a percentage of the money I'd spent on beverages during the week. It is an odd system but it works for both parties, apparently.

When I sat down at my desk again it occurred to me that Ms. Washburn might want a bottle of the diet soda she prefers so I asked her. She complimented me on remembering to ask but said it was too early in the morning for such a beverage and that she wasn't thirsty anyway. Ms. Washburn, I know, attends a gymnasium three nights each week and does not follow my in-office regimen.

"So what's our plan?" she asked. "Do we call all the Reuben Hoenigs and hope we get lucky?"

There is a colloquial, less polite definition to the term "get lucky," but I was fairly confident that was not what Ms. Washburn meant. "If you would agree to take three of the phone calls, I will do the others," I said. Ms. Washburn, knowing that I am uncomfortable on the phone, has been urging me to practice more, so I have made an effort. I intended to give her all the numbers in the United States and hope that the Hoenigs in the European countries did not speak English, thus making the calls short and less stressful.

She smiled, acknowledging the concession I was making. "But you get at least one in America." Perhaps when a woman has kissed you, it is sometimes more difficult to disguise your intentions from her. There is no scientific data to support this observation, but I have found it to be true.

I nodded, conceding the point. "First we should examine the letter itself for any indicators it might contain." I picked up the envelope and turned on the desk lamp to better illuminate the surface. I have a magnifying mirror in my lower desk drawer and took it out with a slight feeling of embarrassment. Magnifiers are an investigative cliché. But in this instance it was necessary.

Ms. Washburn walked to my desk and stood behind my chair, looking over my shoulder. I was aware of her presence but my attention was focused on the envelope. I removed the two pages and again smoothed them out carefully on the surface of my desk, side by side. I felt the best information, if there was any, would come from the envelope, so I held that back and examined the pages of the letter first.

"What are we looking for?" Ms. Washburn said quietly. She was very close behind me and no doubt wanted to avoid startling me. She would tell me later that she thought the moment held a certain solemnity to it, but I was not aware of any particular emotional charge. I was searching for data.

"We won't know until we find it," I answered. "I am not a handwriting analyst so there will be little I can discern from the script itself. Perhaps the paper holds some secrets we can discover."

"It's not stationery," Ms. Washburn noted. "It doesn't have an imprint."

I looked closely through the magnifier, which stands on its own on the desk. "You are correct, Ms. Washburn. And it holds no watermark that might help identify where it was purchased. This is stock paper, perhaps from an academic notebook, no doubt bought in bulk. There is nothing especially distinctive about it."

"What about the ink?"

I examined it. "Nothing special. Not from a fountain pen, certainly. A ballpoint, again probably one of many. Perhaps my father works in an office supply store or selling for a paper company. He did once sell musical instruments, and I suppose a salesman can work with any product. There has been a very long gap in our knowledge of him, which makes even an educated guess very difficult to make."

"What was the postmark on the envelope?" Ms. Washburn asked. "Wouldn't that at least tell us the city he mailed it in?"

"Because my mother insists Reuben is not a dishonest man, we can probably eliminate the notion that he would have used one of the websites designed to postmark a piece of mail in a location other than the one in which the mailer is living," I said. "I examined the postmark on the envelope. Please take a look and tell me what you see."

Ms. Washburn pointed at the envelope and I nodded that it was indeed my intention that she should pick it up. No crime had been committed that we knew about and there was no reason to think fingerprints would be an issue. Besides, the envelope had already been handled by postal sorters, a mail carrier, my mother, and myself. Another set of prints would not add very much to the confusion. Ms. Washburn raised the envelope to a level where she could examine it closely.

"It's smudged," she said. "The city is pretty much unreadable to the naked eye, but I think the state is either California or Georgia. Maybe Colorado. Does the magnifier help at all?"

"Let's see," I answered. Ms. Washburn handed me the envelope and I placed it under the large lens for better visibility.

After a few moments Ms. Washburn cleared her throat. That is a sign that the person making the sound would like someone's attention, although to me it always sounds like he or she wants a drink. I looked up at her.

"Can you move over just a little so I can see too?" she asked.

The thought had not occurred to me. Moving to one side might slightly diminish my view of the envelope. I decided if it was important to Ms. Washburn I would allow her an angle and take a better look at the envelope myself after she had returned to her desk. This is one way in which I have learned to consider another person's feelings, something I have spent many hours discussing with Dr. Mancuso.

With enlargement due to the lens, it was clear the city name included two words, but they were not intelligible. The state was more clear with this magnification.

"California," Ms. Washburn said.

"Yes," I said. It wasn't necessary to affirm Ms. Washburn's statement, I knew, but I have been told that people find it odd when one doesn't respond to something they say. If there is nothing to add there doesn't seem to be a point to an answer, but it is easier in some cases to simply comply with convention.

California is the most populous state in America. It takes up a large percentage of the country's West Coast, from the border with Mexico to the Pacific Northwest states of Oregon and Washington. Its coastline, I had once noted, reaches for 840 miles. Its population is slightly under 39 million. Finding one man in the state would actually be more difficult than locating the proverbial needle in a haystack. Assuming it was one needle of hay and not a steel one used for sewing, which would shine in sunlight and be simpler to find.

Finding Reuben Hoenig without more detailed information would be a considerably difficult task.

"Can you read the zip code?" Ms. Washburn asked.

"This magnifier is meant for stamp collectors looking for imperfections in very small printings, but all it does to a smudged ink mark is to make it larger," I said. I sat back. There is a certain eyestrain that results from using a magnifying glass under bright light and it does not take a long time to set in. "Unfortunately the only easily legible digits are nine and zero, which are extremely common in California."

Ms. Washburn moved to my left and leaned over a little more severely. "Mind if I take a look?" she asked.

I saw no reason her eyes would be more adept at deciphering obscured ink than mine, but there was no harm in letting her try. Ms. Washburn has proven very talented in a number of areas and there was no reason to dissuade her. "Feel free," I said.

She stood and looked at me for a long moment. "You need to let me in, Samuel."

It took a moment to realize what she meant. My first thought— which was interesting upon reflection later—was that Ms. Washburn wanted to kiss me again. I did not have time to make a decision about that before I realized she was asking for access to the magnifying glass on my desk. I nodded and stood, giving her a clear path to my chair. She did not sit, but leaned over the desk and looked directly into the lens.

Ms. Washburn did not say anything for seven seconds as she stared intently into the glass. Then without taking her gaze away she reached for a small pad of paper I keep on the right side of my desktop. She reached behind her right ear for a pen she had stored there, something I have not told her I find slightly nauseating. I am trying to accommodate Ms. Washburn. I am her employer but I want her to think of Question Answered as her home base as well.

She wrote without looking at the pad. I watched her hand, which wrote, "9-0" and then hesitated. I moved my gaze to her face. She was intent on the lens, squinting in an attempt to see the other digits more clearly. Again without looking down she wrote, "6" and hesitated. After a moment, the pen wrote "86" on the pad and she looked at me.

"I'm pretty sure," she said.

"You rarely fail to reaffirm my wisdom in hiring you, Ms. Washburn," I said.

She smiled with an edge of something else I did not recognize. "It's nice how you can turn a compliment for me into something that shows off your own intelligence, Samuel." She laughed lightly and added, "Thank you."

"I did not mean to—" I began.

Ms. Washburn waved a hand. "Don't worry about it. So where is your father?" She pointed at the note on the pad.

"I'm afraid we still don't know for certain," I answered. I sat back down in my chair and looked up at Ms. Washburn, who was not yet heading back to her desk as I had expected. "The zip code you wrote down is not in California. In fact it is located in Mexico."

She folded her arms. "Mexico? Do they have zip codes there?"

"Yes. It is essentially the same system as that in the United States. This one is in an area called San Isidro."

Ms. Washburn shook her head, but not in a negative fashion. "The day we met you told me you had memorized every phone exchange in North America and some in Western Europe. Do you memorize zip codes, too? We need to get you a hobby, Samuel."

"How would a hobby differ from what I do?" I asked.

She smiled crookedly. "We're veering off topic again. So you know zip codes and this one is in Mexico. How about..." She looked again at the note she'd written. "How about nine-one-six-oh-six? I couldn't decide whether that was a zero or an eight."

"That would be in North Hollywood, California," I told her. "And that is far more likely the area in which to look for my father."

"The area? Not the town itself?" Now Ms. Washburn did move back toward her desk and sat down. She started typing on her computer keyboard.

"Just because the mail went through the North Hollywood post office does not mean we can be certain the person who mailed it lives there," I pointed out. "If it was my father who mailed it, he might have been on his way to or from his home when he mailed the letter. It is also possible he asked someone else to mail the envelope for him. We don't know enough about the process to be definitive. We must avoid reaching a premature conclusion."

"Yes, but it gives us a direction, an area," Ms. Washburn argued. "It's not very likely that your father drove from Denver to mail a letter and then turned around and drove back."

"Perhaps not, but it is possible. He also could be in the Los Angeles area on a business trip."

"So what's our next step?"

I put the magnifying lens back in the desk drawer and returned the letter to the envelope in the hope that I had not damaged it in any way, certainly not noticeably. Then I slipped the envelope into my jacket pocket to return to our house and Mother's nightstand before she could notice it missing. These manual tasks, although not emergent, were helping me to think more clearly.

"No doubt we should begin with calling the six possible Reuben Hoenigs we have managed to identify," I said. "If, as I expect, none of them is revealed to be my father, we need to gather more information about him to determine why he might be living under another name and where that possibility might lead us in establishing his location."

We spent the next twenty-seven minutes (not including my next exercise session) in that pursuit. While I was able to reach both numbers assigned to me in Europe, neither person answered the phone—it was evening where the men were located while morning in New Jersey—the messages I left after voice mail prompts in languages I did not understand were short and probably incomprehensible to the targeted recipients.

The third man on my list, the Reuben Hoenig in Billings, Montana, did answer the phone. That time zone was two hours behind mine so it was earlier in the morning but I had not expected the man to sound like I had awoken him with the call. "Yeah?" he said by way of a greeting.

"Is this Mr. Reuben Hoenig?" I asked after a moment of contemplation. In my experience, "yeah" was a form of "yes," which would indicate that I had asked a question whose answer could be found in the affirmative. I had said nothing at all to this man yet. I had heard the word used as a form of, "Why are you speaking to me?" and assumed this was one of those instances.

"Who wants to know?" the voice asked. Again, it took me a moment to decipher the inquiry. Would he slip into a different identity depending on the person asking? Wasn't he the same person all the time? It was confusing. I decided, looking at Ms. Washburn, who was on the phone to another Reuben Hoenig, that I should simply press on. It seemed he was asking for my name, so it made sense to tell him who was calling.

"Allow me to introduce myself," I said. "I am Samuel Hoenig, the proprietor of Questions Answered in Piscataway, New Jersey."

"I don't want to buy anything," the man said.

"I am not selling anything," I countered.

"They all say that."

"Who?"

"People who are selling something."

That seemed contradictory. "I am not selling anything, I can assure you," I told the still-unidentified man. "I do not wish for you to give me any money. I am simply looking for Reuben Hoenig."

I heard a rustling sound through the telephone. Perhaps the man was getting out of bed. "Who did you say you are?"

"I am Samuel Hoenig, proprietor of—"

The man spoke before I could finish the reiteration he had requested. "Is this because we have the same last name?" he asked. "Are we related or something?"

"I am not sure," I told him. "That is one of the reasons I am calling. Are you Reuben Hoenig?"

"I suppose so."

That answer wasn't at all helpful. Did the man in Montana not know who he was? Amnesia is an extremely rare disorder, usually brought on by a severe blow to the head or some other trauma and is most often temporary. "You're not certain?" I asked.

"Of course I'm certain." Now the man sounded slightly irritated, which did not seem logical. He had said he supposed he was Reuben Hoenig but apparently I was meant to understand he was stating his name with certainty. I have never been to Montana, but I did not think the English language was spoken differently there.

"So you are Reuben Hoenig." Perhaps if I stated, rather than asked, the answer would be clearer.

"Yes, for god's sake. What do you want?"

That was clearer, but I seemed to be annoying this Reuben Hoenig more now. "I am trying to locate a man named Reuben Hoenig who lived in Piscataway, New Jersey, until twenty-seven years ago. Are you that man?"

"No."

Certainly that was definitive. "My apologies for disturbing you then, sir," I said. "Do you know anyone else with that name? I am endeavoring to locate my father." I have been told by Mother and Dr. Mancuso that people tend to respond more favorably when one personalizes the problem at hand. It is meant to arouse a sympathetic impulse.

35

"I've never been to New Jersey," the man said. He disconnected the call without saying goodbye, which I found mildly surprising. I put the telephone receiver back in its cradle and looked at Ms. Washburn, who was still speaking into her phone but noticed my glance and shook her head negatively. She had not found my father, either.

It was the result I had expected but it was still something of a disappointment. Our efforts would have to move in another direction now.

For reasons I could not have explained I retrieved the envelope from my jacket pocket and spread the letter out on the desk again. I decided that reading it for content rather than subliminal information might be helpful. Ms. Washburn would say I had no better ideas, and she would be right.

The element that seemed most imperative was my father's suggestion that this might be the last communication Mother would ever receive from him. That was expressed more than once but never explained. There were a number of possible motivations behind such a tactic, but I thought perhaps a consultation with Dr. Mancuso would best help me identify those I might not consider on my own.

Ms. Washburn hung up the phone and her shoulders slumped a bit. "Nobody on the list is panning out," she said. "I guessed that you didn't find your father from those, either, did you?"

I shook my head. "I did not expect to, so it is not a serious disappointment. Ms. Washburn, can you imagine why my father, in writing this letter, would twice announce that this might be the last time my mother will ever hear from him?"

Her eyes narrowed, which with Ms. Washburn indicates she has questions about my meaning. "I imagine he thinks he won't be able to write again," she said. Her tone indicated there was more to my question that she did not yet comprehend.

"I understand the meaning of the words," I explained, "but it's the motivation behind writing them that puzzles me. Why does a man write to his estranged wife, whom he apparently has never divorced, after an interval of years to tell her she won't hear from him again? Particularly since he never actually explains why future communication will not be possible. That seems a strange message to send. It did seem to have a profound effect on my mother. I am trying to grasp what drives a person to send that message without further details."

"So you want to know about your father's possible motive," Ms. Washburn said. I believed I had said that already, but was aware this was Ms. Washburn's way to clarify the issue.

"That's right. If it is going to be the last time he writes to Mother, doesn't it make sense to say why that is happening? And if he is desperate to communicate with her one last time, why wait in this day of instantaneous communication to send a letter via postal service. From California, that delivery probably took about a week, although the date on the postmark is illegible. Why make that the point of the letter?"

Ms. Washburn frowned. "I didn't actually read the letter and I don't want to; that's private between your parents. But was that really the main message he was sending? You said he talked a lot about the job your mother did raising you and how sorry he was that he hadn't been there for that."

"Yes, but he could have written to her with that sentiment anytime in the past decade and had roughly the same effect. Besides, he doesn't know what kind of man I have become; his only source of information is my mother, and as you well know she is hardly objective on the subject."

"I think anyone observing would say your mother should be proud of the way you turned out, Samuel," Ms. Washburn said. I thought that might be intended as a compliment, but it was aimed at Mother, not at me, so I did not accept it for my own.

"Perhaps," I answered. "But it does not answer the question at hand. Why would he write and say such a thing, then announce this might be the last communication for their lifetimes?"

Ms. Washburn stood up and consulted the digital clock I have hung on the post between our desks. "Well, it's just about time to see the only person we know who has actually met your father, Samuel. Let's go talk to you mother."

Of course. It was lunchtime.

FOUR

Ms. WASHBURN HAS A standing invitation to accompany me to lunch at my mother's house. Since on most days she is the one to drive me home in the afternoon, she is often present anyway, and besides she and Mother have formed a bond I don't entirely understand but which appears to be quite amiable.

Today, however, I think Ms. Washburn saw the afternoon meal as an opportunity to ask the questions of Mother that I—either because it would not occur to me or because it is difficult with one's parent—would not easily ask.

If that sentiment had been voiced I would have disagreed, although it was possible there were some areas I would not have considered independently. Sometimes I do not consider emotional aspects of an issue that another person would believe to be obvious.

We had told Mother of our slow progress in locating my father, and I had returned the letter to her, confessing my borrowing it without asking first. Mother had said simply that she assumed I would need the letter to aid in answering the question and had not concerned herself with it being missing.

Now Ms. Washburn, eating a tuna sandwich at our kitchen table, wiped her mouth with a napkin and looked at Mother. "I think I need a better sense of your husband, Vivian. Samuel and I have been trying to figure out what his state of mind might be. I don't know if that will help narrow down his location, but it might give us some sign of what we can do that will."

"Samuel should know about his father anyway," my mother said without looking in my direction. It is not often she speaks about me without acknowledging my presence in the room. I wondered if she was actually somewhat irritated with me for entering her bedroom to borrow the letter from my father.

Ms. Washburn nodded. "There shouldn't be that kind of gap in his background; you're right. What can you tell us?"

Mother sat back; she had taken only two bites from her own tuna sandwich. Ms. Washburn would tell me later she thought Mother might be worried about my father and therefore eating less heartily than usual. "I met Reuben at a dance my friend Joanne talked me into going to at a synagogue. I don't know what it was about him, but he just had this swagger about him that I thought was interesting. But he was very quiet and shy when we started to talk. He loved old movies and so did I, so we bonded on that."

This thread of conversation did not seem to be leading to any information that would give me some idea of how to find my father in or near North Hollywood, California. But through many previous questions I had discovered that the key information sometimes reveals itself in unexpected areas, so I ate some of the turkey sandwich Mother had made for me and listened to Ms. Washburn carefully direct my mother through her recollection.

"Did you date for a long time before you were married?" she asked.

Mother, whose line of sight seemed to be directed at the molding over the kitchen door, shook her head. "Three months," she answered. "Reuben wanted to be married soon and I was head over heels for him. My parents objected until they met him and then they were thrilled."

I had met my mother's parents only once, when I was twelve years old and not yet "diagnosed" with Asperger's Syndrome. They had flown in from their home in Hollywood, Florida, and visited with Mother and me for three days on their way to Colorado to see my mother's sister, Aunt Jane. I was going through what Mother would have described as a "difficult phase," and from what I could recall of them, it was hard to imagine her parents being thrilled about anything. Mostly what I could recall was looks of disapproval for me and Mother. Years later when Mother informed me that her mother, then her father had died, I had not felt anything out of the ordinary; I had barely known them.

"Reuben just had a way of charming you, making you believe in him," Mother went on. "He's a kind soul; he really wants to help everyone he knows. But sometimes he's less than careful about the way he goes about doing it, and that can lead to trouble."

That seemed to be a signal. "What kind of trouble, Mother?" I asked.

My mother continued to look at the top of the doorway with a look she would no doubt have described as "out into space." She was thinking about my father and their early life together, it seemed obvious, and she was smiling. It would seem natural for a woman whose husband had left her with a small "special needs" child to resent that man and harbor unpleasant feelings for him. Mother appeared instead to have clung tightly to her regard for my father and was apparently trying to convince Ms. Washburn, if not both of us, that he was actually a man driven to what he'd done by his strong desire to help his family, which seemed unlikely.

"He never got into anything with the police, Samuel," she said with a slight hint of rebuke in her voice. "I told you that."

"You told me he hadn't gone to jail," I corrected. "That didn't mean he'd never been arrested or charged with a crime. I wanted to make the point clear."

"You made it clear," she replied with a tone I could not identify. Then Mother said to Ms. Washburn, "Reuben was so anxious to be successful, so much in a hurry to show me I was right to believe in him, that he rushed into things without thinking sometimes. Once he was going to start a company with a friend of his to film people's weddings just at the time video was starting but was expensive. Reuben just didn't want to wait for the price to come down. He thought he could convince people film was better."

It occurred to me that my father had impulse control issues but I decided saying that would be counterproductive in this conversation. Mother was trying strenuously to paint a positive portrait of my father. If I were to illuminate his faults, she would spend more time contradicting me than giving Ms. Washburn information that might eventually become useful. I resolved not to ask another question nor to make another comment and to give Ms. Washburn the lead. She does well under such circumstances.

"Does he have any relatives, Vivian?" Ms. Washburn asked. "Someone he might have been in contact with all these years?"

Mother shook her head. "When he left and I didn't hear from him for such a long time, I tried calling his brother, who was the only one left. Arthur lived in Chicago in those days, and he said he hadn't heard from Reuben either. He promised to get in touch if Reuben called or wrote, but he never did."

I had never known I had an uncle named Arthur in Chicago, but my plan remained the same. I listened.

"Was he close to his brother?" Ms. Washburn asked.

"No. Arthur was a lot older; he'd be close to eighty now. But they sort of grew up in two different families. Arthur is really Reuben's half brother. Their father divorced Arthur's mother and married Reuben's three years before Reuben was born. I never met either of his parents or his stepmother."

Ms. Washburn's tone became gentler, indicating she knew she was approaching a sensitive subject and wanted to be sure she said nothing to upset Mother. I felt my hands, under the table now that I had finished my turkey sandwich, ball into fists at the thought that this could be difficult. I do not respond well to emotional scenes.

"Vivian, Samuel told me some of what he read in Reuben's letter to you. A couple of times he says this might be the last time you hear from him. Do you know why that would be?"

Mother looked at me quickly, then at Ms. Washburn. Her face showed some stress at the corners of her eyes and mouth. "Isn't it obvious?" she asked. "Clearly, Reuben is dying."

FIVE

DESPITE MS. WASHBURN AND me proposing any number of possible scenarios under which my father might write that he would not be communicating with my mother again—a change in lifestyle, perhaps a new marriage, a lack of interest after decades of separation—she would not be moved off her belief that my father was somehow about to lose his life.

This seemed somewhat irrational to me. No matter what his motives or the circumstances under which he had left, the fact was that Reuben Hoenig had not lived under the same roof as my mother for twenty-seven years. His personality, from what I could glean through Mother's remembrances, which were certain to be biased, was a flighty and impulsive one. The idea that he had contacted Mother at all after this much time was an indicator that the man would simply indulge any thought that occurred to him and felt like the right thing to do at that moment.

But the matter at hand was his location. That was the question Mother had asked me. My father's motivations or intentions were not relevant. The key was discerning if Reuben Hoenig had any people on the planet he might contact other than Mother.

His brother Arthur, she had said, had been living in Chicago, Illinois, when she had last communicated with him. That was a place to start, if Arthur was still alive.

I asked Mother for any contact information on other people who had known my father so the process of searching online could be streamlined or bypassed completely based on the currency of her data. She had written out a list after consulting a paper address book she keeps stuffed with envelopes, return addresses, index cards, Post-It notes, and other effluvia she has managed to accumulate over the years. It is a highly inefficient style of record keeping.

Ms. Washburn and I said our goodbyes and she drove me back to the Questions Answered office without any conversation during the ride. I am a nervous passenger and Ms. Washburn is a very good driver. I let her concentrate on the road during the short drive.

Once inside the offices, though, Ms. Washburn began as if we had not had a break in conversation at all. "Do you think your uncle Arthur would have contacted your mother if something really serious was going on?"

I sat down behind my desk and revitalized my desktop computer. "Until forty minutes ago I had no idea I had an uncle named Arthur," I reminded her. "I have no way of analyzing the man's personality or predicting his actions."

"It was an academic question, Samuel. Would a man do something like that?"

The answer appeared to be obvious. "It would depend upon the man. Perhaps we should call Arthur Hoenig and find out."

Ms. Washburn fixed me in her gaze. "Perhaps *you* should call Arthur Hoenig. You are his nephew."

I did not see how a blood relationship would make a difference in extracting information from an elderly man I had never met, but it has become evident over time that trying to successfully persuade Ms. Washburn with logic when she is arguing with emotion is usually a lost cause. I am not fond of calling strangers on the phone, or talking to strangers at all for that matter, but I did need the information if Arthur Hoenig had it and calling was more time efficient than having a prolonged conversation with Ms. Washburn that would eventually lead to my calling him anyway.

From Mother's handwritten notes I dialed the phone number in Chicago and listened to five rings before the phone was engaged. A man's voice said, "Hello?" It was a question spoken as if it was a wonderment or a source of some disgruntlement that another person had chosen to dial his number. I understood the sentiment but went on.

"Allow me to introduce myself," I said.

The man disconnected the call.

I looked at Ms. Washburn. "I believe the phrase is, he hung up on me," I said.

Her face registered surprise. "Really!"

"Perhaps you should call," I suggested. "Maybe I said something wrong." I couldn't think of what that might be, but that is often the case in my conversations with the supposedly neurotypical.

"I didn't hear you say anything wrong," Ms. Washburn insisted. "Try again, but just say, 'Hello, this is Samuel Hoenig.'"

"That is not the way I introduce myself," I reminded her.

"I know. Maybe in this case your name will make a difference to him. Even though you had never heard of him before today, I'll bet your mother has mentioned you to him more than once." Ms. Washburn looked at her computer screen. "I'll listen to your end of the call and let you know if you're going in the wrong direction, okay?"

If anyone other than Ms. Washburn had suggested listening to me make a phone call to verify my ability to do so, I would have been insulted. But because I trust her judgment I nodded and touched the redial button on my phone.

This time the man answered after only three rings, but his greeting was more gruff and his voice more harsh. "Yeah?"

"Hello, this is Samuel Hoenig," I said. Then I realized I did not know what I should say next because the conversation was not falling within my established parameters.

"*Samuel* Hoenig?" the man said. "Are you Reuben's boy?"

That was a confusing question. If Arthur Hoenig was indeed the man on the other end of the conversation, was he asking whether I would take my father's side in an argument? Was he suggesting that I was not an adult male? Did he mean to be in some way denigrating or insulting? His tone was indeed raspy and direct, but his intentions were mysterious.

"I am the son of Reuben Hoenig, if that is the question you are asking," I said.

"What?"

"I believe the answer to your question is, yes," I answered.

"You're Reuben's son."

It seemed difficult for the man to believe. I felt I already knew his name but was obligated to prove my thesis. "Are you Arthur Hoenig?" I asked, having already adequately established my own identity.

"Yeah. Reuben is my brother." Again, that was a piece of information that I had inferred but not confirmed. "What do you want?"

I appreciated my uncle's directness. "I am trying to locate my father," I said. "Do you have a current address for him in California?" Ms. Washburn, whom I knew had been listening carefully, looked up at that. She knew I had not actually established beyond question that my father was in California, but as an interrogatory technique it is sometimes helpful to assume knowledge and have it confirmed or denied rather than ask and have the subject be untruthful.

"Why are you looking for him?" Arthur asked. It was not an answer to my question, which was irritating. My left hand, not clutching the telephone receiver, tightened on the desk.

"I am his son," I said. That was true, although it was not the reason I was seeking Reuben Hoenig's address. This gave Arthur just as little information as he had given me by answering with a question. "Do you know where he is?"

"Yeah, I know," Arthur answered. I waited for more and there was silence on the line. I silently berated myself for wording my question badly. I felt my head vibrate on my neck in an involuntary expression of my frustration.

"Would you please tell me where?" I asked, getting the words out through clenched teeth. Ms. Washburn's expression, seen peripherally, appeared to be concerned.

There was a pause on Arthur's end of the conversation and I hoped he had not had a heart attack and died from the stress of the situation. I understood he was not a young man and such things can happen. If he died I would lose a potential source of information that could lead to the answering of Mother's question.

"No, I don't think I'm going to tell you," he answered finally.

It was my turn to delay speaking while my thoughts flooded with contradictory impulses. Why would a man refuse to answer such a question? If Arthur did not provide my father's address, how would I find it? Was there any way to convince him that he should provide the information even if he did not wish to do so?

"What is your favorite song by the Beatles?" I asked him. My first guess would have been "Mean Mr. Mustard."

"What?" That was the second time my uncle had demanded I repeat myself in this conversation. If Arthur had a hearing problem, he certainly could have obtained for his phone a device that increases the volume of the incoming audio. If he did not, he was either stalling for time or legitimately confused.

I did not repeat the question, assuming Arthur was simply attempting to get more time to think. There are 309 songs listed as having been released on recordings by the Beatles. No doubt there are many more on unreleased tapes, alternate takes, bootleg recordings, and song segments that could be included in the question. It is not an easy one to answer, so I understood his need for additional thought.

"I don't listen to the Beatles," he said.

That hardly seemed likely. Arthur, if now in his late seventies, would have been a youth in his twenties when the original recordings were released in the United Kingdom and in America. Even if they were not his favorite band—an opinion I am aware is held by some people although I do not understand it—surely he would have heard the recordings and formed an opinion in the ensuing decades.

"Nonetheless," I persisted as Ms. Washburn looked on. "If you had to choose one song by the Beatles, what would it be?"

"I listened to Elvis," Arthur said. "I liked 'Jailhouse Rock.'"

"The Beatles," I insisted. "One song by the Beatles. Please."

"Why?" Arthur sounded genuinely mystified by the question. I find that odd, but it is not atypical. I have posed the question to a great deal of people I meet. It is a device I employ to better understand a person's psyche. Since I know the recordings of the Beatles very well, I can reference the song a subject chooses and divine some insight into his or her character. It is not a completely scientific method, but it is surprisingly effective much of the time.

"It will be of great use to me," I answered. The idea that I would use it to analyze his personality seemed a detail better left unspoken. I have found that to be the case in the past.

"I heard you were weird," Arthur told me. Again, that was not the first time I'd heard such a statement, although I did wonder who might have told him about me. Certainly my mother had not expressed the opinion that I am "weird."

"Can you name a song, please?" There was no point in responding to his comment.

"Oh, fine. Write down 'Nowhere Man.'"

That made sense. A person who believes himself to be alone and isolated, not connecting to society. That helped me understand my uncle better and led to a tactic I could employ.

"My father sent a letter to my mother and it has upset her," I said. "She doesn't hear from him very often and worries about his welfare. If I could contact him it would be helpful for me, for her, and for your brother, I believe. It might even help you."

"Me? How?" Now Arthur sounded interested.

"I assume he has been in touch with you somewhat regularly," I said. "If you tell me where he is he can communicate with my mother and me and come to you for help less often."

Arthur thought that over. "I don't think I'm going to do that," he said slowly.

I had not expected that response so I had no answer ready. I sat and was silent.

"I'll tell you what I *will* do," Arthur continued after a moment. That gave me the feeling he was going to be helpful in some way, and I felt my forearms relax on the arms of my chair. "I'll get in touch with Reuben and tell him you're looking for him. I'll give him your phone number because I have it now on my phone. And if he wants to talk to you, he'll call you. How's that?"

Ms. Washburn had not been able to hear Arthur's side of the conversation. I felt the need for some guidance, so I said, despite already having the information, "You want to contact my father and give him my phone number so he can call me if he decides to do so?" I made it sound like a question so my uncle would not be able to discern that I was repeating it for Ms. Washburn's benefit.

"You got someone there listening?" he asked.

Perhaps I was not as cagey as I had thought. But Ms. Washburn was not listening, at least not to Arthur, so I said, "No." I did look at her, and she nodded her approval. "But if that is the plan, I will agree. Please get in touch with my father and tell him it is urgent I speak to him. In fact, if he would like to text me his address, that would be even better."

"Why?" Arthur asked. "Do you want to go there?"

"I definitely do not," I said truthfully.

"Then you don't need his address unless you're sending him flowers. You're not sending him flowers, are you?"

"No, I am not."

"I'll give him your phone number, boy. What he does with it is his business." Arthur let out a long breath, almost a sigh. "So how's your mom?" he asked. "She still a looker?"

I had no idea what he meant by that. I knew Mother did look at things, but I seriously doubted that was the question being asked. So I stayed silent.

"I guess I shouldn't have asked that," Arthur went on. "Well, it's almost time for *Cake Boss*." He disconnected the call.

I replaced the receiver on its cradle and looked at Ms. Washburn. "My uncle Arthur is a confusing man," I said.

"Why am I not surprised?"

SIX

My FATHER DID NOT call. We waited an hour, including three exercise sessions and three bottles of spring water for me, one diet soda for Ms. Washburn, but the phone in the Questions Answered office did not ring. Ms. Washburn appeared to be working on collecting information that might help, and was absorbed in her work so I did not interrupt her.

I knew there were alternate tactics I could try, but my mind was occupied with the idea of my father calling. I have sometimes missed the sound of a ringing telephone if engrossed in some other pursuit and did not want to have that happen now. If Reuben Hoenig called I could answer my mother's question and move on. That was my single goal at this moment.

So I spent time answering the few emails I had received that were worthy of attention. Most proclaimed that I had won some clearly bogus lottery (there is no such thing as the Coca-Cola Lottery) and were deleted immediately. Others were general information posts from a list I have joined, ASpire, which consists of other people whose behaviors have identified them as having Asperger's Syndrome. I do not post on the list very often but I do read some of the entries and find that I tend to compare myself to the person posting, picturing a wide spectrum of autism and trying to determine whether the posting person is closer to "normal" or further to the right than I am. I realize I should not be competitive in those areas and don't know which side I would prefer to be on, but I confess that I do make the comparison.

Ms. Washburn entered something into her computer and stood up. She stretched, having sat for longer than I would have. She does not exercise every twenty minutes, although she appears to be in excellent condition.

"I'm on to something, Samuel," she said. I recognized this expression as meaning she had found an avenue of investigation that we had not previously considered. It had taken some time to learn many of these imprecise word chains, but it saves a good deal of time in more conversations than one might expect. It's really more of an exercise in memorization than analysis of syntax. "I've been tracing your father's progress from the time he left New Jersey twenty-seven years ago, and although I have a lot of gaps, I think I see a pattern. He might very well be living under a new name."

I stood and walked to her station, assuming she would want to show me her research on the computer screen at her desk. But Ms. Washburn remained standing and stretched her right hand behind her head, then tilting to the left, a move I believe intended to loosen her shoulder. "What have you found that leads you to that conclusion?" I asked.

"There are records of Reuben Hoenig living here in Piscataway at that time, which makes sense," Ms. Washburn said, her flexibility allowing her to speak with her head almost at the height of her waist. She straightened up and reversed the stretch. "His name was on the mortgage for your house and never came off, even after your mother paid it off. The deed and the title to your house are in both their names."

I couldn't understand why immediately, but that information made me feel a bit angry. "How does that lead to your belief that my father took another name?" I asked.

"It leads to a trail," Ms. Washburn said. "It's not a straight line. From here the next records I could find of your father are from Tulsa, Oklahoma, just like your mother said. He surfaced there a month or so after he left here and went to work for a company called Round 'Em Up, like in the movie *City Slickers*."

I must have stared at her blankly because the title was not familiar.

"Well, don't worry about it. The idea was that this company would bring tourists out there and make believe they were on a cattle drive. They'd bring the cattle to another location on their vacations, and then the next group would come and bring them back."

"That seems extremely inefficient," I pointed out. "The cattle simply move back and forth between two ranches."

"It's the experience, Samuel." Ms. Washburn stood straight and performed a yoga move centering her hands in her midsection and breathing slowly and deliberately. She did not close her eyes, but it looked like she should. "Anyway, that's not important. Your father, according to his employment records, only lasted in that job, marketing to travel agents, for five months."

"Why would travel agents want to move cattle from one ranch to another?" I asked.

Ms. Washburn relaxed the pose and sat down in her chair again, apparently refreshed. "Again, don't worry about that part. The point is that your father shows up again, three weeks after his employment ended at Round 'Em Up, in Portland, Oregon."

"Portland?" I asked. "My mother said he'd been in Seattle, Washington."

"Eventually," Ms. Washburn said. "It's only about a three-hour drive from Portland to Seattle. In Portland your father was working for a company that sold parts to manufacturers of payphones. He was earning pretty well, too, but again he left soon, only three months later, and that's when he went to Seattle."

"I appreciate the effort, Ms. Washburn," I said. It is good to say something complimentary to a person before pointing out a problem. "But this has all been merely an elaboration on information we already had. I do not understand how it leads to my father being in the area of North Hollywood, California, and living, as you say, under an assumed name. What did you find that led you to that conclusion?"

"Ah. That's the interesting part." I would have expected it would be, but said nothing. Ms. Washburn rubbed her hands together and typed on her keyboard. "Look here."

I leaned over her shoulder to get a better vantage point for her computer screen. Projected on it was a chart of statistics. At the top was the logo of a corporation, although from this angle I could not make it out. Flat screens like that on Ms. Washburn's computer are directionally based and therefore are clearly visible only to a person sitting directly in front of them.

"This is a copy of some payroll records from the Rayborn Corporation of Seattle, Washington," Ms. Washburn said. "I think these radio stations digitized their records and maybe didn't realize they were accessible from the outside. They're from the same year your father was working there as an advertising salesman for a radio station, KRQL, a very low-wattage AM station that at the time had programming about local news and some sports. As you can see, your father's name is listed among the employees who were paid every two weeks." She pointed at a spot on the image which did display the name Reuben Hoenig.

"So you have established that he worked for Rayborn while in Seattle," I said. I did not ask again how that led to a move to Southern California under a name that was not his own because it had become clear that Ms. Washburn wanted to convey that information in her own way, which I had found was usually effective. I would let her talk. It's not always easy for me to do, but in Ms. Washburn's case I have found it is often the best plan.

"Yes, and then all of a sudden he stops getting paid, but he's never taken off the books." Ms. Washburn scrolled down to a second screen. "See, this is the same payroll a month later. Your father's name is on it but there is no amount next to the name."

"That is odd. Why keep a man on the payroll if he is not being paid?"

"That's what I was wondering. But look at the handwritten scroll next to his name."

"I'm not able to read it," I told her. Cursive writing is at best a challenge for me, but cursive writing on an image from twenty years before, on a screen at the wrong angle, was impossible.

"It says, 'Trans. Mendoza.' In the records of Rayborn were references to a Mendoza Communications, which owned a few small stations in Southern California in a town called Reseda."

I did not have to consult a map. "Reseda, California, is less than a thirty-minute drive from North Hollywood," I said.

"You've obviously never driven in the Los Angeles area, but yes, they're very close," Ms. Washburn said. I did not feel it was necessary to remind her I had never traveled outside the tri-state area of New Jersey, New York, and Pennsylvania.

"And here's the thing: Less than a week after your father disappears from the Rayborn payroll, another man named George Kaplan appears on the Mendoza payroll, with the notation that he was transferred from Seattle."

My hand went to my temples, which is something that happens unconsciously when I am thinking. "There were no other transfers from Seattle to Reseda at that time?" I asked.

"No other transfers to Reseda that *year*," Ms. Washburn emphasized. "And the payroll records show Reuben Hoenig on the roster without pay while George Kaplan starts on the payroll the second he goes to Reseda."

It didn't seem to be adding up. "How could they transfer Kaplan to Reseda if he hadn't been on the payroll before the transfer?" I asked.

"The same way they could stop paying your father and keep him listed as an employee," Ms. Washburn said. "If he went to California under the name George Kaplan."

"Can you find an address for George Kaplan?" I asked Ms. Washburn.

She began typing into her system as the phone on my desk rang. I walked over and checked the Caller ID feature, which showed a number I did not recognize.

It was a California exchange, based in the Los Angeles area.

"Ms. Washburn, please monitor this call," I said.

She looked up. "Is it your father?"

"I don't know. Please pick up when I pick up."

Ms. Washburn's eyebrows lowered. "Samuel, are you sure you want me to hear—"

"Please."

I reached for the received and saw her do the same. I nodded and we picked up our desk phones simultaneously.

"Questions Answered," I said. I have trained myself to do so, as the statement really does not mean anything as the opening to a conversation.

The voice on the other end was male and harsh, as if its owner had a mildly sore throat. "Is this Sam Hoenig?" it asked.

I did not introduce myself, as the question had been posed. "I am Samuel Hoenig," I said. "Proprietor of Questions Answered. How may I help you?"

Ms. Washburn looked at me with something like confusion on her face. She said nothing, although I was certain she had employed the mute feature on her phone.

"This is Reuben Hoenig, your father," the man said.

It was what I had expected, of course. But the words sounded strange. I was not able to adequately analyze the problem, other than I had never heard anyone identify himself to me that way before. But that was not the issue at hand right now.

"Would you please give me your address?" I asked. It was the simplest and fastest way to answer Mother's question. Ms. Washburn's expression, however, became more serious, bordering on disapproval.

"What?" Once again my conversation seemed to have taken someone by surprise. I did not know what another person might have said to the father he had not seen since the age of four.

"Your address, please. My mother has requested that I find it, and I promised her I would do so. Please tell me your address." I reached for the pad of notepaper and the pen I kept to my right hand side on the desk.

"I'm not going to tell you my address," the man answered.

That seemed strange. "Why not?" I asked.

"Because I don't want your mother to know where I am," he said.

That was even less reasonable than his previous statement. "Mr. Hoenig," I said, "I am unable to think of a reason you wouldn't want your wife to know your location. I am aware that you are somewhere near North Hollywood or Reseda, California, but my mother has requested your exact location. She is concerned about you based on your own words and feels it is important to get in touch with you directly. If you will not give me your address, may I assume that the telephone number you called on is your own private cellular telephone?"

"Why do you talk like that?" the man asked.

I speak in the same way that everyone else who speaks does, with thoughts coming from my brain and through my vocal system, so the question had the effect of making me pause momentarily to think. Ms. Washburn, I noticed, frowned at the question, probably considering Reuben Hoenig to be rude.

Still, it was not a sentiment I had never heard expressed before, so after a moment I realized what he was really asking. "There are those who would say I have a disorder known as Asperger's Syndrome or a 'high-functioning' form of autism," I explained. "Now may I have your address, or should I give my mother this phone number?"

"It's not my phone," the man said, although even my somewhat undeveloped ability to read tone of voice told me he was lying. "Sam, you have to realize I don't want your mother to be able to find me. It's been a long time and she's not part of my life anymore. Neither are you. So tell her to stop trying to find me and move on with her life, okay?"

I did not care for the way he was casually speaking about my mother, whom he had left more than a quarter-century earlier. "This contact was not initiated by my mother," I reminded him. "This began because you sent her a letter in the mail."

"A letter!" The man appeared to have some difficulty remembering or misunderstood what I was saying. "When?"

I saw no reason to answer the question. "Sir, I have made a promise to my mother that I would find you, and I will. If you refuse to give me your location information, I will be forced to acquire it through other means."

"What?"

"I will find you whether you tell me where you are, or not," I explained. "It will be easier if you tell me."

"Are you threatening me?" he asked.

"I do not believe I am," I said. "It would depend on your definition of a threat. If you are afraid of my being able to find you, then I suppose it is a threat, because I will find you. If you think I'm suggesting you might come to some form of bodily harm—"

The man disconnected the call.

After a moment I replaced the receiver and considered the idea that more than one person had ended a phone call with me very abruptly today. I looked at Ms. Washburn, who was also putting her phone back onto its cradle.

"Well, that did not go very well, Samuel," she said. "I'm sorry."

"I don't see how it was your fault."

"It's something people say. Your father was rude."

"No, he wasn't." I told Ms. Washburn. "My father did not display any behavior at all. The man on the phone was not my father."

SEVEN

"How do you know he wasn't your father?" Mother asked.

We were sitting in the living room of my mother's house, she on the sofa with Ms. Washburn, who had driven me home, on the opposite side. I was seated in the armchair where I could see both women most clearly. I had not been home more than ten minutes and Ms. Washburn had said we should give Mother this news in person like any other client. It was one hour and twenty-three minutes before we would normally be eating dinner. The sun was still visible in the front window behind Mother and Ms. Washburn from my vantage point.

I had not explained my reasoning to Ms. Washburn because she had insisted upon leaving immediately and we usually do not converse in the car while she is driving. In addition, she had said she wanted to hear my explanation at the same time as Mother. I am not sure what her rationale behind that sentiment was, but I assumed it was valid.

"There were a number of gaps in his conversation that made such an indication," I answered. "He reacted with some surprise, which I believe was genuine, when I referred to the letter you received from him yesterday. Apparently he was not aware it had been sent, and possibly not aware it had been written. You are certain, I assume, that you recognize my father's handwriting on that letter."

Mother nodded. "No question," she said.

"I expected as much. So if my father wrote that letter and the man on the phone was unaware that it existed, the man was not my father."

"Could he have some kind of medical condition, a memory issue that might have made him shaky about the letter?" Ms. Washburn asked.

"It is always possible, but better not to make that assumption," I said. "We could decide that anyone we speak to has memory issues and then nothing they say would have any credibility at all."

Mother seemed to wince a bit at the thought. "But Reuben did say this would be the last time I'd hear from him," she said. "I think he's dying or he wouldn't have said that. Something that serious could involve neurological conditions."

"There was more that convinced me," I told them. "He asked me why I speak the way I do."

They sat for a moment and looked at me. I thought the point had been made clearly, but it was obvious Ms. Washburn and Mother did not share that belief. "Surely my father knew I was not a typical boy, even when he left," I continued when I made that realization. "I know I had not received a diagnosis at four, Mother, but I still contend my 'unusual' behavior was a factor in my father's decision to leave New Jersey."

"Oh, Samuel," Mother began.

I did not let her finish. "You are not hurting my feelings, Mother. I am aware that I was not an easy child to raise because I would deal with situations in ways that other children wouldn't. For some people that is a challenge, and that is how you saw it. You met the challenge. My father was, in my estimation, a person for whom it would have been more difficult to handle. I don't believe I am the only reason he left us, but I do think my behavior was not helping to keep him here."

"But your father knowing you were different when you were four would not translate into his knowing how you speak now," Ms. Washburn argued. "He hasn't spoken to you in more than twenty-five years. How does his question prove that the man on the phone wasn't your father?"

"He did not have to have conversations with me to know about my progress," I suggested. I turned toward my mother. "You wrote to my father periodically for all the years he has been away. You did until you no longer had a working address for him, which was after I was 'diagnosed' with an autism spectrum 'disorder.' I assume in all that time my name came up in your letters. Did you speak to him on the phone as well?"

"Early on," Mother said. "Since he moved out of Seattle I haven't had an address or a phone number and I haven't been able to find one."

"But when you were in contact, you told him about me, didn't you?"

"Of course. He's your father."

"And I imagine that my style of speech, particularly when I was younger, was something that came up when the doctors and school administrators were trying to classify me," I continued.

"I didn't leave anything out," Mother said.

"Then he would know, if not exactly what my conversational style is, at least that there was an issue," I said. "He might note that I do not speak like most people, but he would certainly know why that is the case. The man on the phone was not my father."

Ms. Washburn stood up and began walking slowly around the room. This is not a practice designed to elevate the heart rate, like my circuits around the Questions Answered office, but is more a device Ms. Washburn uses to help her think.

"But I don't understand," she began. "What possible reason would the man on the phone have to try and put himself across as your father? And why would your uncle Arthur call him and not your father when that's what he said he would do?"

"How is Arthur?" Mother asked.

"Coarse and bad-tempered," I said. Mother nodded. I looked at Ms. Washburn, who was holding her hands out in front of her as if searching for something casually. "To answer your question, I have no idea why my uncle would direct my query to someone other than my father, but he clearly did, and he did so knowingly because he would have recognized my father's voice on the telephone."

"Do you want me to call Arthur?" Mother asked.

I had actually considered the idea but I shook my head negatively. "I don't believe he would give you my father's address either. He specifically said he felt my father did not want you to have it, but now that the man on the phone has been proven not to be my father there is no way to be sure that is his true intention. In any event, if Arthur was willing only to contact my father—or the man pretending to be my father—on my behalf, I see no reason he would do anything other than that for you."

"I could confront him with the lie he told," Mother suggested. "I've known Arthur a long time and you don't, which is my fault, Samuel. I apologize."

That struck me as unnecessary. "My life is no more enriched to know of him than it was before today," I said. "There is no need for an apology. But I think letting the man in California, if that's where he was, know that we are aware he is pretending to be someone other than himself would be a strategic error. Let's not give up the one advantage we have here. Ms. Washburn and I can use other methods to find Reuben Hoenig."

"Like what?" Ms. Washburn had not stopped walking around the room. She had touched nothing but had examined everything here, although her eyes did not seem to be registering what she saw and had seen before. She was thinking.

"We can begin with George Kaplan," I said. "Tracing him would be a major step forward in answering the question."

"George Kaplan?" Mother said, looking up at Ms. Washburn. "What about George Kaplan?"

Ms. Washburn explained, in a great deal of detail, how she had traced my father's employment records to Reseda, California, after he had left Seattle, Washington, and how the name George Kaplan had appeared on a transfer record at the same time, although no such person had been listed on employee records before that date.

"Why do you ask about the name like that?" Ms. Washburn asked Mother. "Do you recognize it?"

"George Kaplan is a name in the movie *North by Northwest*," Mother said. "He's a fictional man made up by the spies. He doesn't exist, but everybody thinks he does and that's why Cary Grant gets chased all over the country."

I had not seen the film. "Is he a major character in the motion picture?" I asked. "Is there something about his personality that could be significant in our search for my father?"

Mother shook her head. "He's not in the movie at all. He has no real personality. They talk about him until it's discovered he was made up."

Ms. Washburn's eyes registered concern. "He doesn't exist?" Perhaps she was trying to determine Reuben Hoenig's motivation for using the name, but I had another issue that was confounding me.

"If he is not a character on the screen, why do you remember his name so well?" I asked Mother.

"I must have seen it fifty times," Mother said. "*North by Northwest* is your father's favorite movie."

———————

"Would you care to listen to an album by the Beatles?" I asked Ms. Washburn.

Because we had no new information to help answer Mother's question, and because dinner was still scheduled for almost an hour in the future, I had asked Ms. Washburn if she would stay and help me do further research while Mother cooked. Mother had invited Ms. Washburn to stay for dinner. I felt the extra work would make up for the time we had lost leaving the Questions Answered office early. I did pay Ms. Washburn for a full day, after all.

Ms. Washburn had agreed, so now we were in my attic apartment where my computer equipment would help us with our research. It was the first time Ms. Washburn had been there.

She looked around the room, which is fairly large but with a pitched ceiling, for a while, smiling in an odd fashion when she passed my collection of vintage corkscrews, a remnant of a previous special interest of mine that I now found only mildly interesting. She asked no questions initially but seemed to be taking great care to memorize the space and its contents.

"Sure," she said. I did not ask her for a preference, as she had not indicated one, and selected *Help!*, from the motion picture of the same name. It was my joke; I felt we could use all the assistance we could get at this moment. "Do you only listen to the Beatles, Samuel? I don't think I've ever heard you mention another musician."

"The Beatles are one of my most long-standing special interests," I said, "but I have music from many other artists. Would you prefer to listen to another type of music?"

"No, this is fine." She walked to the far end of the room near my bed and spent twelve seconds looking at the nightstand. Then she walked back to the area where my desk and three flat-screen computer monitors were assembled. "What are we working on specifically?"

"George Kaplan. If the name is taken from the Alfred Hitchcock film *North by Northwest*, as my mother suggested, there is a very good chance my father did choose to call himself by that name." I sat down in my usual spot behind the desk and realized I had only one chair in the room. Mother has had some issues with her knees and does not climb the stairs to my apartment, so there had never been a need for another seat until now. I stood up.

"What's wrong?" Ms. Washburn asked.

"There is only one chair. You should take it," I said.

"Oh, that's not necessary."

"I would not be comfortable sitting if you could not," I told her. I probably would have been comfortable, but it is not polite to say so.

Ms. Washburn reached into the bag she carries and took out her laptop computer. She walked across the apartment and sat down on the edge of my bed. "I'll work here," she said. She opened the laptop and started to boot it up.

For a moment I considered protesting, thinking it would be more polite for me to give up my seat, but Ms. Washburn looked quite comfortable where she was and I was certainly used to the position I had taken. I sat down at my desk again.

"If you look for George Kaplan in the North Hollywood area, I'll research the number that called your phone," Ms. Washburn said. "Let's see if we can find out who is pretending to be your father, and maybe why."

I agreed to the plan, although I did not immediately turn to my computer screen. Seeing Ms. Washburn on the edge of my bed was very odd; it was certainly not what I was used to seeing when I looked in that direction. I tried to analyze why the difference was significant but could not find a likely cause.

"Is that okay?" she asked, presumably because I had not answered or begun seeing to the task at hand.

"Certainly." I turned toward my desk to find any records of a George Kaplan in the North Hollywood, California, area. I began with a more general search and found surprisingly few men by that name, although there were numerous others scattered all over the country. One was a man of 108 years, grandson of a slave, who lived in Indiana. After that most of the references were to the character in *North by Northwest*.

When I narrowed the search to the Southern California area the search became more promising. There were no George Kaplans listed in area phone directories, but that was not unusual. Many people now go without a landline phone entirely, and cellular phones are not listed in directories.

There was, however, a business called Kaplan Enterprises which listed as its proprietor a "G. Kaplan." The business was located in North Hollywood.

By itself that was certainly not positive confirmation of any of the theories I had been forming: First, that my father was using the name George Kaplan instead of his own, and second, that the G. Kaplan who owned an as-yet-unspecified business in the area in question was named George. There was no definitive connection between the two.

The last employment record I had for my father was with Mendoza Communications, which operated radio stations in the region. Given his history of leaving jobs, it was not an enormous leap of logic to postulate that he had also put Mendoza Communications behind him. Indeed, given the age my father must have been by now, it was far from certain that he had not retired.

Looking into Kaplan Enterprises, it appeared to be a concern that bought blocks of advertising time on television and radio channels and then sold them—at a profit—to advertisers based on the best time slots and highest viewership statistics. It was a legitimate, or at least legal, business that I would imagine held some uncertainty in that it bought a product at what would normally be considered retail price and then attempted to sell it for a higher cost to the end user.

That would seem to be in sync with the business George Kaplan (and in Seattle, Reuben Hoenig) had been involved with, but it did not provide conclusive evidence. The proof was accumulating, but it was all circumstantial.

"I'm not really finding much with the phone number," Ms. Washburn reported from my left. I did not turn my head to look although there was nothing of particular interest on my screen. "It might be a burner phone or just not listed. But the number itself does show up on a few sites that talk about annoying sales calls. They report that number as calling randomly and trying to sell something without being clear about what."

I shared with her my findings on the dealings of Kaplan Enterprises. I kept looking at my screen and searching on various sites for George Kaplan, but found only the same few references.

"It sounds like that George Kaplan could be the head of the business and might be your father based on what we found in the Mendoza payroll records," Ms. Washburn said.

"I would say it's possible but we have not proven it yet," I responded.

There was a pause and I imagined I could feel Ms. Washburn's gaze on the back of my neck. "Samuel, why aren't you looking at me?" she asked.

I did not turn my head. "I beg your pardon?"

"You heard me. You're staring at your screen like it holds the meaning of life but you're not hitting any keys. You're going out of your way not to look at me when you talk. So what's going on? Are you uncomfortable having me up here in your room?"

I found it was not difficult, after all, to turn and face Ms. Washburn, who had pushed herself onto my bed and was propping her head on one hand while lying almost prone, her laptop computer in front of her eyes. That was slightly disturbing, as the blanket had been displaced in spots, but I faced her and said, "I am not uncomfortable. And this is my apartment."

Ms. Washburn nodded. "My mistake," she said.

"It is an understandable one."

She sat up and leaned toward the foot of the bed. "You're sure you're not uncomfortable? You can't be used to having anyone but yourself up here."

"We are working," I said. "The location of our research is not a relevant variable."

"Of course. About the cell phone. Do you think it's worth pursuing? It seems like whoever uses it is just cold-calling people about some vague business proposition. We could call back on my phone. Whoever the man is behind this, if he is George Kaplan or not, wouldn't recognize the number and might pick up thinking it's a potential client."

"That is a very good idea," I said. "Please get out your cellular phone."

Ms. Washburn did, and I read her the number of the last incoming call at the Questions Answered office. I had already placed my iPhone on my desk, just to the left of my keyboard, because I have a concern about losing it and want to be certain I can glance down and see it whenever I am working. When I am somewhere other than my attic apartment or the Questions Answered office, I will carry the iPhone in the left hip pocket of my trousers and tap it regularly to ensure its continued presence in a known location. I have misplaced items in the past and find it very upsetting.

Ms. Washburn tapped the digits into her cellular phone. We waited for a response as the number rang six times.

Then Ms. Washburn's eyes widened slightly and I heard a voice on the other end of the conversation, although I could not hear what was being said. I was momentarily frustrated that there was no extension to Ms. Washburn's cellular phone allowing me to listen in.

"Yes," she said, her voice slightly nervous. I did not know why she would feel that way until a moment later she said, "I'm calling because there was a call on this phone and I didn't recognize the number." She was pretending to be a potential client of Kaplan Enterprises.

Ms. Washburn listened for eighteen seconds, which is a long time for one person to speak uninterrupted. She made a point of establishing eye contact with me and nodded; yes, this was the same man I had spoken to earlier today who had claimed to be my father.

"Well, what would I be buying?" she asked the man, and there was a response of twelve seconds this time.

It was very disappointing not to hear what the man was saying. I stood and walked to the bed. I stood next to Ms. Washburn, who was still sitting at the foot, leaning slightly back. She was listening closely, then looked up and gestured that I should sit next to her so she could tilt the phone into a position that would allow us both to hear.

I sat very carefully, doing my best not to interfere with the laptop computer, but I could not lean in close enough to clearly hear both ends of the conversation. Ms. Washburn's eyebrows dropped a bit, a sign that she was thinking.

"Do you mind if I put you on speakerphone?" she asked the man. "My husband is here and I'd like him to hear about your proposal."

For a moment I wondered if Simon Taylor, Ms. Washburn's ex-husband, had entered the room, but that was an absurd thought and lasted less than one second. I realized then that I was being cast in the role of Ms. Washburn's husband and had no time to think about it. If I was to speak to the man using Kaplan Enterprises's cellular phone, I would have to modulate my voice, something that is not easy for me. I did not want him to recognize my voice from our earlier conversation, during which he had tried to convince me he was Reuben Hoenig.

"Thank you," she said, which I assumed meant the man had agreed to her request.

She touched the screen of her cellular phone and I heard the same gruff voice, trying this time to sound friendly, say, "Are we all here now?" It was a ridiculous question, since he was the only participant in the conversation present in his location.

I decided not to try a wildly different voice from my own because it would probably sound false, so I simply mumbled, "Yes."

Ms. Washburn nodded, understanding my reluctance to speak loudly. "We're here," she told the man. "I'm sorry; I don't think I got your name." This was an expression. Ms. Washburn was not suggesting she should now own the man's name and use it for herself.

"I'm George Kaplan," he said. "I own the business. And what is your name, honey?"

The idea that this person, whose name was probably *not* George Kaplan, was presumptuous enough to address a woman he had not met with an expression of endearment was somehow irritating to me. Ms. Washburn looked at me and responded to what must have been my facial expression with her right hand, palm down, pushed in a downward motion and shaking her head, indicating I should not be offended by "George Kaplan's" presumed familiarity with her.

"I'm Patricia Longbow," she said. "You can call me Patty." I must have looked surprised because Ms. Washburn stifled a small laugh.

"Hi, Patty. It's nice to meet you. And what is your name, Patty's husband?"

Ms. Washburn shook her head quickly, indicating I should not introduce myself as Samuel Hoenig, which would have been my first reflex, but I was in no need of reminders. "I am Paul," I said quietly and quickly. The Paul McCartney song "The Night Before" was playing on the *Help!* album at that moment.

"Hi, Paul. Now, to bring you up to speed, let me give you the skinny on what I was telling your lovely wife."

There were so many things wrong with that statement I did not know where to begin. My speed was not going to increase or decrease based on the man's statement. There is no such object as a "skinny." Ms. Washburn was not actually my wife, although the bogus Kaplan could not have known that. And there was no way for him to know without using a video feature on the phone whether she was in fact physically attractive or not according to societal standards.

"Yes, please do," I mumbled.

"It's all about speculation," Kaplan said. "It's about making a lot of money. I can't guarantee anything, but I can tell you about some clients who have more than doubled their investment in a matter of days."

"And what we'd do is buy advertising time?" Ms. Washburn said. "That seems strange because we don't have anything we want to advertise." She looked at me and I nodded back. I understood the scene we were playing. I am not comfortable pretending to be someone other than myself, but playing a version of myself with a different name was only mildly bothersome. It helped that Ms. Washburn was, by necessity, doing most of the talking on our end of the conversation.

I did my best to avoid talking directly to her, however, because I was not certain how a husband would address a wife. I knew it would be wrong to call her Ms. Longbow.

"That's right," the man answered. "You're not buying to advertise anything for yourself. You buy the time from us and then sell it to a list of clients who *do* have something they want to get in front of a lot of people. You charge whatever you want for the time, which means you can make as much money as you want."

There were so many flaws in that plan it was difficult to know where to begin. "Is that legal?" Ms. Washburn asked. "It sounds too good to be true." It did not sound good at all to me, but her eyes held a hint of mischief, indicating she knew what she said was not true. I assumed it was what the false Kaplan would want to hear.

That proved to be true. "It's perfectly legal," he said, although I would later find out the practice was legal only in some states. "We even supply you with a list of clients we know will be interested in the time slots you buy from us."

Ms. Washburn's mouth twitched. She was trying to decide what to do next.

I said, "Why don't you sell them the time slots yourself?"

Ms. Washburn shook her head slightly, but it was too late. Perhaps she was concerned that my voice would be recognized, but it was also possible I'd said something inappropriate. It is hard for me to know.

"We have so much volume we'd have to hire too many salespeople," the man said. The answer was practiced; he'd obviously heard this question many times before. Clearly he was now lying. "Frankly, we use you as a sales staff and let you set your own salary based on the rates you charge your clients."

"And what is your rate of markup?" I asked, now forgetting I was playing the role of Paul Longbow (unless Ms. Washburn's character had not taken her husband's name when they married). "What do you pay to buy the time slots and how much do you charge for them?"

Ms. Washburn closed her eyes. I knew now that I'd made a serious error. I felt my jaw tremor and I bit hard on my lips. I felt my right hand begin to move back and forth rapidly.

"Who is this?" Kaplan asked. "Are you ... is this ...?" There was another pause. "Don't call here again." He disconnected the call.

I felt my eyes roll up and my hands clench into fists. I'd acted so stupidly that I had forfeited the interview and ruined Ms. Washburn's cellular phone number to call the man back again.

Then I felt her touch my right hand. I looked down and her hand was on mine. "It's okay, Samuel," she said. "We weren't going to find out much more anyway."

I kept looking at the hand. My anger with myself subsided and was replaced with the thought that this might be a good time to suggest kissing again.

Instead, my mother texted me with the news that dinner was ready.

EIGHT

Ms. Washburn stayed through dinner, which I served at our dining room table. Mother's knee was clearly causing her more pain than usual so I insisted she sit at the table and allow me to serve. Mother does not like to cede that much control under normal circumstances, but tonight she did not argue.

We told her about our findings and the second phone call with the man who had pretended to be my father earlier in the day. Mother listened as she ate, roast beef and baked potato. There was also broccoli, which I dutifully took onto my plate.

"This is very confusing," Mother said. "This man is pretending to be Reuben, but under the name George Kaplan, and he's trying to sell advertising time he's already bought so that you can sell it to someone else?"

"I doubt he expects any of his buyers to sell the television and radio time they have purchased," I said. "If it was sellable he would no doubt be able to make a profit on the time slots himself. This is a way for this man, whomever he might be, to sell off a product he knows is worthless and trick innocent investors into believing they have a chance to become wealthy."

"That shouldn't be legal," Mother said, shaking her head. "But what does it have to do with finding your father, Samuel?"

I finished chewing the bite of food I had taken (I abhor watching people speak with food in their mouths) and said, "If Reuben Hoenig is involved in the scheme, and if it is illegal in the state of California, it is possible he had some reason to think he would not be able to contact you again."

Mother blanched. "You think someone might kill him?" Her voiced sounded choked.

"Of course not," Ms. Washburn said in what was intended to be a soothing tone.

But that wasn't accurate. "It is not possible to be certain about either possibility," I told Mother. "We do not yet know enough about the people involved and how desperate they might be. He might be in danger. But he might not. There is no way to be sure at this moment."

Mother looked concerned, which I supposed was predictable but not necessarily rational. She lowered her eyebrows in thought and cleared her throat. "How close are you to finding his address?" she asked.

"It has proven to be elusive," I admitted. "We know he was, at least, in the North Hollywood area but the addition of a man falsely claiming to be Reuben Hoenig has complicated matters. Ms. Washburn and I need to dig deeper into public records to find his current location. And that hinges on the assumption that he is now using the name George Kaplan, which is not confirmed."

Again it seemed to take a moment for Mother to process what I'd said. "So what are you prepared to do?" she asked.

This confused me. I knew Mother understood my methods because she had seen them at work many times, long before I had opened the Questions Answered office. She was not asking about how I collect data and come to a conclusion. She seemed to be making some other point through her question.

I looked at Ms. Washburn, who had sat back in her chair and was watching Mother's face. She looked slightly surprised and a bit worried, if I was reading her expression correctly.

"Mother," I said, "are you questioning the effort Ms. Washburn and I are investing in your question?"

"Oh, no," she answered. "I believe you're trying as hard as you can." That was something of a relief, as I would least want to disappoint my mother more than any other client. "But I am questioning your motivation."

Ms. Washburn's attention shifted quickly toward me.

"My motivation?" I asked. "You believe that this question carries a lower priority than most in my mind? I assure you that is not the case. I am treating this question as I treat every question I have been asked since I opened the Questions Answered office."

Ms. Washburn nodded. "That's right, Vivian," she said. "Samuel has been acting exactly as he always does when we have a question: He's very serious about finding the right answer."

Mother wiped her mouth with a napkin although I could see nothing on her lips that required removal. She leaned forward with her elbows on the table and her hands, clasped in front of her, supporting her head.

"That's just it," she said. "I would think this question would be special. I expected that you wouldn't treat it like any other job you've been offered. I would think that finding your father would have some importance to you beyond just answering a question I asked."

Any number of impulses were coming to me simultaneously. I had to process conflicting and confusing thoughts. Why would Mother expect me to change my methods for a question when the ones I always used had been almost uniformly successful? Had I done something to suggest I would deviate from my normal pattern inadvertently? Was I actually trying not to answer the question for some reason? I felt the manifestations of what Mother calls a "meltdown" coming on: head shaking, fingers flailing, hands flapping at my sides. I was blinking and found it difficult to stop.

"I didn't mean to upset you," Mother said.

Ms. Washburn, seeing my state of agitation, stood and walked to my side. She put her hand on my upper arm, which focused my attention and stopped some of the larger "stimming" actions. I felt my mood slightly dissipate. Even in that moment I saw Mother watching and looking directly at Ms. Washburn's hand. Her gaze moved to Ms. Washburn's face when she spoke.

"Vivian, of all people you should know that Samuel attacks a question the same way because that's how his mind works. The circumstances of the question don't factor into his choices." Ms. Washburn pulled her chair toward mine and sat next to me, but when she saw that I was regaining control of my body, she removed her hand from my arm. "I don't understand why you'd think he would act differently."

Mother's face, which showed concern, forced itself into a smile. She looked at me. "I'm sorry, Samuel," she said. "I didn't mean to accuse you of anything. I'm very upset about this whole business with your father and I'm anxious for something to happen quickly. I don't think it's your fault. Do you understand? Can you forgive me?"

I pondered her questions. I did understand the words Mother was saying, but doubted they represented the point of her asking. She wanted to know if I could empathize with her emotions, and I was not sure that would be possible. The second question was easier to answer so I addressed it first.

"I see nothing to forgive," I said. "You have done nothing intentionally to hurt my feelings. You do not need forgiveness, Mother." I looked at Ms. Washburn and nodded my thanks. I could tell she understood. She was becoming the only person I knew—including my mother—with whom I could communicate nonverbally.

"Thank you, Samuel," Mother said. "I didn't mean to question your methods. I'm sure what you're doing will help find your father. But if this Kaplan man is a dead end, what is there left to do?"

I will confess that I took a certain amount of pride in the fact that it was Ms. Washburn who responded. I have done my best to include her in every aspect of the Questions Answered business and that meant showing her how I go about researching a question. So when she could analyze and plan the next steps before I could speak, I felt she had absorbed what she'd seen exceptionally well.

"Kaplan isn't a dead end," she told Mother. "Just because we couldn't keep him on the phone doesn't mean we can't find the address of his business. That could give us a jumping-off point. And we have some other leads."

I reached into my pocket to confirm that my iPhone was still there and it gave me an idea. "Mother," I said, "you can help us with this question, at least in ensuring that we have been correct about one assumption. Would you mind listening to something?"

Mother's eyes narrowed in puzzlement. "What can I do?" she asked.

I held out the phone. "I was recording some of the conversation Ms. Washburn and I had with the man who identified himself as George Kaplan. You can tell us whether it is indeed my father's voice."

Mother blinked. She did not move, thinking. "Go ahead," she said.

Ms. Washburn looked at me but I could not read her expression. This seemed like the most obvious of tasks; I would play the recording and Mother could confirm what we already suspected. But I am empathetic enough to understand that there was an emotional charge over the situation even if I could not identify it.

I negotiated to the application and played the section of recording. "Hi, Patty," the man's voice said in a surprisingly clear tone. "And what is your name, Patty's husband?"

Mother held up her hand, palm out, almost as soon as the first word was played. She shook her head. "That's not your father," she told me.

"You are certain?"

"Absolutely. I'd know his voice, especially over a phone, and that wasn't it." Mother let out a long breath as if relieved. I could not imagine what she might have found so upsetting that she had to brace herself, but that she was releasing pent-up tension was palpable.

"Did you recognize the man's voice?" Ms. Washburn asked. It was the very question I was about to pose.

Mother shook her head again. "I've never heard that voice before."

"Very well," I said. "We have eliminated one possibility." I put the phone back in my pocket and patted it again.

"Samuel," Mother said quietly, "we need to find your father soon. I think something is very wrong and he needs our help."

It occurred to me that there had been many times Mother especially could have used some assistance from my father and did not receive it. But there was no point in arguing with her when she had her mind set the way it was now. My mother can be a very stubborn woman when she believes the reason to be important.

"I understand your desire for a prompt answer," I said truthfully. I did understand Mother's concern but I did not share it. That would not have an impact on my efforts to answer the question. "But there is no shortcut that will provide us with an address more quickly."

Ms. Washburn was clearly doing something with an application on her phone. I did not distract her and assumed she would make her actions clear when the time was appropriate.

"I think what I need to see from you is some passion for the project," Mother said. "I know how you feel about your father but he is still your father."

That did not seem to make much sense. "He has always been my father in the biological sense," I said. "You can't expect me to harbor warm emotional feelings for someone I barely remember. I haven't seen Reuben Hoenig in twenty-seven years."

"Neither have I," Mother said. I was aware of that fact and did not see its relevance.

Luckily Ms. Washburn interrupted the conversation. "I have an address on Kaplan Enterprises," she said. "It's in Reseda. From the Google Earth image I'd have to say it's located in somebody's house."

She turned her phone to show me the photograph taken for the Google Earth project, which claims to document virtually every area on the planet. Reseda seemed like a very working-class community from the image, with a one-story home centered in the viewer. It was brown with a stucco exterior and a bare area where the lawn would have been, but it was devoid of any vegetation at all.

"That is Kaplan Enterprises?" I asked, although it was fairly clear Ms. Washburn had been making that point. It was somewhat surprising that a business would have its headquarters in this structure, but there was certainly no physical limitation on the kind of commerce Kaplan had claimed to be conducting. There would be no need for the extra cost of office space.

"That's it," Ms. Washburn said. "Assuming the address is right, but I'm betting it is."

"May I see?" Mother held out her hand and Ms. Washburn passed the phone to her. Mother examined it carefully. Ms. Washburn turned it to a horizontal position to maximize the size of the image. Mother looked at it closely and her expression became even more serious than it had been until now. "Is it possible to see this bigger?" she asked.

Ms. Washburn and I passed a somewhat confused look but the tote bag Ms. Washburn keeps with her was handy and she extracted her laptop computer from it and turned it on. After the computer had successfully booted up its software applications, she navigated to the proper page, which took two minutes and sixteen seconds. No one said a word while she did her work.

"Here," Ms. Washburn said, turning the notebook computer's screen toward Mother. "Do you see something that makes a difference?"

"Yes," Mother said. I stood and walked toward her, standing behind her chair to see when she pointed at the screen. Ms. Washburn did the same. She indicated a spot in the home being displayed, in the front window. There was a dark silhouette behind a sheer white curtain.

"That's your father, Samuel," Mother said.

NINE

THE IDEA THAT MOTHER could identify, through a grainy image on a computer screen taken through a curtain and seen only in shadow, the figure of a person—I could not even definitely say it was male—as my father was illogical. But I could not convince my mother of that fact.

"I recognize him," she said firmly. "I know that man and I know what he looks like. That's your father. You know where he is."

Since that would have seemed to end the business of answering Mother's question, I could have agreed with her, written down the address and moved on to my next client. But the argument was so deeply flawed that I did not feel comfortable doing so.

"Mother," I said, "the shadow on that curtain is barely even recognizable as to gender or gross physical characteristics. You have not seen Reuben Hoenig in twenty-seven years, so you have no idea how he has aged. There is no discernible facial information in this photograph. And even if we could determine that the figure is indeed your husband, the image was taken at least a year ago and probably less recently. We have no reason to believe that Reuben Hoenig, if he was at that address when the picture was taken, would still be there."

"That's him," Mother insisted, as if her certainty were enough to disprove all the arguments I had just made. "That's your father. Now you need to go to California and help him, Samuel."

Ms. Washburn, who had not attempted to influence the conversation at all, made a small choking sound.

Because my personality traits indicate some aspects of an autism-spectrum disorder, it is something of a given that I do not travel. Routine and a comfortable reliance on predictability are very important to me. Travel removes all of that and replaces it with random happenings, a complete loss of control over one's personal situation, and surroundings that are not at all familiar and can contain virtually any danger or discomfort. I had never been inside an airplane. I had been inside airports only to escort Mother when she was traveling. I had never left the state of New Jersey other than to go to New York City on rare occasions and once to travel into Pennsylvania, an experience I found very disquieting.

"I see no reason to go anywhere," I told Mother. "You asked Ms. Washburn and me to find Reuben Hoenig's address. I do not believe we have verifiably accomplished that goal, but if you are willing to accept this house as an answer to your question, I will accede to your wishes. However, there is no practical reason for me to travel away from home. That will not verify the address. I have been asked no other question."

Mother's eyes brightened and I saw her reach into a pocket on the apron she was wearing, but I held up a finger to stop her because I had seen her do something very similar before.

"Please don't reach for some money and ask me a second question, Mother," I said. "You know the rules I have set up for Questions Answered, and I can't ignore them even for you."

Her face dimmed. Her shoulders slumped. I thought she might start to cry, the last thing I would ever want to cause.

"Samuel," Mother said, "I don't think you understand exactly how important this is to me. The letter says your father has gotten himself into some kind of trouble and he believes he might never be able to communicate with us again. I won't allow that. I won't allow it for me, I won't allow it for your father, and I won't allow it for you. I've gone too long without making it an issue; you should know your father. It's my fault you don't, and now that there's a crisis it's time to correct that problem."

I had sat in a chair to Mother's left and taken her hand, a gesture she usually finds comforting in some way. But I could not agree to her terms now because they simply made no sense. "There is no evidence that Reuben Hoenig is in crisis," I said.

"Why won't you call him your father?" she asked, her voice distressed.

"Because I have never felt like I had a father," I told her. "It is true that biologically he fits that description, which I assume because you have told me it is so and I have no reason to disbelieve you. But you raised me, Mother. You have been my family. Reuben Hoenig has never attempted to contact me. I feel nothing for him. And the letter you received does not change that fact. Indeed, your assumption that there is some dire situation into which he has fallen is not borne out by the words he wrote. He simply wrote that you should not expect to hear from him again. It is possible that he does not want to have any further contact."

Mother shook her head violently. "I will not believe that. Something is desperately wrong and you need to fly out there to help him." She turned to make direct eye contact with me, which I had been trying to avoid. "I know him, Samuel. It's true that you don't, so you need to rely on my instincts because you have no facts. I'm aware of how difficult it is for you to think about flying three thousand miles across the country." (The actual distance is 2,452 miles as estimated by the

Federal Aviation Administration.) "But this is family and family has to be important. You're strong, Samuel. You're capable of more than you think you are." Rather unfairly in my view, she turned toward Ms. Washburn. "Janet, convince him. You understand, don't you?"

Before she could answer, I said, "Please don't ask Ms. Washburn to take sides between us in an argument, Mother. It is not fair to her."

I think Ms. Washburn looked relieved.

"You're right. Do you see how upset I am, Samuel? I would never do that to Janet if I was thinking straight." Mother closed her eyes tightly, perhaps in an attempt to fight off or to conjure tears; it was difficult to know which. "Do you see?"

Clearly, I could see. My vision was unimpaired by what had been said. But I was at a loss to decipher Mother's meaning here. "Do I see?" I repeated to her.

"That this is very important to me."

"Of course I am aware of that," I answered. "You have made it quite clear. But if you feel there is some problem with Reuben Hoenig and only by going to California can it be fixed, surely you should be the one to go. You know him and you obviously have an emotional stake in the matter that I lack." It was the obvious and most factual analysis of the situation.

Somehow these truths eluded Mother. She looked as if I had insulted her. "You know I can't do that, Samuel," she said in a low voice. "My health won't permit it."

Mother's heart problem in the past had been very disturbing for me, and it had taken two years before I was willing to leave her alone in the house again. But since that time I had seen her regain her strength and return to the level of activity she had known before. Indeed, she now made sure to walk at least a mile every day to maintain aerobic fitness and was more careful about her diet than before she had been hospitalized. So to hear her say now that her health was again an issue stopped me from replying as I processed the information.

"Your health," I said.

"Oh, I'm all right," Mother said. "But my knees aren't going to stand up to a trip to Los Angeles and I'm not as young as I used to be. Even if I could get out there, if there's some kind of situation your father has gotten into, what could I do?"

I was having some difficulty understanding what it was Mother expected me to do if I were to travel to the Los Angeles area and find Reuben Hoenig. Perhaps she felt that if he was in some physical danger my training in tae kwon do might be an asset, but I had not kept up my training and could not be considered at all a master of the form even when I had kept current.

"What could *I* do?" I asked. "I research questions, Mother. I am not a bodyguard."

"Samuel." My mother's word sounded more like a moan.

Ms. Washburn drew a breath, causing Mother and me to instinctively look in her direction. She shook her head. "This is a family matter," she said. "It's not something I should be involved with."

If she was not interested in voicing an opinion I would support that decision, but Mother looked at Ms. Washburn and said, "You are family, Janet. Say what's on your mind. Nobody will think ill of you."

I was not sure how Mother could predict what anyone would think, but it was equally difficult to imagine a circumstance under which I would think badly of Ms. Washburn, so I did not question or argue. I looked at Ms. Washburn.

"We've done everything we can from here, Samuel," she said. "We need to go to California."

I had not expected that pronouncement. I'm sure my facial expression was exhibiting surprise, because Ms. Washburn again put her hand on mine as if to calm my rising emotion. She was misreading the situation; I was not becoming upset because she had disagreed with my assessment.

I was realizing two things: First, that now I would probably be traveling to find Reuben Hoenig more than 2,400 miles away, which was exactly what I had not wanted to do.

Second, Ms. Washburn was including herself on the trip. Perhaps I was going to North Hollywood, California, but in my discomfort I would continue to have a familiar face at my side.

But that second point was not strongly registering in my mind yet. I was simply picturing the difficulties of traveling and they were not pleasant ideas for someone like me to face.

I looked from Ms. Washburn's face, which was concerned, to Mother's, which was guardedly hopeful, if I was interpreting it correctly. What I was about to do would require meticulous planning and an unusual amount of courage on my part, which is not something I often find myself needing to display.

"Very well," I said. "We will go to California."

Immediately I began to regret the decision.

TEN

WHEN THE PUBLIC ADDRESS system, which seemed unnecessary since the woman speaking into the microphone was less than ten feet from us—announced our flight was ready to board, I did not move.

Ms. Washburn stood up and reached for the tote bag she always uses to carry her laptop computer. The bag was now overstuffed with extra items she would not need on a normal day. She had added extra toiletries, a small pillow, an eyeshade, a book, a change of undergarments (a piece of information I would have been more comfortable without), and three protein bars. "They don't feed you on the plane anymore," she had told me.

I knew that fact, having spent the past three days reviewing and researching airline and hotel procedures and searching for facts that might have made this excursion unnecessary. I had unfortunately found none of the latter and now Ms. Washburn and I were sitting in Terminal C at Newark Liberty International Airport. To be more accurate, Ms. Washburn was standing and I was still sitting.

I was wishing this were a normal day.

"It's okay, Samuel," Ms. Washburn said quietly. "Air travel is statistically much safer than car travel." That fact did not bring me solace; I have accepted the necessity of automobile travel but have never become comfortable with it. I do not drive a car, but now I wished I could pilot an airliner. Ceding that level of control was a terrifying thought. I wondered if I could sit in the cockpit with the captain to observe his technique and all safety measures.

That was a joke.

"I am aware of the statistics," I said. Against my will, I stood up and picked up the small backpack I had taken for the plane ride. After having consulted various sources for the size of a bag to place under the seat in front of a passenger I had purchased the backpack, which fit the parameters of 19 inches wide by 9.5 inches tall as specified by the airline Ms. Washburn had selected for us to use.

Having consented to this trip—while still believing it was unnecessary and ill-advised—I had suggested taking at least two months to research the air travel involved and the area in which Ms. Washburn had booked two hotel rooms near Reseda but actually in Canoga Park, California. Given the reportedly deplorable state of mass transportation in the area, Ms. Washburn had secured a rental car reservation for the three days we would be in Southern California. I had agreed to no more than that amount of time, concluding that if we were unsuccessful in finding Reuben Hoenig in three days, the problem would not be one of time but attributable to a lack of reliable data.

None of this planning held any comfort for me. The idea of being that far from home for that long a period of time was frankly terrifying, and more than once I had considered informing Mother that I would not make the trip. I even thought of letting Ms. Washburn go alone and monitoring her progress by phone and computer, but that seemed somehow cowardly and I did not voice the suggestion.

I submerged myself in the best possible preparation for what I felt was a doomed expedition. The size of the baggage allowed was only the beginning. While a passenger is also entitled to have one suitcase of 9 inches by 14 inches by 22 inches that can be stored in what the airlines refer to as an "overhead compartment," I had chosen to pack one wheeled bag Mother kept in our basement for her sporadic travels. I had never needed it before. It was larger than the overhead bag specifications, which would require me to pay the airline a fee to store the luggage while I was on the flight. That seemed an odd thing for which to require payment but there are no airlines making this flight that would waive the fee so I paid it and planned to pack strategically.

Given that this was not a leisure trip, I made sure the backpack I purchased could reasonably store my MacBook laptop computer. I would need more than my iPhone after reaching California and was not comfortable with Ms. Washburn's notebook computer for both of us. That was the first thing I packed.

In accordance with the advice given by a number of websites, I also packed toothpaste and a toothbrush in special cases I obtained at the local drug store. Then I put the cases inside a sealable plastic bag to ensure there would be no leakage in or out. One small bottle of shampoo, under the 3.4-ounce limit allowed by the Transportation Security Administration, was also well sealed and placed in a separate plastic bag.

The front pocket of the backpack held my driver's license and my passport, despite the fact that we would not be leaving the country on the flight. If for some reason Ms. Washburn and I found it necessary to travel to Mexico to find Reuben Hoenig, the passport would be essential. I considered that an unlikely possibility but one must plan for unlikely possibilities when traveling so far.

Online sources also recommended a change of underwear, which I did not pack in the bag to accompany me in the passenger compartment. If my suitcase was not brought with us to Los Angeles, a lack of proper undergarments would not be my first priority. Those can be purchased in any city. I would be considerably more concerned about such items as the laptop computer, which holds all my personal data, the passport, and the water bottle, which I had brought to the airport empty and filled from bottles of spring water I had purchased after passing through the security checkpoint.

That itself had been a major source of anxiety for me. If I had been called for a "random search," as the Transportation Security Administration terms it, I do not think I would have been able to contain my anxiety. I had been careful not to wear a belt or carry any coins or metal objects with me when leaving for the airport. The passenger in line ahead of me, a middle-aged man in a Los Angeles Dodgers t-shirt and cargo shorts, had been required to empty all his pockets and had then been probed with a metal-detecting electronic wand after passing through the metal detector. A very unpleasant beeping noise, which caused me to cover my ears with my hands, had resulted from his stepping into the device, and an employee of the Transportation Security Administration had run the electronic wand over the man's body, which caused him to look confused and made me break out in a cold sweat. The sunglasses he had hung on the round collar of his shirt had proven to be the trigger for the beeping and the man was allowed to go on his way.

I was very grateful that no such sound was emitted after I passed through, put my hands up as instructed, and was scanned by a fluoroscope to prove I was not carrying anything not permitted onto the plane. Ms. Washburn, the next passenger after me, was also not "flagged" for any special treatment.

Now at the gate, I took a very deep breath. This was the moment I had been dreading, although other passengers seemed to have been virtually uncontained in their anticipation. Ms. Washburn looked at me. "It'll be fine," she said. "Come on. Everybody's getting ahead of us in line."

I stood still and looked at her. "Aren't our seats reserved?" I asked. "Why is it important to be on the plane sooner?"

Ms. Washburn smiled. "Yes, our seats are reserved," she said. "But the overhead bins aren't, and there won't be room for our bags up there if we don't get on right away. Don't worry, Samuel." She held out her hand.

I did not take it. "I don't have a bag to put into the overhead bin," I reminded her. "You go ahead. I'll join you shortly."

Her eyes narrowed. "I'm not sure you will." The hand gesture was repeated. "Come on, Samuel."

There was a short discussion after which we boarded the plane. The inside of the aircraft was extremely cramped and narrow, two things that do not appeal to people like me. I think Ms. Washburn noticed my breathing becoming shallow and frequent. She looked up at my face as I followed her down the aisle toward our seats.

"You're white as a sheet, Samuel," she said. "Are you all right?"

"I don't think so. Perhaps we shouldn't go."

She avoided smiling, but I believe it took some effort. "Nice try." Ms. Washburn opened the overhead bin above our seats and found it full with other passengers' baggage. The thought of mingling my belongings with so many strangers' made me feel relieved I had not brought anything to store in there. Ms. Washburn sighed. "No place to put this one."

She walked down the aisle a bit farther and found an open bin where she stored the bag she had brought. "Is that ethical?" I asked when she returned to the aisle containing our seats. "Now some other passenger will have no storage space."

"It's the rule of the jungle on an airplane, Samuel," Ms. Washburn answered. "Do you want the window seat or the one in the middle?" She gestured toward the row.

"This is my first time on an airplane," I reminded her. "I do not know which is better, but I am fairly sure it will not help me to see clearly out the window as we travel."

"Some people find the middle seat a little confining," Ms. Washburn warned. "Will that bother you?"

"The whole trip bothers me." I was acting more irritable than I should have, but my anxiety level was not falling as the takeoff time approached. "We can find Reuben Hoenig from home."

A man in sweatpants and a jersey bearing the logo of the New York Rangers hockey team stood in the aisle behind me and pushed a little into my back. "Let's go, pal," he said. "You're holding everybody up."

"I am trying to decide whether I should take the window seat or the middle seat," I informed him.

"Window," the man said. "Now, sit."

"I don't think you understand," I explained. "This is my first flight and I am trying to determine what is the safer alternative."

"Doesn't matter," he answered. "If the plane goes down, we're all dead no matter what seat you're in. Sit."

"Come on, Samuel," Ms. Washburn said, again taking my hand. "I'll take the window."

It took a great deal of effort to sit in the center seat after Ms. Washburn positioned herself in the tight quarters and maneuvered her tote bag under the seat in front of her. I stared at the man in the Rangers jersey for a moment and then sat down in my designated spot.

"I do not understand hockey fans," I told her after I had carefully placed my bag in the area specified. I would have preferred to hold it, but a flight attendant passing by said that was not an option, "for your own safety." I did not see how a small backpack was going to be a threat to my safety, but the attendant moved on before I could ask her the question.

A small man took the aisle seat next to me just as the flight door closed. He stared straight ahead and had no baggage with him. I thought it would have been best for me to have acted as he did, but it was too late now. I would have the backpack washed when we arrived in Los Angeles.

It is probably best to omit the details of the takeoff. I was in an agitated state, which some people in the plane appeared not to comprehend. Ms. Washburn tried to explain, but it was hard to hear over the engine noise and my own vocalizations.

Once the plane had reached its cruising altitude and I realized there would be another five hours on this aircraft before we landed, I became more acclimated to the surroundings, although I was never comfortable. But it would have been considerably more difficult to have the airline abort the flight and return to New Jersey than to contain myself until we reached California, so I opted for the latter.

Ms. Washburn took out her laptop computer despite the fact that there was no Internet access on this flight. She was searching through notes on the question we were researching, she said, because she thought she'd missed something in the conversation I'd had with my uncle Arthur and it was bothering her. "I have the time now," she said.

Given little to do, I still did not remove my MacBook because I was concerned about draining its battery before we arrived in Canoga Park. I wanted to read the magazine in the seat pocket facing me, but it had been well thumbed by previous passengers so I asked the flight attendant for a fresh copy, which she supplied. The articles were not especially enlightening.

The man in the aisle seat next to me put on a pair of eye shades and leaned his seat back to the point that I believed the woman sitting behind him could see the bald spot on the back of his head. He soon began to snore loudly and frequently.

I found it difficult to close my eyes during the flight. The motion of the aircraft was unpredictable. The sound of the engines coupled with the air conditioning and cabin pressure made sleep virtually impossible. I was trapped in a seat between Ms. Washburn, whose laptop computer's screen was glowing dimly, and the sleeping man to my right, who added to the noise and commandeered the armrest between us. I pulled my own arms close in to my torso, sat straight and tried very hard not to think about the 35,000 feet of air between my body and the ground.

Looking forward to spending time in a hotel room that was not my own didn't calm me down at all. The total lack of control over my life this trip would necessitate was not only inconvenient; it was alarming. And the only way to return to the life I very much preferred would be to go through this process again in the opposite direction.

It was very difficult not to cry out. A few times I felt myself shake with frustration. Ms. Washburn noticed once, put her hand on my triceps and told me there was nothing to worry about. I appreciated the sentiment, but she was mistaken—there was a great deal to worry about.

Out of sheer boredom coupled with anxiety, if that is possible, I forced myself to concentrate on the question we were flying to Los Angeles to answer for Mother. The few facts we had managed to establish so far indicated that at some time in the past year or two Reuben Hoenig—who had left New Jersey twenty-seven years before and arrived in Reseda, California, by way of Tulsa, Oklahoma, and Seattle, Washington—might have been standing in the window of a structure owned by Kaplan Enterprises, a company which bought and sold advertising time on radio and television. The legality of that enterprise was questionable but probably verifiable. I would ask Ms. Washburn to check with an attorney in California on the possible difficulties such an operation might face.

According to employee records from Mendoza Communications it appeared—again, without confirmation—that Reuben Hoenig was now operating under the name George Kaplan. This name was taken from an Alfred Hitchcock film, *North by Northwest*, which my mother said was a favorite of Reuben's. The reasons behind that change were not clear. One obvious possibility, given the text of the letter my mother had received, was that Reuben had found himself in some kind of legal difficulty in Seattle and needed an alternate identity, which might have precipitated his transfer to Mendoza in Reseda.

But we had absolutely no facts that were clearly established other than that my mother had received a letter she said was in her husband's handwriting.

The fact that Arthur Hoenig, my uncle living in Chicago, had first refused to supply an address for his brother and then contacted someone in the Los Angeles area—either Reuben or the man who had impersonated him on the telephone—to alert him to my call, was confusing. If Reuben was interested in hearing from Mother and by extension me, he would not have needed the intermediary. If he was not interested in contact, he could easily have ignored Arthur's message and avoided any further communication.

So it was puzzling that someone pretending to be Reuben called my cellular phone and then answered Ms. Washburn's under the name George Kaplan, which we had assumed Reuben was using.

The complete lack of verifiable information about this question was almost as worrisome as the rattling of the airplane and the snoring of the little man in the aisle seat. I would have liked to have done some walking up and down the aisle, particularly with the possibility of deep vein thrombosis, which can cause life-threatening blood clots on a cross-country flight. But his presence made it difficult to move.

I knew hydration was a priority and had my water bottle filled in the backpack. I was careful not to drink too much, as the idea of using an airplane restroom was not in any way acceptable. I also did some sitting ankle turns and other exercises that I had discovered on various online sites.

"Look at this," Ms. Washburn said as I was contemplating climbing over the snoring man to do some walking in the aisle. She turned her laptop computer screen toward me and tilted it up for me to get a better viewing angle.

The screen showed a map of Reseda, California, and was delineated in terms of the neighborhood's zoning. Reseda is actually a part of Los Angeles itself, not a separate community. So the local laws pertaining to Reseda would be those of the city as a whole.

"Look at the zoning for the street where Kaplan Enterprises is located," Ms. Washburn said. "It's zoned as a residential area."

"Yet George Kaplan, whomever he may be, is operating a business out of that property," I said, nodding. "Not a huge offense, really. People are running businesses from their homes much more frequently now than they did before. If Kaplan Enterprises doesn't have a large number of employees or use any heavy machinery, it's unlikely that would be a legal problem."

"Not usually, but look here." Ms. Washburn pointed at a spot on the map's legend in the bottom right-hand corner. It read, "Property assessment 2014, pending."

I didn't immediately understand the significance. "If the properties were assessed for taxation in 2014, the property would be taxed under that estimate," I said.

"But it's pending," Ms. Washburn countered. "I did some research after I noticed that. The real assessments are due this year, maybe as soon as next month. And with the water problems the area is having, the city is looking to raise as much tax money as it can. So a business running out of a house might be assessed higher than it would have been then."

"If it is assessed as a business," I said.

"Exactly."

I considered the fact. "Is this really about the local assessment of a house?" I asked.

ELEVEN

I ASSUMED AN EXPERIENCE traveler would have considered the rest of our cross-country flight routine. For me it held stretches of excruciating boredom punctuated by moments of extreme discomfort and infrequent swells of alarm.

Still, we arrived at Los Angeles International Airport on time and "taxied" for a long period before arriving at Gate 37B. I was anxious to leave the aircraft as soon as possible, but Ms. Washburn pointed out that it had been necessary to store her bag in a bin behind the row in which we sat, so even after the snoring man (who had awakened virtually at the moment the airplane's wheels touched the runway) had trundled up the aisle and off the aircraft, we had stayed behind until she could retrieve it. I felt this was a result of her stowing her luggage inefficiently but did not voice that opinion.

After finding my bag at the carousel in the luggage area—something with which I was more familiar, having done so with Mother after she traveled—Ms. Washburn successfully navigated us to the car rental shuttle area. After six minutes the proper van arrived to take us to the facility on airport property where the transaction could be completed. There was yet another line before reaching the counter, where Ms. Washburn showed various forms of identification and signed seven insurance waivers before being directed to a bright blue Kia Soul in a nondescript parking area.

Ms. Washburn had brought the portable Global Positioning System unit she usually uses in her Kia Spectra in New Jersey, and because there was no mounting device for it in the rental car—the company prefers one pay extra for a vehicle equipped with the capability—asked me to hold it and program it with the address of the hotel in which she had reserved rooms. I took the relevant information from a printout she furnished and Ms. Washburn steered out of the rental car parking area and began driving to Canoga Park.

The trip, from information derived on the Global Positioning System device, would be one of 26.3 miles, but it took 57 minutes to navigate the startling amount of traffic. We spoke very little other than for me to reiterate or elaborate on instructions given by the voice emanating from the device.

"I thought New Jersey traffic was bad," Ms. Washburn said at one juncture. I would have concurred but I wanted her to concentrate on the road and the enormous number of vehicles inhabiting it.

We reached the hotel and I watched as Ms. Washburn approached the desk in the lobby where check-in is accomplished. Since this was my first stay in a hotel I had done some research on the subject, but this facility did not seem to have employees who carried one's luggage to the room. Ms. Washburn and I were responsible for our own. Each of us was given a key card for a room, and Ms. Washburn reiterated that they be adjacent rooms, which the employee behind the counter assured her they were.

Ms. Washburn showed me how to use the key card because it was not the same as a debit card used in a store. I opened the door to Room 306 and entered behind Ms. Washburn. It is polite to let the lady enter first.

"Do you want this to be your room?" she asked once we had both wheeled our larger cases inside. "It is okay?"

I had thought the room assignments had been predetermined. "How will the other room differ?" I asked.

"Probably it won't at all."

I assessed the room. It was not the same as the elaborate suites I have seen in motion pictures, but it appeared to be clean and did not bear many traces of previous guests. I had asked Ms. Washburn if we could reserve rooms that had never accommodated anyone else but she said that was not possible "unless you're there the minute they finish building the place." It was not my first choice but the room seemed the best possible alternative.

It held a rather large bed, much wider than the one I have at home, a desk with a chair not dissimilar to mine in the attic apartment. A low armoire had a flat-screen television mounted on top and a taller dresser had four drawers at its bottom and two doors above. There was also a small refrigerator that, when I opened it, held a number of small items including a bottle of spring water which I began to reach for.

"Never take anything out of the honor bar," Ms. Washburn warned, and I retracted my hand. "They'll charge you an arm and a leg for that stuff. We can get water bottles in a drug store or something and you can put those in the fridge."

I considered the adage about a company taking one's limbs in exchange for a product rather nauseating, but did not mention my slight revulsion to Ms. Washburn. Instead I nodded and closed the door of the small refrigerator.

The bathroom required closer inspection but there appeared to be no obvious signs of unsanitary conditions. Even the drinking vessels were covered in plastic. I turned toward Ms. Washburn. "I believe this room will be satisfactory," I said. I would have preferred to reverse the trip and fly home to sleep tonight but knew that was not possible.

"I'll unpack in my room and then maybe we can plot strategy and find some dinner," Ms. Washburn said, reaching for the handle of her wheeled suitcase. "How does that sound to you?"

It sounded like Ms. Washburn's normal conversational tone. "It is fine," I said. "Should I come with you?"

She smiled a crooked smile I did not understand. "Why don't you unpack and I'll text you when I'm ready to leave," she suggested. "We need a break."

"I am not going to unpack," I said. "I prefer to leave my belongings in my own bag."

Ms. Washburn hesitated briefly and nodded. "Well, I *am* going to unpack. You can lie down for a while or whatever you like. I'll text you, Samuel." She turned and wheeled her suitcase out of my room.

I did not intend to place my clothing into the drawers provided by the hotel because I had no idea who had been using that furniture before me or how recently and thoroughly it had been cleaned. There was some utility to removing the three plastic bags I had packed containing my toothpaste and toothbrush as well as a few toiletries. Those I placed, sealed, on the counter next to the sink in the bathroom.

The sun was beginning to set when I walked out and stood in the center of the room. I had seen hotel rooms depicted in motion pictures and television programs of course, but I had not been prepared for the somewhat clinical smell of the carpet and the walls, something that must have been overwhelming because I do not have a strong sense of smell.

I walked to the large windows overlooking the parking lot of the hotel. If I looked up I could see the Santa Monica Mountains in the distance. Closer to where I stood lights were beginning to glow. The sky was clear and a darkening blue without a cloud to be seen. I had never felt so isolated before.

I decided that Ms. Washburn's advice, which had always proven to be helpful, was worth following. I lay down on the bed without removing the bedspread or rearranging the pillows. It felt like sleeping in someone else's home and my childhood fear of doing the wrong thing was strong in this place. I folded my hands on my midsection and stared at the ceiling, which was unremarkable.

It was going to be a very long four days (including travel back) and three nights.

Nonetheless I must have fallen asleep because the next thing I noticed was the tone from my iPhone indicating that I had received a text message. The room was almost completely dark now except for the lights of the city visible through the windows. I pulled the iPhone out of my pocket and looked at it.

The message read READY FOR DINNER? It was from Ms. Washburn.

We decided to meet in the hallway outside our rooms and then took the elevator to the lobby, although I privately would have been more comfortable with the stairs. Now that we were not carrying any luggage the relative safety of a stairwell, rather than an elevator I had not personally inspected, would have been my preference. Ms. Washburn probably would have acceded to my wishes, but I was trying to seem "normal" on this trip although I wasn't certain why that was a priority.

Ms. Washburn had done some research on her cellular phone and discovered a restaurant called Just Nice within walking distance of the hotel. I would have preferred to find an outlet of a national chain like Applebee's, but Ms. Washburn said there were none within a reasonable distance and certainly not one to which we could walk. I decided not to double-check her research on the subject.

The restaurant was small and had a menu consisting of recognizable foods, which is a priority for me. I did have to ask that my small sirloin steak be served without kale or plantains and the server, who informed us his name was Blaine, said that would not be a problem.

Ms. Washburn ordered a diet soda and I drank water, which we had to request because of the area's severe drought. Once Blaine left to take our orders to the kitchen, Ms. Washburn asked what our plan for the next morning would be.

"The most direct option is for you to drive to the address we have for Kaplan Enterprises and see if Reuben Hoenig is there, although I consider that to be unlikely," I answered. "It is probably also worth investigating the idea of visiting the local office of the Reseda Neighborhood Council, since its records online are not very complete. The city of Los Angeles governs Reseda but its public records are voluminous to say the least. This is a small neighborhood. Someone interested enough in its welfare to staff the council office might know about many residents and certainly about the zoning issue you discovered on the plane."

Ms. Washburn considered that and agreed. "Can we go to the Chinese Theatre on Hollywood Boulevard?" she asked.

That seemed an odd request. "Is there some connection to finding Reuben Hoenig at the Chinese Theatre that I have overlooked?" I asked.

She shook her head. "I've always wanted to see the footprints in concrete," she said. "I've never been to Los Angeles before."

"This is not a sightseeing trip," I told Ms. Washburn. "We are here to answer Mother's question."

"Why can't we do both?"

Blaine brought a basket of rolls and Ms. Washburn's diet soda along with my water. He quickly retreated again and each of us drank from our glasses, although I wiped mine with my napkin before doing so and Ms. Washburn did not. I am not a germophobe but I do not like to take chances when dealing with people I do not know personally. The person washing glasses might have been in a hostile mood.

"Are there other side excursions you've been planning without telling me?" I asked when we were alone again.

"I'd like to go on a studio tour," Ms. Washburn answered, not realizing I was asking sarcastically because I have difficulty modulating my tone. She must have seen a pained look on my face. "If we have the time."

"I had no idea you were interested in the filmmaking process," I told her. "I do not think that business will have a connection to finding Reuben."

Ms. Washburn chose not to follow that thread of conversation. "You know, it would make your mother happy if you referred to him as your father."

That seemed a strange point to bring up at this moment. "My mother is not here," I reminded Ms. Washburn.

She closed her eyes momentarily and leaned back in her chair. "I know, Samuel. I assume you called her when we got to the hotel?"

That was not actually a question but Ms. Washburn's vocal inflection implied that it was, so I responded in kind. "Mother knew the time the plane was scheduled to land and is perfectly capable of finding the airline information online," I said. "She trusts your ability to drive a car and she knows we have a Global Positioning System device. Surely she knows we have found the hotel."

Ms. Washburn smiled slightly. "I'm going to take that for a no. Samuel, your mother isn't used to having you away from home, especially at night. She'd probably like to hear your voice."

That made little sense to me, but I trust Ms. Washburn's judgment on such matters so I took out my iPhone, which was in the left hip pocket of my trousers, where I keep it whenever I am awake. I considered calling Mother, then looked at Ms. Washburn.

"It is three hours later in New Jersey than it is here," I noted. "But Mother is probably not asleep yet. Do you think it would be jarring for her to hear the phone ring at this hour?"

Ms. Washburn's smile broadened a bit. "Very good, Samuel. You're thinking about your mother's feelings. Yes, perhaps it would be a little bit of a shock when she's getting used to being in an empty house. Maybe you should just text her."

Just as Blaine was arriving with our dinners I finished sending Mother the redundant information that we had arrived safely in Los Angeles. I then devoted my attention to the food on my plate, and did not find any reason to send it back to the kitchen. Ms. Washburn had chosen the restaurant well.

Perhaps being distracted by the dinner was the reason I did not notice until the next morning that Mother had not responded to my text.

That was odd.

TWELVE

"Did you call her this morning?" Ms. Washburn asked as she drove the Kia Soul on Sherman Way toward Reseda. Since there were virtually no turns necessary at all until we were in Reseda, the Global Positioning System device was not making any sound and Ms. Washburn felt comfortable enough to have a conversation.

My sensibility was slightly more nervous but I knew Ms. Washburn was confident and she was driving. I touched the iPhone in my pocket to assure myself it was there.

"Yes. I called this morning before I texted you and I called again just before we left. Both times Mother's voice mail came on immediately, which indicates her phone is turned off or the voice mailbox is full. No one ever calls Mother except me and her sister, Aunt Jane, so my guess is the telephone is turned off and she is not answering the landline at the house."

The drive would be short, even in heavy traffic. The Global Positioning System device, which I held in my right hand, was estimating it would take us three minutes to arrive at the address on Jamieson Avenue in Reseda. With the traffic, it was more likely to take eight if I was calculating correctly.

"Maybe you should call Aunt Jane," Ms. Washburn suggested. "Is her number programmed into your phone?"

Our progress was slow but it was undeniable. We had moved forward by two blocks in the past three minutes. "There is a right turn coming up on Victory Boulevard," I informed Ms. Washburn. "Yes, I have Aunt Jane's phone number. I am not certain the situation is serious enough to call her, or that she would have information I do not have. If she calls Mother, she too will be connected directly to voice mail or reach the house phone, which is not being answered."

"Give it a few hours," Ms. Washburn suggested. "Maybe your mother just didn't charge her phone last night and she's out shopping for groceries or something. After we check out this house we came to see, maybe you'll have news to give her anyway."

The Global Positioning System device reported the upcoming turn onto Victory Boulevard, and after another minute Ms. Washburn was able to turn right. We would not be on this street long. There were more turns coming before we reached our destination. I decided not to speak until we were there.

The side streets were less crowded, so the remainder of the drive took only one minute. We arrived at the house on Jamieson Avenue and Ms. Washburn found a parking space across the street. When we got out of the Kia Soul we were standing almost exactly at the same vantage point as the image we had seen on Google Earth.

"The house has not been painted lately," I noted. "The color is exactly the same as the computer image we saw."

"There's a car in the driveway," Ms. Washburn pointed out. "I'm guessing somebody is home. Shall we?" She gestured toward the house and I nodded.

We walked across the street and up to the front door. The house was not especially notable physically; it was a one-story home with a basement, judging from the casement windows cut into the foundation. This building had not been constructed on a concrete slab, as some in the neighborhood were. There was a rather tired-looking palm tree on the right side and the left consisted of the gravel driveway and a side door. Looking inside the front window I could see no obvious movement. The semi-sheer curtains that had been in the Google Earth image had been replaced with more substantial ones so there was less visibility into the front room.

There were also odd dark rings, small and crude, at strategic points under most of the windows. It looked like holes had been drilled there, which was perplexing.

"I'll ring the bell," Ms. Washburn said. I am not given to touching doorbells, but Ms. Washburn had been attempting to break me of that revulsion. In conceding to make the move now she was sparing me an unpleasant moment. I wondered about her motivation.

She pushed the doorbell button and we waited for sixteen seconds, not a highly unusual amount of time for someone to reach the entrance from another area of a house. Ms. Washburn and I did not speak during the interval. I was thinking about the possibility of answering Mother's question immediately and flying home later today. Airline schedules were monopolizing my thoughts. I have not asked Ms. Washburn what she was thinking.

When the door opened there stood behind it a woman in her mid- to late twenties. She had brown hair at shoulder length and was dressed in a plain pink t-shirt and a pair of jeans. She looked first at Ms. Washburn, then at me. Her face looked surprised.

"Yeah?" she said.

I extended my hand. "Allow me to introduce—" I began.

Ms. Washburn spoke over my attempt at a greeting. "Is this Kaplan Enterprises?" she asked.

I halted my speech and looked at her, but Ms. Washburn did not offer a glance at all to help me interpret her intentions. I decided it was best to trust her judgment and retracted my hand.

"What?" the young woman said.

Ms. Washburn repeated the question.

"You want George?" the woman asked.

"If he's home," Ms. Washburn said.

The young woman's eyes displayed a certain vacancy and slowly she seemed to come to a response. "Oh no, he's not home," she said.

Ms. Washburn's face was betraying no particular emotion I could identify. "How about Reuben Hoenig?" she asked.

"Who?"

That seemed to dispel any notion that Reuben was a fixture at the house, at least not under his given name. If he had taken the name George Kaplan not only professionally but in all walks of life, it was possible he was the man the young woman claimed was not here. If not, George Kaplan, who presumably would be the man with whom Ms. Washburn and I spoke on the phone, might know where Reuben was today.

But my chances of getting on an airplane back to New Jersey seemed to be diminishing.

"Reuben Hoenig," Ms. Washburn repeated. "Are you saying you've never heard the name before?"

Again the young woman seemed to come to an answer gradually. "That's it," she said. "I've never heard the name."

This was clearly not an especially bright young woman and I would have to caution Ms. Washburn later on the danger of giving a subject an answer to a question when one wants an honest response. I leaned forward to try to establish a rapport with the young woman.

"Reuben Hoenig is my father and I have not seen him in twenty-seven years," I said. "Are you sure you have never heard of him?"

People will sometimes respond to a personal plea rather than a professional one.

The young woman snorted. "Sure," she said. I did not understand what she meant by that.

"Can we come in?" Ms. Washburn asked. I understood she was speaking colloquially and knew the proper question would have begun with the word *may.* "We were supposed to meet George Kaplan here." That was not true unless considered from a very specific viewpoint, but immediately the young woman shook her head.

"You can't come in," she said. "George doesn't allow it."

"I thought George wasn't here," Ms. Washburn reminded her.

Two seconds before the response. "Um, he isn't, but he still doesn't want you to come in."

Sometimes it is more difficult to defeat an opponent who is not intelligent. They tend to stick to their initial defense no matter how clearly one demolishes its logic. Unmovable in an interrogation is a position that is very hard to best.

But Ms. Washburn simply walked into the house past the young woman and her look toward me indicated I should do the same. I followed Ms. Washburn after a moment even as the young woman said, "Hey!"

"It's okay," Ms. Washburn told her. "We're not here to bother anybody or cause any trouble. We just want to see George Kaplan and talk to him for a moment. Now, can you get in touch with him and let him know we're here?"

The room was very sparely furnished. There was a standing pole lamp in one corner that illuminated the room, given that the drapes on the windows allowed in very little light. There was a folding chair of the type normally reserved for outdoor activities standing next to the lamp, unfolded and unoccupied at the moment. Otherwise, the room was empty. A glance into the next room, which was a kitchen, showed only an open pizza box with no food in it. There were no

113

utensils on the counters, no table at which to eat. The hum of a refrigerator was the only sound coming from the interior of the house, but there was the sound of another machine, possibly in the basement.

It was quite clear that no one lived here.

The young woman relaxed her shoulders in a gesture of compliance. "Look," she said. "I know what you're here for. Will you go after I give it to you?"

"I assure you we are here to see George Kaplan," I said.

"People are here to see George all the time," the woman responded. "I know what they come for, and I can give it to you. He just didn't tell me you were coming, that's all, or I would have been ready. Hang on."

Neither of us protested as she walked into the kitchen and through it to a room beyond it in the house.

"Maybe we should leave," I said to Ms. Washburn. "George Kaplan is not here."

"How do you know?" she answered. "She hasn't told us the truth about anything. Why should we believe that part?"

"I don't know, but I am concerned that she went into another room to get a gun." I had seen homes like this in motion pictures and television programs. They rarely housed happy families.

"I hadn't thought of that." Ms. Washburn suddenly looked nervously in the direction the young woman had walked. "Do you think we should leave?"

I believed that would be an overreaction but did not have the time to state my opinion because the young woman re-entered the kitchen from the back room. She was, to my mild relief, not carrying a weapon of any kind nor was she accompanied by another person. Instead, she was carrying a small package wrapped in colorful paper with a shiny blue sheen.

"She's giving us a present," Ms. Washburn said. I believe she was speaking to herself.

The young woman walked to us and extended the package to Ms. Washburn. "Here," she said. Nothing more.

Ms. Washburn, probably by instinct, took the package from her hand. I considered asking the young woman if the package contained drugs because I did not want to be caught with such a parcel. But my social skills training led me to believe the question would be seen as rude. It was a difficult choice to make but I remained silent. Ms. Washburn did not seem to share my belief because she held the package casually.

"We really are here to see George Kaplan," I repeated.

"Oh my god!" The young woman sounded exasperated. "Look, you got what you came for. Now just go, okay?" She pointed toward the front door.

Apparently my mention of Kaplan was also rude, although I could not discern exactly why the young woman would react in such a fashion. I looked to Ms. Washburn, who was already turned toward the door. I followed her.

The young woman opened it with an air of impatience and we walked back out onto the suburban street. I looked at her as we stepped into the sunlight from the rather claustrophobic atmosphere of the empty front room.

"May I give you my cellular telephone number? If Mr. Kaplan comes back, he can call me."

The young woman slammed the door in my face.

I looked at Ms. Washburn. "Did I say something wrong?" I asked.

She held up a hand palm out. "No, Samuel. That girl really just wanted us to leave and that had nothing to do with you."

I stood and surveyed the area for a moment because I had no immediate idea of a next move. "Perhaps we should visit the office of the neighborhood association next," I said finally.

Ms. Washburn nodded and we walked back to the Kia Soul. Ms. Washburn pressed the proper button on the key fob to unlock the doors and we both seated ourselves inside. I reached for the Global Positioning System device while Ms. Washburn started the engine and the air conditioner began pushing cool air through the vents, which was a bit of a relief, although the mechanical sound was an irritant.

"What is the address of the office?" I asked Ms. Washburn.

"In a second," she said, reaching for the brightly wrapped package, which she had placed on the center console. "First let's see what kind of gift she was so anxious to give us."

After dismissing the notion that the package was filled with drugs, I had partially forgotten about it. My concern about committing a social faux pas had overridden my curiosity. "Yes," I agreed. "I wonder what George Kaplan gives to everyone who rings his doorbell."

Ms. Washburn was already tearing the wrapping paper, which made me slightly uncomfortable. I prefer to carefully remove any adhesive tape and unfold the paper cautiously. Ms. Washburn clearly was more concerned with the outcome than the process in such cases. I made a mental note of that fact in the event I ever had occasion to give Ms. Washburn a gift.

Almost immediately she gasped. My visual angle did not allow me a view so I asked, "What is it?"

She turned the partially opened package toward me.

It contained a great deal of money. From what I could see there were four stacks of $50 bills, each bearing the image of President Ulysses S. Grant. Each stack probably held two hundred bills.

"What's this all about?" Ms. Washburn asked.

"It's about forty thousand dollars," I answered.

"I wonder what she would have given us if she liked us," Ms. Washburn said.

THIRTEEN

Ms. Washburn dissuaded me from walking back to the home of Kaplan Enterprises and returning the money.

"At this point, that girl thinks she gave this money to the right people," she said. "There's no reason for her to set off any alarms. That's an expression, Samuel. I mean that she won't immediately call George Kaplan or Reuben Hoenig or someone else and inform him that there are two people walking around with forty thousand of his dollars for no particular reason. She doesn't know who we are. We didn't give her our names."

A person does not actually transfer his or her name to someone else simply by saying so, and that had been a difficult axiom for me to grasp initially. Now I barely registered any confusion at all.

"Perhaps not, but this is not our cash," I pointed out. "We have done nothing to earn it."

"We don't have to keep it, but it might turn out to be evidence later." She engaged the transmission of the vehicle and released the parking brake. In seconds we were moving down Jamieson Avenue.

"Where are you driving?" I asked. "I have not programmed the Global Positioning System device yet." I reached for the printout Ms. Washburn had brought with the address of the local neighborhood commission so I could enter the information into the device.

"I want to get out of her sight in case she's watching from the house," Ms. Washburn answered. "That money is our leverage over her. I don't want her to get the license plate number on this car. We can pull over a few blocks from here."

She maneuvered the Kia Soul for three blocks to Enfield Avenue and parked the car in an empty space on the street. Neither of us had said anything as she drove.

Ms. Washburn placed the transmission in the Park mode and turned toward me. "Okay, Samuel," she said. "What's our plan?"

I thought I had made it clear that my plan would be to return the money to the woman at the Kaplan Enterprises facility, but Ms. Washburn was obviously not expecting me to reitcrate that suggestion. The circumstances had changed. We had arrived seeking Reuben Hoenig and had left with $40,000 we did not seek but no more specific information on Reuben's whereabouts.

"My guess is that the money was not earned in a traditional fashion," I began, musing for myself aloud so I could work my way through the problem. "It might be stolen. It might have been taken in exchange for illegal drugs. It is possible Kaplan Enterprises is involved in any number of criminal activities that deal almost exclusively in cash."

"That doesn't tell me what we're going to do next," Ms. Washburn pointed out.

"You know how I work," I reminded her, then continued to pursue my train of thought. "Given that the money was likely obtained illegally or at least illicitly, it is quite likely that the loss will not be reported to the authorities."

Ms. Washburn almost snorted. "That's for sure."

"That means we have some time to decide what we want to do," I reasoned. "We should proceed as if we had not suddenly been handed these funds and take our time to think the matter through."

"So we go to the neighborhood council?" Ms. Washburn said. Her tone betrayed no skepticism. She was not disagreeing with me, merely asking for instructions.

"Yes." I gave her the address of the Reseda Neighborhood Council and she turned her attention to driving after I programmed the information into the Global Positioning System device. It was a very short drive.

The council was housed in the same building as a Bank of America branch, its entrance just to the left of the street-facing Automated Teller Machine affiliated with the bank. We had not called ahead and I wondered as Ms. Washburn and I approached whether anyone would be staffing the council if there was no pressing business.

But the front door was open and Ms. Washburn and I walked in. I had been taught to hold the door for a woman so Ms. Washburn entered ahead of me. She did not react in any way upon entering, and when I walked in I could see there was no reason to do so.

The council headquarters was a single room that looked like the local branch of a political campaign office. There were binders occupying every inch of shelf space. The floor was carpeted with inexpensive wall-to-wall fiber. Rather than a desk or a counter, there was a table in the center of the room. A woman in her forties of Latin descent sat behind it and looked slightly surprised to see guests walking in.

"The bank's next door," she said.

"We are aware of that," I assured her. I extended my right hand. "Allow me to introduce myself. I am Samuel Hoenig, proprietor of Questions Answered, and this is my associate, Ms. Washburn."

The woman looked at my hand for a moment and then took it briefly. I appreciated her not holding on long; for me the contact is more than I really desire. It is the gesture that is significant in such interactions. "We're not buying anything," the woman said.

"That suits us, as we are not selling anything," I told her. "We are trying to locate a man who might live in Reseda and thought you might be able to give us some direction in that area."

"Police station is on Vanowen," she answered. "We don't do missing people here. This is a community council. We have enough trouble just trying to help senior citizens find the right place to vote."

Ms. Washburn took a step forward. "This isn't exactly a missing person," she explained. "Samuel here is looking for his father and we thought maybe someone in a neighborhood organization might know him. Reuben Hoenig?"

The woman shrugged. "Never heard of him."

"Do you know anything about Mendoza Communications? We think Reuben might be working there, Ms. . . ." Making her voice trail off at the end of the sentence was apparently a way that Ms. Washburn used to ask the woman her name. It was the first time I had understood that particular practice although I had heard it before.

"I'm Carmen Sanchez," she said. "I've heard of Mendoza, but I don't think they have an office in Reseda anymore. I think they moved out four or five years ago. They used to own a couple of radio stations in the area but they sold out to some big corporation and started creating websites for people or something online."

There was only one more area in which Ms. Sanchez could possibly have helpful information. "Are you aware of Kaplan Enterprises?" I asked her.

Ms. Sanchez's face looked like she had detected an unpleasant odor. I almost asked her if that was the case because I could not be counted on to notice such a thing, but Ms. Washburn was not reacting the same way so I decided Ms. Sanchez's expression was in response to my question.

"If your dad is working for that Kaplan guy, good luck to you," she said. "I've gotten nothing but complaints since they moved in two years ago."

"What kind of complaints?" Ms. Washburn asked.

"Guy keeps that house like a fortress," Ms. Sanchez told us. "No open windows. Not a word to the neighbors. That wouldn't be so bad; you don't have to be friendly if you don't want to. But more than one person has seen the barrel of a rifle sticking out through holes drilled in the walls. They don't make noise, but people are coming in and out of that house all day and all night. Might be a drug house."

"Has no one called the police?" I asked.

Ms. Sanchez shrugged. "For what? We don't know anything. No noise complaints. Maybe they saw guns, maybe not. It's not illegal to own a gun. Far as I know they haven't shot anybody. Just seems weird."

"If you think people are selling drugs there…" Ms. Washburn began.

Ms. Sanchez held up a hand. "The key word there is *think*. We don't know anything. It's not our job to report our suspicions when we have no proof. The neighborhood council just promotes Reseda, that's all. We're not the cops and we're not your mother. What you do here, assuming you don't hurt anybody else, is your own business."

"What *can* you tell us?" Ms. Washburn asked. It was undoubtedly a final effort.

"There's a street fair coming up Sunday," Ms. Sanchez told her. "There'll be a bounce room, pony rides, and free popcorn."

I handed her one of the Questions Answered business cards Ms. Washburn had suggested I have printed. "If anyone mentions the name Reuben Hoenig at the street fair or any other time, will you call me?" I asked.

Ms. Sanchez looked at the card as if deciding whether it was safe to handle it. She took it from my fingers and looked away as she stored it in her wallet, which she took from a purse she had left on the floor. "If they do, but I wouldn't count on it."

"Why not?" I asked.

"There are seventy-five thousand people living in Reseda," she answered. "What are the odds one name will come up?"

Actually, the high population density in Reseda would be something of a statistical asset for finding Reuben Hoenig if he were in fact there. A higher number of people who can know something increases the chances that someone will have the information needed.

Ms. Sanchez wished us good luck, which I supposed had some significance although I do not believe in luck as a concept. Every occurrence is traceable to a series of occurrences that came before it and caused it to happen. But I was not in the mood to debate the point with Ms. Sanchez. Mostly, I believe her good wishes were a ploy to persuade Ms. Washburn and me to leave the council office and by that measure they were quite effective.

We walked back to the Kia Soul, whose bright blue color was very difficult to mistake on the sun-drenched street. The air was starting to become hot and thick with humidity. It occurred to me that it was cooler and drier in New Jersey. In three days I would be on the aircraft heading east. It was worth remembering.

"Maybe you should try calling your mother again," Ms. Washburn suggested as we got into the Kia Soul.

I had not forgotten but the reminder was welcome; I do not always know what the appropriate amount of time to wait might be in any given social situation. I tend to act on things when I think of them, and if it is a subject I think about frequently I can take action far too often. I reached into my pocket and pulled out the iPhone.

Ms. Washburn started the engine and was asking me about our next destination when Mother's voice mail message played into my ear. I held up a hand and Ms. Washburn stopped talking.

I left my third message on Mother's voice mail and replaced the phone in my pocket.

"Is there anyone else you can call?" Ms. Washburn asked. "A friend of your mother's or a neighbor who can look in?"

"I can't call Mike the taxicab driver, I'm afraid. He is not in proximity," I said.

"No, I guess not. Anyone else? A neighbor who knows your mother?"

"There is Mrs. Schiff next door," I answered. "But Mother gave me her phone number only to use in an emergency. I am not certain this situation qualifies."

Ms. Washburn let the air conditioning flow over her for a moment, leaning in toward the vent. "An emergency doesn't have to be a dire situation, Samuel. It can just be a moment when you need someone to help you. Mrs. Schiff can certainly knock on the door and make sure your mother is all right, can't she?"

Her reasoning was impeccable. I found the contact information for Mrs. Schiff and, although I considered asking Ms. Washburn to make the call for me, drew in a breath and pushed the icon to make the call.

Mrs. Schiff answered after the fourth ring. I looked at the time on the screen of my iPhone and made the mental adjustment for the East Coast. "Good morning, Mrs. Schiff," I said. "This is Samuel Hoenig calling."

"Hello, Samuel," she answered. Ms. Washburn could probably hear her voice from the driver's seat; Mrs. Schiff spoke quite loudly. "Is something wrong?"

That was a disturbing question. "Why do you think so?" I asked.

"You've never called me before and you live right next door," was the reply. "If everything was all right and you just wanted to talk, you could walk over to my house."

"That is true," I admitted, "but the circumstances are not typical. I am in Reseda, California."

There was a significant pause of three seconds. "You are?"

"Yes. And I have been unable to contact my mother. Her cellular phone is sending my call directly to voice mail and she is not answering the landline inside the house."

"Oh." I could hear some sounds that indicated movement on Mrs. Schiff's part. "I'm walking out onto my porch," she said. I heard the door hinges creak a bit as she opened it, then louder footsteps as Mrs. Schiff stepped onto the wooden porch.

"Your mother's car is not in the driveway," she reported. "Do you want me to go over and knock on the door?"

"Please do," I said. Ms. Washburn nodded so I added, "That would be very helpful."

There was the sound of walking and Mrs. Schiff's breathing became slightly more labored. The houses are not far apart at all so it took only eight seconds for her to reach Mother's front door.

"All right, I'm approaching the door," she said. "I'm going to ring the doorbell."

Ms. Washburn stifled a smile. "I feel like I'm at Mission Control," she said.

"Please let me know if my mother answers the ring," I told Mrs. Schiff.

"First thing," she agreed. "So far, nothing." It had been three seconds since she had said she was ringing the doorbell. Mother would have had to stand next to the door to answer that quickly. I chose not to point out that fact. I reminded myself that Mrs. Schiff was doing this on my behalf.

"I'm still waiting," she reported.

Ms. Washburn's face was no longer amused. She whispered to me, "If her car isn't there, she's probably not home."

That opinion was borne out thirty-seven seconds later when Mrs. Schiff, having rung the doorbell a second time, reported no response from my mother. The fingers on my left hand began to clench and open in rhythm. I was aware of the movement but did not attempt to stop it.

"Thank you for trying, Mrs. Schiff," I said after a long moment. I could think of nothing else.

"I'll check in later, Samuel," Mrs. Schiff said. "If I see or hear from your mom, I'll make sure she calls you. Don't worry."

I thanked her again and disconnected the call, but I saw no reason that I should not be worried.

Ms. Washburn must have observed that emotion on my face. "If something really serious had happened, you would already know," she said as we sat in the car and felt the cool air distribute itself throughout the interior. "You are your mother's emergency contact. You'd be the first person they'd get in touch with. I'm sure this is something very simple, like her cell phone breaking. She's probably out right now at the store replacing it."

While there was a good deal of logic in what Ms. Washburn said, I was already scrolling through possible scenarios in my mind. Very few of them were benign.

"You are probably right, Ms. Washburn," I said. "But perhaps we should fly home tonight so I can be certain."

She shook her head. "Not yet, Samuel. We still have work to do. What's our next move?"

I had no chance to answer because my iPhone rang at that moment. Assuming it was some news about Mother I reached for it quickly. But a cursory glance at the screen showed a number with a California area code, one I had seen recently.

It was George Kaplan's number. Disappointed and frustrated, I accepted the call. I did not offer a greeting. I did not have to.

The voice on the other end of the phone was that of the man who had identified himself to Ms. Washburn and me as Kaplan. He did not waste time with his message. He spoke as soon as it was clear that I had opened the line.

"You have something of mine," he said. "I want it back."

FOURTEEN

I touched the screen in the proper area to activate the speaker function so Ms. Washburn could hear the conversation. "What is it I have of yours?" I asked.

Of course, the obvious answer was the package of cash Ms. Washburn had stored in the glove compartment of the Kia Soul. But there was no point in giving this Kaplan, whomever he actually was, an advantage in what was to come. I would make him state his terms as clearly as possible.

With my mother unreachable, I was determined to conclude this business as swiftly as possible and find the next available flight to Newark Liberty International Airport. The urgency of the situation as I saw it had strengthened my resolve and made me slightly less cautious than usual.

"You know what you have," the man said.

Ms. Washburn looked slightly alarmed.

"I have a great many things," I said. "I do not know which one of them is yours, and how I might have acquired it."

Now Ms. Washburn looked very surprised.

When Kaplan spoke again it was in clipped tones, as if through clenched teeth. He was trying, unsuccessfully, to mask his irritation. "You have a package the idiot at my house gave you and I want it back or you're going to have trouble. Is that clear enough?"

"You mean the packet of cash in the amount of approximately forty thousand dollars?" I said. If Kaplan thought this line was not secure and that he was compromising his own operation by speaking on it he would be more inclined to come to an agreement quickly. That was my reasoning.

"Yes." The sound was like the hiss of a rattlesnake, if the recordings found on television programs and in motion pictures are at all accurate. I have not seen a rattlesnake within physical proximity of myself because I would find that very unsettling. Kaplan's response reminded me of such a noise, but not to the point that I would be especially upset about it. Clearly, a human adult male was speaking and not a rattlesnake. "Now give it back to me."

It was time for me to, as the expression states, put my cards on the table. I had no cards and there was certainly no table inside the Kia Soul, but in this case the metaphor was appropriate since the conversation was becoming very much like a game of poker and I was about to make my bid.

"I will be happy to give you back your money," I said. Ms. Washburn looked at my eyes and nodded. "But first you will have to put me in touch with Reuben Hoenig."

Kaplan made a sound like a balloon slowly losing its air. "This again?"

"I have never asked for anything else," I pointed out. "I have forty thousand dollars that the young woman in your house gave my associate and me as a gift. You can have it back. But first you must set up a meeting between me and Reuben Hoenig."

"I can't do that," he said.

I looked at Ms. Washburn. She smiled just a bit and nodded.

I disconnected the call.

"That was very rude of me," I said.

Ms. Washburn chuckled lightly. "Sometimes you have to be rude to get the results you need."

The iPhone rang almost immediately. I reached for the screen, but Ms. Washburn held her finger up. "Let him wait a few rings," she said.

I must have cocked an eyebrow, which is an expression I'm told I exhibit when surprised by something. Ms. Washburn put her hand on mine. "It's okay, Samuel. He's not going away."

The phone rang four more times before Ms. Washburn nodded again. "Now."

I exhaled and pushed the screen to begin the call. "Hello?"

This time the man's voice was a little higher and sounded less patient. "You hung up on me!" I thought the remark irrational. Did George Kaplan or his surrogate believe that I was not aware I had ended the previous call abruptly? So I said nothing. "What's wrong with you?"

I am aware that some people believe I suffer from a disorder of the neurological system. Others think I have a mental illness. There are those uninformed individuals who refer to my personality traits as a "disease." But I felt there was no point in detailing my Asperger's Syndrome for George Kaplan.

"I am in excellent health, I assure you," I told him. "Now. When and where will I meet Reuben Hoenig?"

"I'll find you," the man countered. "I'll find you and take back the money and then I will do something. To you or to your girlfriend."

I looked at Ms. Washburn, who pointed to herself. Then she shook her head in a negative fashion.

"I have no girlfriend," I assured Kaplan. "But I can guarantee that even if you find my associate and me you will never see a dollar of the money we have in our possession. I have the ability to think of hiding places no one else would ever consider. Even my associate would be unable to recover your cash and I certainly will not tell you where I have secured it, until I have met and spoken with Reuben Hoenig." This might be the place to disclose that I hold no special talents as a result of Asperger's Syndrome. But I was fairly certain Kaplan did not know that.

"I can make you tell me." That was not even a credible threat but it did point to an operation considerably more illicit than either Ms. Washburn or I had imagined. I felt a slight tremor in my digestive system but blinked twice to banish the thought.

"Mr. Kaplan, if that is your real name," I said, "you are a businessman. Your sole concern is to create a profit. And the best way to do so is to operate efficiently."

"Yeah. And the most efficient way for me to get that money back is to find you and beat it out of you. So expect that."

I anticipated Kaplan disconnecting quickly so I spoke immediately. "That is not your best option as a businessman," I replied. "It is inefficient, largely because I will not tell you where the money is being kept. I will banish the location from my own mind and forget it, making it impossible, no matter how dire the situation becomes, for me to accommodate you." This, again, was a lie based on the proposition that Kaplan had no idea what Asperger's Syndrome might entail. I gave him no time to consider the preposterous fiction I was creating. "But if you produce Reuben Hoenig I will be glad to give you back every dollar immediately and you can retrieve your property with no loss of time or efficiency. It is, if I am correct in my terminology, a win-win situation." I looked toward Ms. Washburn, who was smiling and raising a thumb in approval.

There was a pause on Kaplan's end of the conversation, and I became confident that the ploy had worked.

"Okay," he said. "I'll get you Hoenig. But you're going to have to wait until tomorrow."

Normally I would have considered that capitulation a victory, but with Mother unresponsive and almost three thousand miles between us I had no time for Kaplan's hesitation. "Why?" I asked.

"I have to locate the guy and convince him to meet with you," he answered. "I have to set up a place and a time that I can be sure won't involve … government agencies I want to keep out of the situation. I can't just make him appear out of the air."

I looked at my wristwatch. I wear a wristwatch despite having the time displayed on my iPhone because I do not have to push a button to make the correct time appear and because it was my custom long before I began carrying a cellular phone. The time now was 11:56 a.m.

"You have until five p.m. today," I said. "If I don't hear back from you before then with a suitable rendezvous arranged before nine p.m. this evening, I will break off all communication between us and disappear with your money. Is that clear?" I knew the statement was simple to understand but I had heard that last phrase uttered many times when people were attempting to make their points emphatically.

This time Kaplan did not argue, although I felt it was against his nature to accept my terms so quickly. That made me suspicious. "Okay," he said. "I'll call you before five. Make sure you have the money with you."

If his intention was to find Ms. Washburn and me and force us to give him the forty thousand dollars without an interview with Reuben Hoenig, it was necessary for me to disabuse him of that notion. "The money is in a safe place right now," I said. "After I have met with Reuben Hoenig I will tell you its location."

Kaplan disconnected.

"He is no longer there," I said to Ms. Washburn. "Does that mean he is not accepting my terms?"

"No," she answered. "It means he knows he can't argue with you and that makes him angry. Be careful with this guy, Samuel. He's not the kind who takes losing kindly."

That struck me as irrelevant. "He is not losing," I suggested. "He is going to get what he wants. We will give him back the money his employee accidentally gave us."

"But he has to give you something for it, and he doesn't like it. Just be careful, okay?" She turned her attention to the dashboard of the Kia Soul. "Where are we going?"

I consulted my watch again. Six minutes had elapsed since I had checked most recently. "Perhaps we should seek out a place to have lunch. Just Nice?"

Unexpectedly, Ms. Washburn shook her head. "I know what you want, Samuel, but we're not going to eat all our meals in Los Angeles at the same restaurant. And I'm not going to spend the next three days looking for an Applebee's. You saw that things worked out well at the place I picked the last time, right?"

I had to admit she was being accurate.

"Good. So you're just going to have to trust me. I saw a little place on the way here this morning. Let's go." And before I could suggest otherwise, she had engaged the Drive gear and was navigating the vehicle back into traffic.

When we were settled in a small, redolent delicatessen called Andy's, I had quelled my rising anxiety with a look at the menu, which indicated there were items served in the establishment that were not foreign to my experience, although many certainly were. Ms. Washburn asked for a hot pastrami sandwich, which I knew I would not want to see while I settled on a turkey sandwich with lettuce and mayonnaise, similar to what I eat for lunch at Mother's house most days.

That was when I tried Mother's cellular phone again. The voice mail did not immediately pick up, which meant that she had at least turned on the phone at some time since I had last called. But it was still taking her messages and she was not answering the phone when it rang.

"Maybe I should call the police," I said to Ms. Washburn.

"They do sometimes check in on seniors," she said, considering. "Is that something that would make your mother uncomfortable?"

It was a valid question. I thought about the answer for a moment. "I don't know. I am certain, though, that if she is in some distress I would not be comfortable having ignored the situation because I was concerned she would be inconvenienced. I am going to call the Piscataway police department."

"I think you're probably right," Ms. Washburn said. "I assume you checked your own voice mail to make sure she hasn't called you? It is odd that she hasn't looked in on you yet."

How Mother could see me from New Jersey when I was in Canoga Park, California, eluded my reason. "I haven't checked," I admitted. "It hadn't occurred to me that Mother might call. She knows where she is."

I looked at the voice mail application on my iPhone and found there was indeed a message from Mother, which made me realize how anxious I had been about it. My stomach loosened itself and I let out a long breath. I activated the playback for Mother's voice mail message.

"Hello, Samuel," she had said two hours before, according to the time stamp on the message screen. "This is your mother. Everything's fine here. I hope you're doing well in California. Please don't call for a day or so because my phone is acting very strange and I won't get your message. You don't need to worry about me. I'll get a new phone and call you when I have it, but I probably won't get out until tomorrow at least. I'll talk to you soon. I miss you, and I don't mean to make you feel bad, but I look forward to you coming home. But I'm very proud of you for going and hope you find your father soon. See you in a few days. Okay, bye."

She disconnected after that, and I found that against my expectations, I did not feel better after having heard her message.

Ms. Washburn had clearly seen that emotion in my facial expression. "What's wrong?" she asked.

"I think we should get tickets for a flight home today," I told her. "My mother is in some very serious danger."

FIFTEEN

"I DON'T UNDERSTAND," Ms. Washburn said.

She had insisted on listening to Mother's voice mail message and although I thought it was rather personal, I had agreed to let her do so. Now she was sitting opposite me with a pastrami sandwich in front of her, laying untouched like my own lunch before me.

"Your mother says everything is fine and that you should go ahead and look for your father," Ms. Washburn continued. "How does that translate into us cancelling the meeting with your father and flying home to rescue her from something she never actually mentioned at all?"

"How would you characterize Mother's voice?" I asked.

Ms. Washburn squinted. "Her voice? She sounded like herself."

"I disagree. I believe she sounded tired and weak. I think she sounded like someone who has been deprived of sleep and who had perhaps been coerced into making that phone call to placate my curiosity and concern."

Ms. Washburn sat back in her chair. "I did not get that at all," she said.

"In addition, the things she said are suspect," I continued.

"She said she was fine but missed you," Ms. Washburn said. "That's understandable. It's not a signal that she's being kept from calling the police to save herself. What time did she make that call?"

I checked once more. "Two hours and twelve minutes ago," I told her.

"That's before eight in the morning on the East Coast. What time does your mother usually get up?"

"She cooks breakfast for us most mornings, and as you know, I leave for my office at 8:35 a.m. Mother is usually awake by seven. It would be highly unusual for her to sleep later, if that's what you were about to suggest."

Ms. Washburn smiled at me, not in a gleeful way. I believe the expression was meant to show sympathy or support. It was not one of those I have memorized for Ms. Washburn's face. "Samuel, I understand your concern," she said. "I do. But you have to understand that these are not normal conditions. Your mother doesn't have to get up at seven because she doesn't need to make breakfast for you. So maybe she slept in a little bit today because she could. That's all I'm saying. She could have sounded tired because she was tired. There are explanations for everything that's worrying you. Jumping to the conclusion that she's in danger is the most extreme reaction you could have. Maybe it's just because you want to go home."

Ms. Washburn understands emotional reactions better than I do. It's not that people whose behavior is on the autism spectrum don't have feelings; it is that we are not sure how to express or cope with those emotions so our responses are sometimes disproportional to the situation. It's also true that we have difficulty deciphering the emotional signals given, consciously or not, by others.

So when Ms. Washburn offers an opinion on such a subject, I tend to defer to her judgment. It was counterintuitive in this case. I thought

Mother was in some kind of difficulty and was trying to hide it from me for reasons I did not know. But Ms. Washburn was correct in her assumption that I was anxious to leave Southern California as soon as possible, and that desire could be clouding my decision.

"I will assume you are right," I told her after a moment. "But if I do not hear from Mother tomorrow, I am going to call the Piscataway police department."

She nodded. "That's fair. Now let's just enjoy our lunch and decide what we're going to do next."

I thought it unlikely I would enjoy the turkey sandwich, but it was necessary to take in nourishment so I ate some more of it. I had purchased a bottle of spring water, reminding me that I had not been exercising every twenty minutes while on the West Coast. It had been physically inconvenient so far but I resolved to look for opportunities as we continued our trip.

Ms. Washburn was chatting about local tourist attractions, a subject that had not occupied my attention and I was feigning interest—something I had learned to do with Dr. Mancuso that was not rude because the other person did not know I was doing it—when my iPhone rang again.

I hoped momentarily the call was from Mother but the incoming number was that of the man we knew as George Kaplan. I showed it to Ms. Washburn.

"I guess you convinced him to act fast," she said. "There goes the trip to Hollywood Boulevard."

I opened the line and immediately Kaplan's voice came through the iPhone, which I held to my ear because the restaurant was too crowded and noisy to use the speaker function. "Six o'clock tonight," he said. "The Hollywood Bowl. Parking Lot B. There's no show there tonight so it'll be empty."

I took on the same persona I'd used the last time I'd spoken to Kaplan. "Six p.m. is acceptable," I said. "But we are not coming to the parking lot of the Hollywood Bowl where we can't be seen. I need a public place where my associate and I can be assured there will be no unexpected difficulty when I meet Reuben Hoenig."

"What do you think, we're gonna get you into a parking lot and bump you off?" Kaplan was actually trying to sound offended after having vaguely threatened Ms. Washburn and me in our previous conversation. "That's who you think you're dealing with?"

"Six p.m. is acceptable," I repeated. "Not the Hollywood Bowl."

Ms. Washburn was looking at me with a quizzical expression; she did not understand my resistance on the point. That was understandable.

Kaplan made a guttural noise in his throat that sounded vaguely like a dog unhappy with the arrival of the postman. "Fine," he said. "Not the Hollywood Bowl. Where, then?"

"Hollywood Boulevard," I said. "The Chinese Theatre."

Ms. Washburn smiled.

SIXTEEN

I was not familiar with the Chinese Theatre or Hollywood Boulevard but I was aware of the exhibit outside the theater bearing the footprints and handprints (and in some cases, other prints) of film celebrities that has been a tourist attraction there for decades. It is considered an honor in the motion picture business to be "immortalized" in the concrete sidewalk outside the theater. I do not understand the custom nor the explanation; a person is no more immortal when he leaves an impression of his hands and feet in wet cement, a fact easily confirmed by noting that the majority of people so honored are now deceased.

Ms. Washburn and I had spent the rest of the afternoon devising our plans for the evening. We returned to Canoga Park and conferred in my room at the hotel, then Ms. Washburn had said she needed to rest a bit because of "jet lag" and she went back to her room to do so. I had not noticed a problem with fatigue and therefore did some Internet research on a lingering question from another client and then rechecked the preparations Ms. Washburn and I had made for the meeting with Reuben Hoenig—and one assumed

George Kaplan—at the Chinese Theatre. I made two telephone calls, one to Mother without receiving a response, and then attached my iPhone to a charger so I could be sure it would be fully functional when I needed it for the meeting.

The afternoon felt like it lasted longer than usual, although that is not technically possible. Time passes at a constant rate.

At thirty minutes past four in the afternoon, Ms. Washburn knocked on the door of my hotel room as planned. Given the astonishing amount of traffic in Los Angeles and our desire to arrive at the destination early it made sense to allot extra time to the trip.

After navigating US 101 (referred to in the area as "The One-Oh-One") and its inevitable delays, Ms. Washburn still brought the Kia Soul to a parking garage near the address of the Chinese Theatre with thirty-seven minutes to spare before our meeting. That would give her the time she desired to see the famed concrete slabs laid out in front of the structure itself.

"I really appreciate your doing this for me, Samuel," she said as we walked on Hollywood Boulevard past the Kodak Theatre, where I had discovered the Academy Awards are handed out each winter.

Her comment puzzled me. "I am happy to accommodate you whenever possible," I told Ms. Washburn, "but I am not doing this for you. I am doing this to answer Mother's question so we can go home."

"I meant changing the site of the meeting so I could see the Chinese Theatre," she explained. "You didn't have to do that."

"I did not want Kaplan to lure us to a location away from view," I said. "This seemed like the most public area possible."

Indeed, the street itself was crowded with pedestrians, very few of whom appeared to be native Angelenos. Many stopped to take pictures of themselves with their telephones. Others simply stared.

The forecourt in front of the building, which had started as Grauman's Chinese Theatre in its Hollywood heyday and was now the TCL Chinese Theatre, was undoubtedly covered in the famous concrete slabs bearing the imprints of many film stars and affiliated celebrities. It was not easy to confirm this fact, however, as the area was almost completely overrun with tourists snapping photographs and pointing at particular slabs with what appeared to be delight.

I felt my elbows tighten involuntarily. I am not fond of crowds or tight spaces.

I glanced away from the forecourt toward the street. People dressed in rather seedy costumes depicting popular culture characters were posing for pictures with children and families. In many cases I saw the people being photographed give the people in the costumes money after the picture was taken.

One such performer, dressed in a red costume meant to evoke the Sesame Street character Elmo was wandering around the area without soliciting photographs. The person in that costume appeared restless, pacing back and forth and not waving hands or leaning in toward children to better facilitate the transfer of funds.

I considered that unusual but not entirely unexpected.

Ms. Washburn strode purposefully toward the exhibits. She had expressed a particular desire to see those commemorating the Marx Brothers and Cary Grant. Ms. Washburn has what I would classify as a special interest in films made before 1990.

My interests run toward the New York Yankees, the Beatles, and the criminal justice system, but I do have some affection for the Marx Brothers. I did not understand, however, how seeing a concrete slab with impressions of their hands (and Groucho Marx's cigar) would enhance that feeling. But given our impending meeting with a man named after a minor character from *North by Northwest*, the Cary Grant exhibit seemed apt.

I stayed back, keeping a very keen eye on Ms. Washburn so as not to lose my sense of her location. I did not know when George Kaplan and Reuben Hoenig would arrive. And I did not know what Kaplan intended to do. Ms. Washburn and I were acting in good faith, even if we had not been foolish enough to assume Kaplan would do the same. I had no idea how ruthless the man could be.

So I watched Ms. Washburn from a distance and never lost sight of her.

She did not seem at all perturbed by the impending event or the idea that it might bring some level of danger. Instead she would point at one of the sidewalk slabs, look over her shoulder, see that I had not moved, and then text me a name: ANTHONY QUINN. FRED ASTAIRE. ELIZABETH TAYLOR. JULIE ANDREWS. MEL BROOKS.

I was glad she was enjoying the moment even if its pleasures eluded me. I took a quick glance at the red Elmo performer, but could not locate the character anywhere. People dressed as Darth Vader, Batman, a character from a Disney animated motion picture I did not recognize, Spider-Man, and Shrek the ogre dominated the tourist traffic.

When I looked back after only a moment, Ms. Washburn was still visible, looking down at the pavement. Most of the people in the forecourt were doing the same, and it made for an amusing tableau. I appreciated it silently.

At precisely six p.m., a black sport utility vehicle arrived in front of the theater. It stopped and three men exited. I did not recognize any of them, but they were clearly scanning the crowd. They were not here to see the sights.

As soon as they closed the front and rear passenger doors the driver moved the sport utility vehicle away, no doubt to avoid a confrontation with one of the many uniformed police officers in the area.

I looked at Ms. Washburn, who was still examining the slabs. I would not walk into the teeming crowd, but texted her that our meeting was about to begin. She looked up from her phone, found my location and headed for me at the same time as the three men did.

Ms. Washburn arrived first but not much ahead. I did not recognize any of the three men who walked to us, but they did not hesitate at all, which indicated they were aware of what Ms. Washburn and I looked like. I chose to dismiss that thought because it was mildly disturbing.

They were led by a man of medium height wearing a dark gray suit incongruous with the sea of tourists in Bermuda shorts and colorful t-shirts bearing slogans of supposed wit. Behind him and to his left was a slimmer, older man in casual trousers and a light blue polo shirt. The third man was large and had dark, bushy eyebrows. He wore a perpetual scowl.

"Samuel Hoenig," the man in the suit said. It was not a question but it did cause me to hesitate briefly because people often say their own names when approaching a new acquaintance. I am aware of only four other people named Samuel Hoenig in the United States. It took less than a second for me to understand this was not one of them.

There was no advantage to denying my identity; the purpose of this meeting was to establish the validity of the person George Kaplan would call Reuben Hoenig and retrieve his address. It was not to gain anything else. "Yes," I said. "Allow me to introduce myself. I am Samuel Hoenig."

The man in the suit and the man with the bushy eyebrows stared at me without comprehension for a moment. The older man smiled strangely.

The man in the suit extended his hand. "George Kaplan," he said. I had anticipated his manner of speech this time and did not believe he was assuming that was my name. I did not accept his hand.

I looked at the older man, who was the only one in the appropriate age group. "Are you Reuben Hoenig?" I asked.

"Don't say anything," Kaplan ordered the older man. "Until I get my money nobody does anything."

"That makes no sense," I told him. "If no one here does anything there is no way for you to receive the cash you are demanding."

Again there was the odd stare. I took the opportunity in the pause. "This is Ms. Washburn, my associate," I told the older man.

He offered his hand and Ms. Washburn took it. "Janet," she told him. "Are you Reuben?"

Kaplan held up his hand as a warning. I saw the man with the bushy eyebrows flinch a bit. His hand seemed to be twitching toward the pocket of the jacket he was wearing. It was a very warm day and the probability was that he did not require an outer garment to concentrate radiated body heat. But he stopped his hand and dropped it to his side again.

"I said, you're not going to find out where your dad is until I get my money," Kaplan said.

"You did not say that," I reminded him. "You said until you get what you refer to as your money, nobody will do anything. That statement still does not make grammatical or logical sense."

"What is the deal with you?" Kaplan asked.

"The deal, as you put it, is that you will get the cash from Ms. Washburn and me once I get to talk to Reuben Hoenig. And since this man is the only one here who is the proper age as described by people who know him, I can only assume this is Reuben." I looked at the older man.

"That's very good," he said. "You established my identity using the facts."

"Stop talking," warned Kaplan.

I turned toward him. "If you want to get the cash, Mr. Kaplan, this is how it will happen. Mr. Hoenig and I will step aside for a moment to have a private conversation. I expect it will require less than three minutes to complete our business. Then we will return to this spot and I will ask Ms. Washburn to retrieve the cash, which we will be perfectly willing to turn over to you. These conditions are not negotiable. So if you will excuse this man and me, we will return shortly."

I turned to walk away from the group and toward the least frantically crowded corner of the forecourt. But I had not completed taking my second step when Kaplan spoke in a harsh, hoarse tone that could not be heard more than a few feet away.

"I get the money now or your dad isn't going to walk away at all," he said. "And neither is your girlfriend."

The man with the bushy eyebrows maneuvered himself to stand behind Ms. Washburn, effectively blocking her path away from the group. This time his hand went to his inside pocket. Ms. Washburn looked angry.

"Perhaps you didn't understand what I just explained," I said to Kaplan. "We have no objection to giving the money to you. But I do not trust you enough to make the transfer before I have the conversation I need to conclude my business in Southern California. So Mr. Hoenig and I are going to walk to that potted plant and speak for a very brief time, and then you will get your money. Is that more understandable?"

"I got it the first time," Kaplan said. "But it's not gonna happen that way. You're going to give me my money and then I'm going to decide whether my friend here decides to let the three of you live past this afternoon."

I looked away from him to avoid eye contact and saw the person in the red Elmo costume again. The costumed person was walking toward us in a circular pattern. This was not uncommon among the performers, as young children were sometimes frightened by large cartoon characters approaching them directly.

"That is not an acceptable arrangement," I said.

"Imagine how much I care," Kaplan said.

Reuben Hoenig appeared to be either medicated or sedated. His reactions were slow and his speech was carefully considered. He mostly stared at the space directly in front of his feet and appeared almost uninterested in the proceedings around him.

"He gives the impression of being a violent person," he said quietly. It was either a warning or an idle observation. It was possible he was not even speaking about Kaplan.

"We're not giving you something for nothing," Ms. Washburn said, taking a step forward and looking stern. "Samuel just wants to talk to his father for a minute and then you'll definitely get your money back. What's your issue?"

I saw the costumed Elmo performer stop circling and get positioned near the man with the bushy eyebrows. The red fur on the Elmo costume had not been recently washed.

"I don't get outplayed," Kaplan said. "You don't get to dictate terms. I get my money and then I decide if you get to talk to your dad. That's the way it's going to play."

I saw no reason to agree to those terms. A three-minute conversation was not equivalent to a forty-thousand-dollar payment.

"I think not," I said. "You have my word that the money will be returned as soon as my conversation with Mr. Hoenig is concluded. That should be good enough for you."

Kaplan folded his arms. "Well, *you* have *my* word that you'll talk to him after I get my forty grand back and not before."

I shook my head. "I believe that my word is more trustworthy than yours," I told him.

"I don't mind telling you I like talking to a man who likes to talk," said Reuben Hoenig. The sentence sounded vaguely familiar but I did not have time to place the wording.

"My way or the highway," Kaplan said. His associate with the generous eyebrows stiffened a bit but remained silent as he had been since arriving. Again, it took me a moment to understand what his axiom meant in context to our conversation. He was saying that if we did not comply with his terms, we should leave.

I looked at Ms. Washburn and shrugged my shoulders. "The highway, then." I turned to walk away from the group and the red Elmo seemed to lose interest, walking away from us.

"You're serious?" Kaplan sputtered.

"Perfectly. But my offer still stands," I said. "I will be glad to give you back your money as soon as I have a brief talk with Mr. Hoenig."

Kaplan looked surprised and angry. His faced was red and as a resident of the area, it was probable that was not due to unusual exposure to the sun. No doubt he had been outdoors every day for months.

"You don't get to beat me," he hissed at me.

Elmo now wandered back to us.

"I am not attempting to do so," I assured him. "My aim is simply to talk to Mr. Hoenig, answer the question I have pending, and give you back your forty thousand dollars. We can both walk away from here with what we want."

"Fine." The word was released rather than spoken. "Go talk. You have two minutes." He gestured with his head toward an unoccupied corner of the forecourt.

I approached Reuben Hoenig and noticed that Ms. Washburn maneuvered herself behind Elmo so anyone trying to get to her would have to deal with him first, which I considered a very intelligent decision.

"May we speak for a moment?" I said to Reuben.

"Very well. We'll talk about the black bird."

That was the speech that made a connection in my mind. Almost everything Reuben Hoenig had said to me had been a quote from the film or the Dashiell Hammett novel *The Maltese Falcon*. For some reason he was speaking almost exclusively in the dialogue from that detective story.

Still he allowed me to lead him to the relatively quiet corner, although no area of the forecourt could be considered secluded or private. No one here, about thirty feet from the gathered group, would be able to hear what was said between us.

"My mother is concerned about you," I said to Reuben. "Please tell me your address."

"My address." Reuben at least did not respond in a Sam Spade reference, but his words were simply an echo of my own. That was not terribly helpful.

"Yes." Perhaps he did not know I was his son. "Vivian Hoenig wants to know where you are living. She received a letter in the mail from you and it contained wording that made her believe you are in danger. Are you in danger?"

"Ah, now you are dangerous." He quoted Hammett again. This was going to be difficult, as *The Maltese Falcon* is not among my special interests and therefore I would not necessarily know every line and its significance.

"What is your favorite Beatles song?" I asked Reuben. Perhaps I could find some insight into Reuben's thought process or some common ground.

The question seemed to stump him just as I saw Kaplan hold up one finger and then point at his wrist. I assumed that was a signal about the amount of time I had been allotted to talk to Reuben. It was hard to be certain because Kaplan's wrist did not have a watch on it, but there seemed to be no alternative explanation.

"Beatles song?" Reuben said.

"Yes. Quickly. If you had to choose one song by the Beatles, what would it be?" I did not know how long the man with the full eyebrows could be held in check before the police in the forecourt noticed.

Reuben Hoenig closed his eyes tightly. His head vibrated a bit as he thought. Then he opened his eyes and smiled. "'Strawberry Fields Forever,'" he said.

I stopped for a moment to absorb that information. Now that I had refocused Reuben's mind perhaps I could gain some information in the seconds I had left. "Your address," I said. "How can my mother reach you?"

"I'll ring four times; long, short, long, short," he said. "And you needn't bother to come to the door. I'll let myself in."

"Reuben, this is not *The Maltese Falcon*," I said with an air of desperation. "Please tell me how I can find you."

He bit his lower lip lightly. "I'm moving around," he said. "I don't have an address."

"Time!" shouted Kaplan. "Get back here *now*!"

"A phone number?" I asked. "Can she call you? Vivian is very worried about you. She thinks you're going to die."

"I am," Reuben Hoenig said. "We all are."

Then he walked off toward Kaplan, who was gesturing insistently. I had no choice but to follow in Reuben Hoenig's path.

It took only eight seconds to arrive back at the central area where Elmo still lurked by the man with the full eyebrows. Kaplan wasted no time on my arrival. "Where's my money?" he demanded.

"It is in a safe place," I assured him. "And Ms. Washburn will be happy to retrieve it for you now. But I will require a longer conversation with Mr. Hoenig after the funds have been delivered." I nodded toward Ms. Washburn and she took a step toward Hollywood Boulevard so she could walk to the parking garage where the rented Kia Soul was waiting.

Kaplan held up a hand and Ms. Washburn, looking surprised, stopped. "I thought you said you were the only one who knew where the money was," he said to me.

"I lied," I told him. "It was a fabrication intended to strengthen my bargaining position and it worked. Now Ms. Washburn will bring you the cash. I don't understand your objection."

"How do I know she's not going to get a cop?" Kaplan asked.

Reuben Hoenig had taken to studying the pavement just ahead of his shoes again.

"If Ms. Washburn or I had intended to call a police officer, we have had ample opportunities to do so right here," I pointed out. "We have not done so. We have no intention of trying to keep the forty thousand dollars. But I am asking for more time with Mr. Hoenig because that conversation was not sufficient to conclude my business."

Ms. Washburn took two more steps toward the street and looked absolutely astonished when Kaplan reached for her arm and stopped her progress. He grabbed both her wrists and pulled them behind her back.

"Hey!" she said.

Taken by surprise, I stepped back.

"She stays here," Kaplan growled. "You want her to go get my money so there must be a reason I don't want her to."

"Then how will you receive the package?" I asked when I regained control. There had been a little hand flapping at my sides, but I had gotten myself back on task again. Dr. Mancuso's methods still worked. "Ms. Washburn was going to get it for you."

"You and I are going together," Kaplan said. "I'll watch you get the money and then we'll come back here."

"They have brothers in her bag," Reuben Hoenig said.

"That is inefficient," I told Kaplan, ignoring the Hammett reference. "Ms. Washburn knows where the package is and how to get it. Besides, if you and I walk off, you'll be leaving her here to call the police at her leisure."

"She'll know that if she calls a cop, I'll kill you," Kaplan said plainly.

Since I had seen no evidence of a weapon on his person, I asked, "Using what?"

"This," Kaplan said. From his sleeve he produced a switchblade knife with a five-inch blade. In extending it from his sleeve had to let go of Ms. Washburn's right arm. He compensated by holding the blade low and close to her torso, disabling her arm.

I felt my jaw close tightly and my neck straighten. These were signs that I was feeling anger. That was inconvenient, as such emotion tends to interfere with my best thought processes.

"When you're slapped you'll take it and like it," Reuben Hoenig said.

"I will go with you," I told Kaplan. "But you must release Ms. Washburn right now."

Kaplan said nothing but pushed hard with both hands on Ms. Washburn's shoulder blades, projecting her forward awkwardly as she again yelled, "Hey!"

She fell forward. I held out my arms and caught her but her momentum carried her hard into my chest and I steadied her there. Then the man with the generous eyebrows moved quickly in my direction and took Ms. Washburn's arm. This time she yelled something less polite.

"That's it," Kaplan said. From the edges of my peripheral vision I saw him nod toward his associate vigorously. That appeared to be a signal so I turned sharply toward where the man was standing, which was immediately behind Ms. Washburn, who was still shouting.

The man ignored her and used one arm to reach around Ms. Washburn's waist, which caused her to make an annoyed sound. The other was reaching into his jacket, where I assumed he had a weapon of some sort concealed.

But he never managed to reach it. Instead, the red Elmo performer appeared behind him, wrapping a large furry right arm around the man, effectively stopping his movement. Elmo's left hand, which was slipped through a slit in the suit around the midsection, was holding a handgun.

"Elmo says don't grab a lady like that unless she asks you to," the performer said in a high squeaky voice. "Elmo says be polite to ladies all the time."

The large man dropped the arm that was reaching for Ms. Washburn and she moved toward me. I did not have a handgun in my pocket, but I am certified in tae kwon do and had taken classes on disarming an assailant. I moved quickly to him.

Kaplan didn't want to make a huge scene and attract attention, particularly from the police officers. He held his knife at belt level and feinted with it, perhaps to remind me that it was there.

"This is not necessary," I said.

"Yes, it is," Kaplan said. "Tell your friend to let him go."

"Not while he is threatening Ms. Washburn."

"I can handle this guy," said the man being held by Elmo. It seemed an almost comical statement considering the furry red arm encircling his chest.

"Elmo doesn't think so."

Kaplan remained silent.

The man with the bushy eyebrows had clenched his jaw severely. "We can get this—" he started to say. Elmo tightened his grip on the man's chest. He reached into the man's inside pocket and took out a pistol. He gestured to me. "Elmo says take the nice man's gun."

"Hey," the man protested.

"Elmo says shut up."

The man stopped speaking. I was not interested in handling a firearm as I am not trained in such things. When I hesitated, Ms. Washburn took it from Elmo's paw and held it on Kaplan, whose eyes narrowed and showed anger. Ms. Washburn hung her purse over her wrist to shield the sight of the pistol from the crowd. Elmo's was low enough to be virtually invisible.

I decided to appeal to him directly. "Let Ms. Washburn go and get the package," I said. "We will give it to you and then we will all leave, but I think Mr. Hoenig will come with me and not with you. Wouldn't you prefer that, Mr. Hoenig?"

"You mean at home?" he mumbled, staring down.

"That's not going to happen," Kaplan said. "Reuben is coming with us and that is not negotiable." Still, he retracted the blade on his knife and put it back into his pocket.

"The man is smart," Elmo said. "Two guns are better than a little knife."

"I believe we have the upper hand in the negotiations," I told Kaplan. "Now, should Ms. Washburn retrieve your cash or not?"

"Absolutely she should," Kaplan answered. "That's my money."

"Agreed." I nodded to Ms. Washburn, who held the gun steady but walked toward the street, giving Kaplan some room.

But when she reached his position Kaplan viciously stuck out his right foot, effectively sweeping Ms. Washburn's legs. She stumbled and Kaplan reached over to get the gun. It dropped to the pavement and made a loud noise but did not fire. Ms. Washburn had applied the safety mechanism, or the man with the bushy eyebrows had before he stashed the weapon in his jacket pocket.

Ms. Washburn reached for the gun but Kaplan, who had not fallen over, was faster. He grabbed it and stuck his hand out to secure Ms. Washburn. She saw what he was attempting to do and rolled away from him. Kaplan stood straight and pointed the pistol, after working the safety off, at Ms. Washburn. I had just enough time to lean over and whisper to Reuben but I wasn't sure he heard me.

"Let's go, Reuben," Kaplan said.

"Elmo isn't letting your man go," said the large furry performer.

"I'll get another," Kaplan said. "I'll be back for my money."

"Let the man go," I said to Elmo. "But don't give him a weapon. Keep your gun aimed at Mr. Kaplan."

"I distrust a man who says *when*," Reuben quoted.

"Samuel," Ms. Washburn began.

"We will be in touch," I said to Kaplan.

"I won't answer. I'll come when you don't expect me." With that he, the man with the impressive eyebrows, and Reuben walked to the curb, where the black car instantly appeared. They got in and it drove away.

I asked Ms. Washburn if she was all right.

"Physically, yes," she answered. "But I'm embarrassed. I never should have let him trip me."

"It was not your fault." I looked at Elmo. "What took you so long?" I asked.

Mike the taxicab driver pulled off the costume head and withdrew his gun inside the costume. "Do you have any idea how hard it is to rent an Elmo costume at the last minute in L.A.?" he asked.

SEVENTEEN

"I believe that Reuben Hoenig has character traits that would indicate Asperger's Syndrome," I told Mike and Ms. Washburn.

We were sitting in the restaurant of the hotel, where I had secured a room for Mike. After he had put off three days of his livelihood at the last minute (an expression I had learned to use only lately) to fly to Los Angeles at my request, it seemed to be the least compensation I could offer. When I had called Mike and explained the situation, he had insisted on making the trip with a handgun legally allowed with a permit, unassembled and unloaded, in the bag he checked for storage by the airline. I had paid Mike's airfare as well.

At Ms. Washburn's suggestion we had vacated the Canoga Park hotel because it was possible Kaplan knew we were staying there. Now that he had vowed to find us when we were unaware of him, it was agreed that new arrangements had to be made. Ms. Washburn used her cellular phone to find another hotel in Burbank. It was considerably more expensive, but seemed the safe choice. I would be sure to accept more questions for income purposes when we arrived home.

"I didn't get a chance to really talk to him, but he seemed to be babbling," Ms. Washburn said. "He said things that didn't really fit the conversation."

"He appears to have a special interest in the novel and the film *The Maltese Falcon*," I said. "But I think he is also either self-medicating or being given some drugs that are affecting his behavior, since Mother never mentioned to me his acting in such a fashion."

"Maybe he didn't act like this thirty years ago," Mike suggested.

"It is a possibility. I have tried to contact my mother again since we arrived here in Burbank but her phone is still referring all calls immediately to voice mail. It is perplexing." I had informed Mike of the entirety of our situation including my inability to contact Mother, which was occupying more of my attention than the question at hand now. I had seen Reuben Hoenig and he seemed to be in no immediate danger. Finding his address might be something of a problem but it was not urgent.

"I'm sure she's fine, Samuel," Ms. Washburn said.

"Why?" I asked. Perhaps Ms. Washburn had information I had not yet received.

She looked stumped for a moment. "Because that seems the most likely thing right now."

Ms. Washburn had been trying to comfort me. I had missed that signal.

"What do we do now?" Mike asked. "We're only here until Saturday, and today's Thursday. Most of the day is gone already."

I had called Mike the day before and asked if he could take a short trip to Los Angeles in case Ms. Washburn and I required assistance, which seemed possible at the time. Mike had agreed and then when he'd arrived called me from the airport. I'd called him back when I could after Kaplan and I had arranged the meeting and Mike and

I had come up with the plan for him to rent a costume. That enabled him to get close to our group without seeming suspicious.

"How do we get your father away from Kaplan and that other man?" Ms. Washburn asked.

"That is not the objective," I reminded her. "Our task is to obtain a means of contact for my mother to use when she wants to communicate with Reuben Hoenig. If his circumstances are acceptable to him at this moment, we have no reason to interfere with them."

Ms. Washburn put down her glass of white wine. "Samuel, your father is being held hostage by Kaplan, maybe by force. Don't you want to help him?"

I realized that many people would be driven by emotion under these circumstances. There are blood ties, I am told, that supersede those of history and incident. I did not feel an obligation to a man who had left my mother with a young son who would be difficult to raise. Perhaps more sessions with Dr. Mancuso focusing specifically on this area would produce something, but there was no time for that now, and Dr. Mancuso was almost three thousand miles away. Trying to achieve a breakthrough would be impractical.

"I see nothing from which Reuben needs to be extracted," I said. "He came with Kaplan willingly, from all indications. He left without resisting physically or verbally. What is interesting is that Kaplan considers him invaluable and would not let us take Reuben away."

"Why do you think he did that?" Mike asked.

Mike is a veteran of the United States military who came home to New Jersey after several tours of duty and bought a Toyota Prius to convert into a taxicab because he does not like to stay in one place very long. We met at Newark Liberty International Airport when I had seen Mother off on a trip to visit her sister Aunt Jane in Colorado. Mike's professionalism—and the fact that his taxicab had never been occupied by another passenger before me—had impressed me and we had eventually become friends. Mike also has a very keen mind that he needs to keep occupied because memories of his wartime experiences are troubling and he prefers to focus on other things. When I have issues involving human interaction, I often consult Mike.

Ms. Washburn has said she thinks it's odd that I do not know Mike's last name but that has never been an issue.

"I believe based on the behavior we have seen that George Kaplan is running an illegal business of some sort from the house we visited in Reseda," I began. "It is a business lucrative enough that people even casually associated with it can be given packages of forty thousand dollars simply on arrival. Because Kaplan seems to require Reuben Hoenig's presence I will venture to speculate that Reuben is in some way an integral part of that business. Kaplan can't afford to lose Reuben. So he might be administering some medication to keep Reuben pliable and that could be enough to squelch any impulse he might have to leave. But much of this is simply guesswork. We don't know enough factually yet."

"We have a day and a half," Ms. Washburn reminded me, "unless we decide to extend our stay."

"That is not feasible professionally or financially," I answered. "I must be back in the office Monday morning."

"Plus, you don't want to be out here any longer than you have to," she countered.

"That is true, but it does not make the other factors less so," I said.

"It brings me back to my original question," Mike said. "What do we do now?"

"I think the most effective way to attack the question is to investigate George Kaplan and his business," I told him. "This will require a good deal of online research I will do in my hotel room tonight. I imagine there will not be much available about him on simple Google searches; covert businesses will be on other areas of the web."

"Can I help with that?" Ms. Washburn asked. She used the word *can* correctly, in that she was asking whether her expertise would be helpful in the research.

"I believe your talents are best suited elsewhere," I told her. "We also need to ascertain whether Reuben Hoenig actually appropriated the name George Kaplan on his move to Southern California, or whether the man we know as Kaplan is actually someone else. The personnel records from Mendoza Communications have shown us that something happened, but we can't be clear on what it was. If we discover the current George Kaplan's real name, we might have some insight into his practices and that could give us some inroads to retrieve contact information for Reuben Hoenig."

"You never refer to him as your dad," Mike noted.

It was a point I had addressed before, but never in his presence, so I tried to ignore the slight feeling of irritation I had experienced. "There is no utility in speaking that way," I said. "I've never known a father."

Mike did not react but seemed to think it over.

"Maybe we should work together in your room," Ms. Washburn suggested. "It'll be more like the way we operate at Questions Answered."

I realized she was attempting to re-create a comfortable work environment for me. But there was something unsettling about being in a hotel room alone with Ms. Washburn that I could not accurately identify. Since I was not able to analyze my feelings I decided to ignore them. "Perhaps that would be a good idea," I said. "Mike, we don't have a computer for you."

"Don't worry about it," he told me. "I'm going to sleep."

"Just us, then," Ms. Washburn said. She looked at me. "You ready?"

I have never been uncomfortable with Ms. Washburn, which is a statement I do not make lightly. I am uncomfortable with almost every person I have ever met. Even Mike, whom I consider a friend, emits an air of incredulousness that sometimes leaves me slightly anxious, wondering if I have said or done something inappropriate. Ms. Washburn has always been unconcerned with pointing out when my behavior is somehow outside the norm and that actually puts me as close to at ease as I can be.

Since I could not accurately analyze the feelings I was having, I saw no way to object to Ms. Washburn's plan. We made plans to meet in my hotel room in twenty minutes to do our research.

Perhaps she was correct and the surroundings would make no difference. It would be similar to our work in the Questions Answered office. There was, indeed, no factual or measureable reason that would not be the case.

But I could not completely banish the slight queasiness in my stomach and the tantalizing feeling that there was something, just out of conscious thought, that was causing my heightened sense of danger. And I realized that my business relationship with Ms. Washburn was the thing I was afraid of losing.

I had explored the new hotel room when we had arrived and set up in exactly the same way as I did in the Canoga Park hotel. This room was slightly larger and cleaner and did not have the overpowering odor that had permeated the other. It was possible, I decided, that this room had been designated as a non-smoking accommodation much less recently than the other.

Ms. Washburn knocked on the door at precisely the time she had said she would, knowing my interest in remaining prompt and my distaste for surprises. She was carrying the bag in which she transports her laptop computer.

"Where should I set up?" she asked, seeing I had opened my MacBook on the desk provided by the hotel. "On the bed?"

"No," I said. "There is a small sofa near the coffee table. That might be better."

"Oh yeah," Ms. Washburn said, looking farther into the room. "The loveseat."

"It is a convertible sofa if an extra bed is needed by the guest," I corrected her.

She smiled and sat down on the sofa. She removed her laptop computer from the bag and opened it on the coffee table. "If I had a phone on the table, I would feel like I was back at Questions Answered," she said.

That was confusing. "This room does not resemble our office," I pointed out.

"You're right." There was no explanation forthcoming.

I decided to immerse myself in the research. I began with some backdoor search engines I have discovered that find things most casual users will not find. I began with the words *Kaplan Enterprises* and, in addition to the same items I had found in more casual searches before were six thousand four hundred and seventy-eight new links concerning George Kaplan and his business practices.

Many of them were false leads, as a cursory glance at the list revealed. Some were simply not about George Kaplan at all but dealt with other people who shared the surname. Others concerned themselves with businesses whose names included the word *Enterprises* and had a mention of someone with the name in a related news article, blog post, or website.

This process of reduction brought the total of new hits to less than three hundred. What was left included references to Kaplan Enterprises purchasing properties in the area, but not so many that it would indicate an enormous financial outlay.

Perhaps this would be a good time to re-examine the issue of kissing with Ms. Washburn. That thought occurred without any direct process. It might be a way to reduce the tension I was feeling with her in the room, something I had never experienced before. On the other hand, even considering the idea of broaching the subject increased my anxiety noticeably. I felt a band of perspiration form around my hairline. I shook a bit without being able to reduce the effect despite knowing it was coming.

On second thought, this might not be the right time or place. Back to the research.

"I've got something," Ms. Washburn said at that moment. "I don't think it's something big, but it's something." She gestured to me indicating I should come to the sofa and sit beside her. "I'm plugged in," she said, pointing to the power cord she had attached to her laptop computer and the wall socket near the sofa.

"Is it about the possibility of a zoning issue on the building in Reseda?" I asked.

Ms. Washburn shook her head negatively. "From all I can tell, that's a dead end," she said. "Nothing's been filed and no complaints have been made. I don't think it's anything."

I stood and walked to her makeshift workstation. She gestured to the seat beside her and reluctantly I sat. I could not stand behind the sofa, which was against the wall, nor could I expect Ms. Washburn to turn her computer toward me when she needed access at the same time as I did.

She showed me the screen. She had navigated to a web page for the United States Department of Labor, which I found immediately interesting. It was not something I would have considered myself. Ms. Washburn proved herself valuable to Questions Answered with virtually every action she took.

"The individual employment records for Mendoza Communications didn't show me anything new," she said. "So I decided to see if the government had any public records showing complaints in their hiring practices, see if there were any legal actions that indicated this name-change thing was something they do on a regular basis."

"Does the government make those records public?" I asked. Sitting this close to Ms. Washburn was undoubtedly distracting me but the question remained unanswered and the information she was giving me definitely had some bearing on our work.

"They have to if they take legal action," she said. "But as far as I can see they never made a complaint against Mendoza."

"I don't understand," I told her. "If there are no complaints, what information is there to be had?"

"There are no complaints against *Mendoza*," Ms. Washburn answered, "but there are complaints against other companies that deal in radio and television advertising time. In fact, there are seven complaints against them, and they are from all over the country. Portland, Oregon. St. Louis, Missouri. Boca Raton, Florida. And yes, one filed in Reseda, California."

"That is somewhat interesting, but probably not very unusual," I said. "Any industry will have some employment complaints filed against companies on a regular basis, I'd think."

"That's right, but I wasn't searching for complaints in the advertising time business," Ms. Washburn said with a sly smile. "I was running a search for the name George Kaplan."

I took a moment to process what I was being told. "You're saying there are seven complaints about companies buying and selling advertising time and they were all filed by George Kaplan?"

"Bingo."

That last word was not a reference to the game played in many churches and social clubs, but a statement that I was correct in what I had surmised. "What is the time frame involved in the complaints?" I asked.

"I didn't look back very far. They all took place within the last four years."

My mind raced a bit. "So it's very unlikely that the man we know as George Kaplan filed all the complaints himself."

"That's right. It appears there are a number of George Kaplans running around the country being hired and fired unfairly," Ms. Washburn said.

I sat back and stopped thinking about kissing her for the moment. "Bingo, indeed," I said.

EIGHTEEN

Ms. WASHBURN AND I spent another three hours digging into parts of the Internet for as much information as we could find about George Kaplan, companies that bought and sold advertising time, and legal challenges to their hiring and firing practices.

During that time, we determined:

There were at least seven complaints filed in seven separate cities in the United States by men whose legal names were all George Kaplan;

The complaints all suggested that the company by which the Kaplan in question had been employed had engaged in fraudulent or unfair business practices, usually involving breach of contract;

Each complaint had been investigated by the Department of Labor of the state in question;

Each complaint had been found valid and disciplinary action had been taken against each of the companies named;

George Kaplan had not profited personally from the complaints;

Five of the seven companies had been forced into bankruptcy due to legal fees and the governmental action taken against them.

Once midnight struck (not literally, as there were no clocks with chimes in the hotel room) Ms. Washburn had said she was tired and needed to go to bed. She stood and said good night and left the hotel room heading for her own.

I prepared myself for sleep as I always do and lay down on the bed, leaving one light on in the bathroom because I was unfamiliar with the layout of the room. I stared up at the ceiling for sixteen minutes thinking about the question I was trying to solve, but my earlier discomfort with Ms. Washburn in the room also crept into my thoughts.

I concentrated on the question first: What was the connection among the seven George Kaplans filing complaints with the Department of Labor? This seemed clearly enough to be a coordinated effort; the idea that seven men named George Kaplan each worked in the same industry, one that I had never heard of before researching this question, that each had encountered a similar kind of workplace violation, that each had thought to file a complaint with the same governmental agency, that all of them had been found valid and that each Kaplan had not gained financially from the proceedings was far too unlikely a coincidence to be deemed plausible.

But if this was a planned initiative, who was behind it? Whose idea had it been, and what was his or her (probably his, given all the George Kaplans) motivation? Surely it was not financial gain.

My mind was starting to slip into a more relaxed and therefore less cognitive state as I considered Ms. Washburn. More to the point, I wondered about my suddenly odd response to her presence. Ms. Washburn had not changed her behavior but my anxiety level was noticeably higher when she and I were alone in the hotel room than it had ever been before, even higher than when she was in danger of having her head cut off.

Suddenly I was noticing the way she looked, which had never occurred to me before. I was paying attention to her proximity when we were working, which was hardly relevant to the work at hand. I was inwardly debating the best time to approach her about kissing again when I possibly should have been concentrating on the fact that my mother remained out of contact thousands of miles away. My priorities were shifting and the worst part was that I didn't understand them.

I don't remember much after that because defying all the clichés about troubling thoughts keeping one awake, I fell asleep and did not wake until my iPhone alarm rang at seven a.m.

As we had previously arranged, Ms. Washburn, Mike, and I met in the lobby of the hotel at eight a.m. with the intention of finding a way to make George Kaplan—the one we had met—come into the open. It would be better to confront Kaplan about Reuben Hoenig on our own terms rather than waiting for a vengeful man to find us.

But I had continued my musing as I showered and dressed that morning and now suggested we find a suitable restaurant to have breakfast first while we discussed plans for our day. We told Mike about our research of the night before and gave him all the information we had uncovered. Then I looked at Ms. Washburn because I wanted to gauge her reaction. "I have a theory," I said. "I believe we should discuss it so I can get your input."

Ms. Washburn did not look surprised, but Mike smiled broadly. "Want to give us a sneak preview?" he asked.

"Food first," Ms. Washburn told him. She is well acquainted with my daily routine, even if it does not typically begin with waking in a hotel room and meeting two people in the lobby. "I've found a place near here."

She took us to a restaurant called the Eye Opener, which devoted itself specifically to breakfast. There had been a mild protest from

Mike about letting Ms. Washburn drive until she pointed out accurately that is was her name on the rental car agreement and she had listed only me as an alternate driver, knowing full well I would never take on such a responsibility. In the past seven years I had driven only enough to keep my skills sharp, twice around the block on which Mother and I live, and had found the experience troubling.

After ordering our meals, we were not silent for long. Mike crossed his arms and looked at me. "Okay, the food's on its way," he said. "So what have you figured out?"

"I don't know if 'figured out' would be the most accurate term," I said. "But I have a theory based on the facts we know and I want to hear if either of you sees a way that it does or does not seem plausible."

Ms. Washburn, who says she is addicted to coffee, took a sip of hers as if to fortify herself. "Let's hear it," she said.

"The idea is based on the part of the question that goes to motivation," I said. "It is clear that with the scheme to place George Kaplans in companies around the country, the Kaplan we know—whatever his real name might be—is trying to accomplish some goal. But because none of the complaints resulted in a financial payment I had a difficult time understanding what the Kaplans were trying to accomplish."

"I'm still having a hard time," said Ms. Washburn. "But you seem to be saying you have an idea."

Mike eyed the plate of sausage and scrambled eggs headed his way as the server, whose name was Linda, placed our orders in front of us. I examined my bowl and the small box of Special K cereal that Linda had brought. "Do you have any one-percent milk?" I asked her. "This is two-percent."

Linda paused after delivering a toasted bagel with cream cheese to Ms. Washburn. "Sure," she said. "I'll be right back."

"One percent instead of two percent?" Mike asked. "You can tell?"

"I would be spending my morning thinking of the extra fat coursing through my veins," I said. "It would be unproductive."

Ms. Washburn smiled, having seen this exchange before. "The motive, Samuel. Why does Kaplan want to file all these complaints with all the other Kaplans all over the country?"

"Think of the outcome," I said. "That was how I came to the answer."

"Oh, let's not go to class, Samuel," Ms. Washburn said as she spread the cream cheese on a half of her bagel. I chose not to look at her hands and had to concentrate on her eyes even if that was not my natural inclination. "Just tell us what you figured out."

I would have preferred to lead Ms. Washburn especially to the same idea and give her the sense of accomplishment, but I decided to accede to her wishes. "The idea was fairly simple, actually," I began. "It was all the Kaplans that distracted me."

"Makes sense." Mike rumbled through a bite of his breakfast. I was very careful not to look at him. I had never eaten with Mike before, and do not care to watch people eat under any set of circumstances. Sausage and eggs simply amplified my distaste. I did not care to think of what they had been fried in.

"What happened was the Kaplans around the country filed small complaints designed to get the Department of Labor in each state, or if they were lucky, the Federal Government, to investigate the practices of other companies doing roughly the same work Mendoza Communications is doing," I explained. "In almost every case the government agency found some impropriety and demanded changes in the company's practices. In a large number of the incidents, the company found misbehaving was forced out of business shortly thereafter."

Ms. Washburn stopped with her coffee mug halfway to her mouth and her eyes widened. "So the goal wasn't to extort other companies into paying the Kaplans to be quiet and there was no reward for bringing the complaints to the Labor Department," she said. Her tone indicated the truth was coming to her fairly quickly. "The idea was to eliminate the competition through the government."

Linda brought my one-percent milk in a small pitcher as I was opening the box of Special K cereal. I thanked her as I have been taught to do and she walked away, which was my preference.

"Exactly," I told Ms. Washburn. "I'd guess that if we researched the income of Mendoza Communications from the time the complaints about employment began until they ended, we would see the revenues rise dramatically as more clients, forced out of the markets they had been trading in, came to the company for its advertising time."

"Why employment complaints?" Mike asked. "That kind of thing won't always result in an investigation that will close a company."

"It got someone inside the competitor first," Ms. Washburn said. I look a bite of Special K with the one-percent milk poured over it and it tasted almost exactly like the cereal I would eat at home. It was possible the one-percent milk was actually fat-free milk, but Mother would say it wasn't worth arguing about.

I tried not to think about Mother. It was already approaching noon in New Jersey and I had left two new messages. Something else I needed to banish from my mind while confronting the issue at hand.

"That's right," I told Ms. Washburn. "Not only did the planting of a false Kaplan begin the possible process of an investigation, it also gained Mendoza Communications valuable information on the inner workings of the competition."

"So how does this help us find your dad, Samuel?" Mike the taxi-cab driver is nothing if not direct. He is an excellent resource for staying on task and on topic.

Ms. Washburn, who was facing the door of Eye Opener, looked up from her plate and seemed a bit surprised. "I don't think that's going to be a problem," she said.

171

I looked at her for a moment until she gestured with her head toward the door. Then I turned to look in the direction she had indicated.

Entering the small restaurant were George Kaplan and his heavily eyebrowed associate. Reuben Hoenig was nowhere to be seen.

"Not exactly," I said.

NINETEEN

"How could they have found us?" Ms. Washburn said quietly as the two men walked toward our table. "*We* didn't even know we were coming here until a half hour ago."

"I texted Kaplan," I informed her. "Better to have them come when we expected them than at some random moment."

"Janet and I didn't expect them," Mike pointed out. He was correct; that had been an oversight on my part.

Kaplan reached the table first and stood over my left shoulder. "You have an offer to make?" he said. His social skills required a good deal of revision, I thought. Perhaps a good therapist or a weekly group meeting would be of help to him.

"I see no reason to change the offer I have already made," I said. "We will be glad to give you the forty thousand dollars in cash when you allow me to speak at length to Reuben Hoenig. But he must not be on his current regimen of medication because that makes conversation with him more difficult." I looked toward the door. "Did you bring him with you?"

Involuntarily Kaplan glanced at the door too. Then his face took on a sheepish quality and he looked back at me. "No, of *course* I didn't

173

bring him with me." His voice had a hoarse, urgent quality. "And stop saying how much money we're talking about when people can hear you."

That made no sense. There was little point to speaking when no one could hear me. Why would I even consider altering the volume of my voice to the point that it would be inaudible?

"When can you bring him to us?" I asked. "It must be sometime today because we are flying back to the East Coast tomorrow morning."

Mike winced just a bit. I thought he was reacting to what I'd said but could not be certain. I would ask him later.

"I'm not bringing him to you," Kaplan said. "You're not giving me anything you didn't already offer."

I already knew that; perhaps Kaplan was behaving this way because I had done something rude. I don't always notice.

"Would you care to join us?" I asked him. "We can get an extra chair from Linda for your associate."

Kaplan sneered. "No, I don't want to *join* you. You don't seem to understand how this works. This is a business negotiation. If you want something from me, you have to offer something I want. You want your dad. I want my money. But you've already welched on one offer. You got to talk to him and I got nothing."

I had anticipated this tactic. I reached into my pocket and retrieved a bound packet of cash I had extracted from the money Kaplan's associate in the Reseda house had given Ms. Washburn and me the day before. "You may have this for the conversation I had with Reuben Hoenig yesterday," I said. "I believe that is fair compensation. For the rest I must see Mr. Hoenig unmedicated and without a time limit. Is that agreeable?"

Perhaps forgetting his declaration of a minute before, Kaplan sat on the empty chair at our table. His bushy-browed associate remained standing.

"No, it's not *agreeable*," he said. "Our deal was you talked to your dad and I got my money. This isn't all my money."

"No, but Samuel didn't have a whole conversation with his father," Ms. Washburn pointed out. "You get what you get until that happens, Mr. Kaplan."

"Watch your mouth, lady," Kaplan said. I felt a flash of anger at the way he was treating Ms. Washburn.

She merely sat back, ignored her bagel, and folded her arms. "What is your real name, anyway?" she asked. "George Kaplan is the name Reuben Hoenig got when he left Seattle. How'd you end up with it?"

Kaplan made a guttural noise. His associate took his hands out of the pockets of his trousers.

Mike unfolded his arms.

"If you wish to negotiate terms, I will make a counteroffer," I told Kaplan in an effort to defuse the situation. I was angry at Kaplan but did not want to see a violent scene erupt in the small restaurant.

He turned his attention to me quickly. "What's your offer?"

"My goal remains unchanged. I want an unlimited conversation with a completely unimpaired Reuben Hoenig. But since you seem to believe the down payment I have given you is insufficient, I will add what I believe businessmen like yourself call a sweetener."

"A sweetener." Kaplan looked amused. I had expected that. "What do you have in mind? Splenda?"

I did not recognize the word so I did not respond to it. Perhaps it was a derogatory name Kaplan was calling me to belittle the competition in some way. "No," I said. "Suppose I don't go through with my plans to tell the Labor Department about the other George Kaplans."

The current George Kaplan did not move a facial muscle for six seconds. When he spoke again, it was in a very low whisper with an edge of coarseness to it. "What did you say?" That was a delaying tactic to give Kaplan time to think. I understood the impulse. He had been surprised with information he was not expecting. It could prove to be damaging to his business and possibly his life, so he was processing and formulating an answer. But even if I did comprehend his hesitancy, I had no reason to indulge it. This was indeed a competition and Kaplan was the opposition.

"I believe you heard me," I said.

"I don't know what you're talking about," he countered. This, too, was merely a method of stalling; Kaplan could not possibly believe I would accept a claim of ignorance.

"Yes, you do," Ms. Washburn said. She is adept at keeping the conversation moving and she clearly understood it was time to increase pressure on Kaplan. "Now, what is it worth to you for us to keep quiet about your operation sending men named George Kaplan around the country and placing them in companies run by your competition?" She was not giving away all the information we had but was making it clear to Kaplan that we were not simply guessing. We had uncovered his scheme and we could, if we wanted to, expose it to the proper authorities.

I was not certain he had done anything illegal, but the way the color drained from his face indicated to me that it was not an unlikely scenario.

Kaplan tried to look calm but there was already perspiration soaking his collar. "It's not worth anything," he said. "We haven't done anything wrong."

"Very well, then," I said, having finished the last of my Special K. "I will return to my original offer of returning the remainder of the cash your associate gave us in exchange for unfettered access to Reuben Hoenig. And we will consider ourselves free to contact any authorities we please to discuss the way you and Mendoza Communications have done business these past few years." I wiped my mouth with the paper napkin supplied and placed it on the table.

I do not signal to servers for the check. I do not wish to interact with strangers when it isn't necessary and I believe the servers consider such gestures somehow demeaning, only because Ms. Washburn has said she felt that way when waiting tables to work her way through college. But Linda came over and asked if we needed anything else and Ms. Washburn indicated the bill would be appreciated. Linda, an efficient server, produced it immediately and left the table.

Since this was a business trip I paid for the entire check. Ms. Washburn and Mike the taxicab driver were in Burbank on my behalf and that of Questions Answered. I calculated a 20 percent tip and included it in the cash—not that given to us by Kaplan's associate—I left on the table. I stood up.

"What time today may I talk to Reuben Hoenig?" I asked Kaplan, who looked agitated.

His mouth opened and closed three times while his eyelids fluttered. I wondered if Kaplan was having a seizure of some sort, but Ms. Washburn, who would normally be concerned at such a possibility, looked absolutely calm.

"You're playing in awfully dangerous waters," Kaplan said finally. Since I do not often play anywhere, but particularly not in water, the expression confused me until I realized he was mixing metaphors. I would decipher his syntax later but I understood he was trying to sound an ominous warning.

"What time?" I repeated. Mike and Ms. Washburn, having stood, began to head toward the door, but I noticed that Mike stayed behind Kaplan's associate.

"I'll call you," Kaplan said. He walked briskly to the door and left without looking back at the three of us, his bushy-browed associate, startled, struggling to keep up his pace.

Ms. Washburn, Mike, and I watched them leave. I saw Mike's shoulders relax as soon as they were outside the restaurant. "Don't go out until I check," he said. "I don't want to walk into something." Assuming correctly we would respect his authority in such matters, Mike walked cautiously out of the restaurant, leaving Ms. Washburn and me behind waiting for his signal.

Unexpectedly I felt Ms. Washburn's hand reaching for mine. I am not fond of being touched when I have not prepared but I did not react. I let her fingers intertwine with my own. The Beatles song "I Want to Hold Your Hand" began to play in my mind.

"You can't do that to me again," she said quietly.

I struggled to understand her statement. She was the one who had reached for my hand; it had not been my idea. Was she upset at my holding her hand? I needed clarification. "Do what?" I asked.

"You texted George Kaplan and told him where we were so he would come in while we were eating," Ms. Washburn said.

"It was an efficient way to expedite the next step in the process of answering the question," I said, although I had explained my motivation earlier.

"I know," she answered. "But you can't do something like that without telling me first. Kaplan is a dangerous man. Something bad could have happened." Her fingers tightened in my hand.

It had not occurred to me that Ms. Washburn would be upset about my method. It made perfect sense to me to contact Kaplan so I had done it. Taking someone else's reaction into account was still a skill I needed to develop.

"I will try not to do that again," I said.

"Okay."

Mike appeared in the front window of Eye Openers and extended his right hand, thumb up. Ms. Washburn and I disentangled our hands and walked outside.

TWENTY

"WE SHOULD HAVE FOLLOWED them," said Mike the taxicab driver.

Ms. Washburn was driving the blue Kia Soul toward the Neighborhood Council building in Reseda in the hope that we might be able to discover something more about George Kaplan's neighbors. Perhaps speaking to them—something Ms. Washburn had suggested but which made me nervous—would unearth useful information before Kaplan called my iPhone and gave us the coordinates for the exchange of cash for Reuben Hoenig, which I hoped would be soon. I had given up hope of leaving the Los Angeles area early but was determined to leave the next day without fail.

"I understand that following Kaplan and his associate might have led us to Reuben Hoenig," I told Mike, "but the idea that we could have gotten to the Kia Soul, which was two blocks away, and then successfully shadowed their movements without being seen is, at best, unlikely. Kaplan will call."

"Yeah, but he'll have time to plan," Mike said. "I don't want this to happen on his terms where he can control the situation."

"It has to happen before two o'clock," Ms. Washburn said, "or I can't go."

That was a surprise. "Why not?" I asked.

"I have a reservation for the Warner Brothers studio tour at two," she answered, a hint of rebellion in her voice, I thought. "It's our last day here and I wanted to see a studio."

"But our business might require you to be present at that time," I protested.

"Sorry, Samuel. I paid sixty-two bucks for this tour. You'll have to plan around me."

Ms. Washburn was treating this trip almost like a vacation, which was uncharacteristic of her. Apparently a person's behavior when traveling can be markedly different that that when in a standard business routine. I preferred the routine.

"Very well," I sighed. "You may have the afternoon off."

"Not that I asked, but thank you, Samuel."

She drove silently and carefully and I considered what we had determined toward answering Mother's question. She had wanted us to discover what Reuben Hoenig's address or contact information was now that he had settled, it seemed, in Southern California. Frankly, given the heat and humidity of the area, the difficulty in going anywhere without driving a vehicle, and the locals we had spent most of our time confronting, I saw little to recommend this area of the country. Others, I knew, would have disagreed with that opinion. They were wrong.

So far we had determined that a man calling himself George Kaplan had established himself with Mendoza Communications, an enterprise that apparently bought advertising time from television and radio stations and resold it to people who were encouraged to believe they could do the same and make a profit—something that was probably not true. Subsequent research had indicated the practice was not illegal, although irregular. Most stations, having sold the time, did not care whether it was filled with paid commercials or plug-in public service announcements because they had already been paid. Advertising agencies, which often bought the time for clients, would not be pleased, but there was no legal recourse. The only people really losing money were the "civilians," as Kaplan had thought Ms. Washburn and me to be, who paid more than market value for time they could not resell.

But there were other Kaplans, men (presumably) who were sent to other cities to work for companies like Mendoza Communications, infiltrate their ranks, familiarize themselves with the companies' business practices, and then report irregular actions to government agencies in the hope of making the competing companies insolvent. Again, nothing illegal, with the possible exception of operating under an assumed name when filing government documents. It was not worth the kind of threats and secrecy Kaplan had been employing.

And then there was the house in Reseda where a casual visitor would be handed a package containing forty thousand dollars in cash. On the surface that was not illegal, but it seemed obvious that some illicit activity was generating the funds being distributed. We had not been able to discover what it might be.

A thought occurred to me so I retrieved my iPhone from my pocket and began pressing on its touchpad.

"Did George Kaplan call?" Mike asked.

I heard his question but was engrossed in the research I was doing. Ms. Washburn said, "I didn't hear it ring."

"Ms. Washburn," I said, "I am going to input a new destination into the Global Positioning System device. You might want to pull over and stop while it calculates the route."

Ms. Washburn did not comment but maneuvered the Kia Soul toward the curb on the right side of the street and stopped. I checked the address on my iPhone screen and made sure I was entering it correctly. After a few moments the device was plotting a route.

"Where are we going?" Ms. Washburn asked.

"To a place called Studio City," I said. "Perhaps you will not need to go on your tour after all."

"Sixty-two dollars, Samuel," she reminded me. The Global Positioning System device began to verbally give directions to the address I had inputted. "I'm going either way. I don't care what the name of this town is. What's in Studio City?"

"A place we should have gone to already," I said. "Number fifteen thirty-two Laurel Canyon Boulevard. I want to see if Mr. Wilson T. Alvarez knows what George Kaplan is doing on his behalf."

"Who's Mr. Wilson T. Alvarez?" Mike asked.

"The chief executive officer of Mendoza Communications. Number fifteen thirty-two Laurel Canyon Boulevard is the company's corporate headquarters, according to its website."

It took Ms. Washburn twenty-eight minutes to drive to Studio City, which was odd, considering it was only fourteen miles from our previous location. I was learning that traffic in the Los Angeles area, notoriously crowded, was even more seriously congested than I had originally anticipated. Every trip's travel time needed to be overestimated by about twice the normal expectation. It was an irritant, but it was predictable and could therefore be included in planning, which helped me tolerate it.

The building housing Mendoza Communications was quite unintimidating. It was a two-story office structure that occupied most of the block and was finished in the same shade of Southwestern adobe that I'd discovered is simulated on many veneers in the Los Angeles area. There was no security at the entrance so we walked in uninterrupted.

A directory in the lobby indicated no fewer than six businesses housed in the facility, but Mendoza Communications was listed in Suite 204. "Maybe this is just their administrative office," Ms. Washburn suggested as we mounted the central staircase from the lobby to the upstairs suites.

"Perhaps, but since the business deals largely, if not exclusively, with a theoretical product, it has no need for warehouse space," I told her. "I would suppose this is the entire operation."

Again there was no obstacle to our entering when we located Suite 204 and turned the doorknob. Mike insisted on walking in first, although there was absolutely no indication of any danger. He takes his responsibilities (assigned or self-imposed) seriously and wanted to best facilitate Ms. Washburn and me doing the best job we could.

Of course there was no one lying in wait for us and I saw Mike relax his shoulders a bit once he was able to scan the facility. It was an extended bullpen area of perhaps eight work stations with a reception desk at the front. Behind it sat a young African-American woman with a very serious demeanor.

"Allow me to introduce myself," I said to the woman. "I am Samuel Hoenig, proprietor of Questions Answered. I am here to see Mr. Wilson T. Alvarez."

The woman behind the desk did not move for a moment, then blinked. "You have an appointment?" she asked.

"We do not," I told her honestly. "We are attempting to answer a question that involves this business and hoped he might be able to enlighten us in a few areas."

Ms. Washburn stepped forward and established eye contact with the young woman. "It will really only take a minute," she said, although I would have estimated a conference time of at least five times that length.

"What do you want to ask him about?" The young woman, whose name was indicated as Taisha Mkombo on a nameplate resting on her desk, directed her question to Ms. Washburn as opposed to me. But she seemed to find Mike the taxicab driver more interesting, and was watching him rather closely. I could not read her expression accurately.

"We have a question about how Mendoza operates," Ms. Washburn answered. "We're not from the police or anything. Nobody's in any trouble. We just need some information. Can we just see him for a minute?"

The area behind the reception desk was a blank wall, but the corner to Ms. Mkombo's left and our right seemed to open to an office. Since the rest of the workspace was devoted to people behind desks, most talking on telephones and wearing headsets, I assumed the sole private office in the facility would be occupied by the chief executive officer. If I spoke loudly enough anything I said would be heard inside that office.

"He's really busy today," Ms. Mkombo said without consulting the computer screen on her desk or a calendar on her blotter. "Why don't you leave a message and he'll call you on Monday?" The last sentence was not a question, but Ms. Mkombo's inflection, one that seemed especially prevalent in this area of the country, indicated that it might be.

"We will not be in Southern California on Monday," I answered before Ms. Washburn could reply. "And it is imperative that we see Mr. Alvarez as soon as possible."

Ms. Mkombo, who had probably been instructed not to allow unannounced visitors in to see her employer, shook her head and attempted to look sad. "I'm sorry," she said. "It's just not possible."

I do not always modulate my conversational voice appropriately. I am not really listening to the tone of my own voice because I am always aware of my intention and my meaning and do not have to interpret it as I speak. But in this case, I consciously emphasized certain words and spoke more loudly than I normally would.

"That is not acceptable!" I shouted. "We must see Mr. Alvarez about *George Kaplan* immediately. The *George Kaplan* affair is of vital importance. We cannot wait to find out about *George Kaplan!*"

As I had expected, a man in his late forties with a seriously receding hairline and a dark mustache emerged from the office behind Ms. Mkombo. He was walking quickly and stopped short of wiping his balding dome with a handkerchief, but looked tense nonetheless.

"Who is shouting?" he asked, despite being able to see me clearly. He did not stare at Ms. Washburn or Mike because it was obvious I was the one shouting the name he'd prefer not to hear at such a high volume.

"I am," I said. It was true, however unnecessary. "Are you Wilson T. Alvarez?"

"Yes. And I'd appreciate it if you'd stop making a scene in my place of business."

I had heard the term "making a scene" many times before, particularly when I was a child. I have never completely accepted its accuracy, as some theatrical scenes can be very quiet and gentle depending on the subject matter. But I have learned to simply assume the common usage and move on.

"I would be happy to speak much more quietly and privately if we can move to your office, Mr. Alvarez," I told him. "I believe you have some idea of what my concern might be based on your reaction to the name George Kaplan." I did not emphasize the sensitive name that time, seeing no advantage in doing so.

"I tried to tell them you were busy," Ms. Mkombo said to her superior.

He waved his hand to declare her concern irrelevant. "We'll talk inside. Make sure we're not disturbed." Then he gestured with the same hand toward his office door, apparently instructing Mike, Ms. Washburn, and me to follow him inside.

We did so and found a rather cramped, sparsely decorated space with the same fluorescent lighting as the rest of the office and two chairs in front of the indistinct desk behind which Mr. Alvarez positioned himself.

I stopped, unsure of what to do. Surely Ms. Washburn should have one of the "guest" chairs, but would it be rude or presumptuous of me to take the other? Would it be insulting for me to offer it to Mike? This kind of interaction is especially difficult for people like me after we have had some social skills training. If I had never met Dr. Mancuso, I would have sat down and never given the matter a thought.

Mike solved the problem by closing the office door behind him at Mr. Alvarez's suggestion and then leaning against the wall in the corner, folding his arms and leaving the extra chair for my use. We exchanged nods and I sat down gratefully. Another in an unending series of difficult human interactions successfully navigated.

"Now," Mr. Alvarez said when we had settled into his office. "What can I do for you nice people?"

I found that a rather bizarre thing to say. Mr. Alvarez had not known any of us long enough to have an impression of our characters. And I had made quite a show of demanding to know about George Kaplan, so asking why we had come to see him was redundant. I wondered if Mr. Alvarez was suffering from some sort of short-term memory disorder.

"We are here to ask about George Kaplan," I reminded him.

He nodded as if reminded of an obscure fact that had been mentioned weeks before. "Of course. And what is it you want to know?"

"We have been doing some research into a question asked by a client of our firm," I said. The fact that the client was my mother, and that she was still not answering her cellular phone or the landline in the house we shared, seemed unnecessary for this conversation. "In doing so, we have run into George Kaplan, or at least one George Kaplan. We are confused as to the type of business he is conducting and why you have asked him to conduct it."

Mr. Alvarez immediately held up both hands, palms out. "Whoa," he said. That is a command for a horse to stop running or walking, so its use in this context was incorrect. "George Kaplan does not work for Mendoza Communications."

That stunned me and apparently had the same effect on Ms. Washburn because she did not respond immediately either. Mike the taxicab driver is a man who prefers to observe and analyze rather than participate in interviews, so his reaction might simply have been a choice to wait and see what would happen.

"He doesn't?" Ms. Washburn said after a moment. "But I saw payroll records indicating that he did work for you. In fact, it appeared that George Kaplan had begun work in the Reseda office of Mendoza Communications a few years ago."

"We have no Reseda office," Mr. Alvarez responded. "We had one and closed it years ago. This is now our only location in Southern California."

I was still trying to work my mind through the ideas Mr. Alvarez was offering. "Does Kaplan work for Rayborn Communications?" I asked.

"No. *I* work for Rayborn. They own Mendoza Communications, bought the company over ten years ago. George Kaplan came down from Seattle a few years back and worked here for about a year, then he left and started his own business. We are actually sort of in competition with him now." Mr. Alvarez leaned back in his desk chair, exhibiting the posture of a very relaxed man.

"Did Kaplan get fired?" Ms. Washburn asked. It was an excellent question.

Mr. Alvarez shook his head. "He wanted to go off and start his own thing, I'm told. I didn't work with him so I don't really know firsthand what happened, but I've never heard that it was contentious or anything."

"So the business of Mendoza Communications is to purchase advertising time and then resell it through third parties at a profit?" I asked. We had speculated that was the case but had never fully confirmed the facts.

"No, that's what Kaplan is doing over in Reseda," Mr. Alvarez answered. "We act basically as an advertising agency, buying the time for our clients when we are instructed to do so and creating campaigns for them when they want to expand their brands."

"Is that what the people out in your office are doing?" Ms. Washburn asked. I had wondered that myself, seeing that most advertising agencies do not solicit clients by phone and that was what the employees in the office bullpen appeared to be practicing.

Mr. Alvarez shrugged. "They're cold-calling to try and find new clients," he admitted. "Radio and TV aren't as important as they used to be. A lot of companies are advertising strictly online. We offer that service, too, but it's not as lucrative. We have a good deal of broadcast time we'd like to get rid of, but the market is slow. The sales staff outside is trying to do something about that."

"So what George Kaplan does is not a standard industry practice?" I said.

"Not really, no. There isn't much upside in it. He has a large amount of outlay in the time he has to buy and then he's got to find people who think they're going to make their fortunes by taking it off his hands and marking up the price. It's not illegal, but most agencies wouldn't even think of doing that. You can get a bad reputation, and George has that."

"Is that why you reacted so strongly when I mentioned his name?"

Mr. Alvarez's face changed expression. His eyebrows dropped. His lips flattened into a horizontal line. When he spoke, his voice was considerably more restrained. This was a complex set of communicational cues happening all at once and I found it difficult to interpret in the moment.

"The thing is, when the corporate office in Seattle informed the people here that George Kaplan was being transferred to Mendoza—and this is strictly hearsay, you understand, because I wasn't here then—the man who came to work here was not the George Kaplan who's doing all this business in Reseda right now."

I suppose Mr. Alvarez expected us to look more surprised than we did. "We are aware there are multiple George Kaplans," I told him. "In fact, that is one of the reasons we have come here today. Can you tell me anything about the man who came here first with the name George Kaplan?"

Mr. Alvarez, perhaps disappointed in our subdued reaction, hesitated, then shook his head. "Like I said, I never worked with him. I don't think anybody who's working here now was in the company at the time, either. But the name George Kaplan has become something of a scourge in the industry."

"Because so many men with that name were planted in other companies and ended up causing them trouble?" Ms. Washburn asked.

Mr. Alvarez blinked, now informed that we were aware of that part of the scheme as well. "Yeah," he said. "It got to the point a couple of years ago where people in the business had been talking to each other enough they could figure out the scam. Anytime someone with the name George Kaplan applied for a job in a communications company, there would be emails all over the place sounding the alarm."

"Do you have the employment file on the man who first came here with that name?" Ms. Washburn asked. "Maybe that could tell us something."

Mr. Alvarez consulted his computer screen. "It's been a while but all our files were digitized last year." He punched various keys and watched his screen closely. "I think it'll be here. I've never even looked at it myself, to tell you the truth. I figured George Kaplan was somebody else's problem now. And he was, all over the country."

"Is the file there?" I asked.

A few more keyboard strokes and Mr. Alvarez nodded. "I just want to make sure there's no proprietary information here. I don't mind helping you find this guy but I'm not putting the company at risk." The fact that we had no interest in harming his company was irrelevant; Mr. Alvarez couldn't be certain of that with three people he had met ten minutes earlier. The fact that we hadn't suggested we were searching for George Kaplan was also unimportant because we hadn't been explicit about our intentions. "Just deleting a couple of documents you don't care about and I do," he continued.

After a moment he turned his computer screen 180 degrees so those of us on the other side of his desk could see the image on it. Most of the split-screen images showed company documents all labeled *Mendoza Communications* with a previous version of the company logo now displayed behind Ms. Mkombo's desk. But one, the company identification card for the employee there named George Kaplan, bore an image of the man who had been transferred from the Seattle headquarters of the Rayborn Corporation.

Ms. Washburn gasped lightly. "Samuel," she said. "That's your father."

TWENTY-ONE

"OUR COURSE OF ACTION should be clear," I said.

"Good. What address?" asked Ms. Washburn.

We sat in the blue Kia Soul outside the offices of Mendoza Communications, where we had examined the employment documents of "George Kaplan," and found remarkably little of interest considering the infamy the name had acquired in subsequent years. This Kaplan had been something of a model employee, had not made any complaint to a government agency regarding his treatment at the company and had, obviously, not brought the business to bankruptcy as a "whistle-blower," a term I understand now but which always brings amusing images and disturbing sounds to my mind when I hear it used.

After looking through the files we had thanked Mr. Alvarez for his time and left the Mendoza Communications offices. We had again retreated to the Kia Soul and Ms. Washburn had, thankfully, engaged the engine and the air conditioner. I looked at her now.

"I believe another visit to the Neighborhood Council is probably pointless," I answered. "It was something I'd suggested because I could not think of an alternative. The information we discovered here changes that."

"Why?" Mike asked from the back seat. "You already knew your father had come here from Seattle and that his paychecks were being made out to George Kaplan. It can't come as much of a surprise to you that he was the Kaplan who seemed to start the ball rolling in this business."

"Indeed not," I agreed. "It is not a surprise that Reuben Hoenig was using the name Kaplan when he arrived here. What is interesting is that it became something of a franchise, passed from man to man, and what we need to discover is how that came to be, considering the records do not indicate scores of George Kaplans *before* Reuben arrived here in that guise."

"We've checked the records pretty carefully," Ms. Washburn said. "I don't know how much more there is we can get in Internet research."

With months to work with and much more powerful computers I believed we could uncover a great deal more information, but under our current time limit I was inclined to agree with Ms. Washburn, and said so. I considered unanswered questions I'd had throughout this affair and remembered one I'd left unexplored before.

"Ms. Washburn," I said, "did you hear a humming noise at the house in Reseda where we received the package containing the forty thousand dollars?"

Ms. Washburn had not yet engaged the transmission of the Kia Soul because we had not yet set a destination. She was checking her cellular phone, possibly for the time (which was also displayed on the dashboard of the Kia Soul) when I asked the question. She looked up and her face took on a thoughtful expression.

"A humming sound?" she asked. "Inside or outside?"

"Inside."

Again, she took four seconds to think. "I can't say," she said. "I really don't have a memory of that part of the visit at all. Why?"

"Because I believe I did hear that sound, almost a mechanical hum, and if I'm correct it might provide very valuable information regarding the question we are attempting to answer. Ms. Washburn, would you mind driving back to the house on Jamieson Avenue?"

The address of Kaplan Enterprises had already been programmed into the Global Positioning System device, so I retrieved it from the proper menu and the device began to direct Ms. Washburn in her navigation. The estimated time of the trip on the display was fourteen minutes and twenty seconds. I assumed it would be closer to twenty-eight minutes.

"I'm starting to get hungry," Mike said from the seat behind me. "We should be thinking about finding a place for lunch."

"You want to eat or go to Jamieson Avenue?" Ms. Washburn asked. "I have to get to Burbank by one thirty."

"I thought the tour was at two," I said.

"They want you there a half-hour early."

I looked at my iPhone; the time was now 11:52. "That doesn't leave us much time," I said. "Perhaps we should go to a restaurant first."

Ms. Washburn, although driving, raised her eyebrows. "Really? I'm surprised you don't want to get to the house first, Samuel."

"If we do that, there is no guarantee that you will have time to get to your tour at the scheduled time," I said. "If you can drop Mike and me at the Jamieson Avenue address, we can take a taxicab back to the hotel."

"Busman's holiday," Mike mumbled.

"Really?" Ms. Washburn sounded genuinely surprised. "You'd do that for me to have the tour? I was under the impression you thought it was stupid."

I was navigating the Global Positioning System device to search for restaurants in the area. "I trust that you are not stupid, Ms. Washburn," I said. "It follows that you will not want to do stupid things. If it means something to you, it is important and should be respected. Mike and I can handle the situation at the Jamieson Avenue house."

Quietly, she said, "That's very sweet of you, Samuel."

I believed I had merely been stating the obvious but did not dispute that with Ms. Washburn. She asked me to read the suggestions from the screen aloud, and together we arrived at the idea of having lunch at a Chili's franchise in Encino, California. Ms. Washburn had previously insisted we stay away from chain restaurants but suggested it once the name was mentioned. I did not ask her why she had changed her thinking on the subject, but was more relaxed than I would have been at an establishment whose menu I could not predict.

Once we had been served, Mike asked about the neighborhood surrounding the Jamieson Avenue house. "Is this going to be a security problem?"

Ms. Washburn considered and said she thought it would not, but I was not as certain. "I'm not concerned about the people outside the house, but we don't know exactly the nature of the business going on inside, and if it is illegal or almost illegal, we might be dealing with some more unpredictable individuals," I told Mike. "Do you have your gun with you?"

Mike's expression suggested I might as well ask if he'd brought his left leg. That is an exaggeration.

"Of course," he said. "I'm fully licensed and I don't think you asked me to come out here so we could try out at the talent agencies."

I did not know what he meant by that, but agreed that was not the reason I had requested his presence. "To minimize the possible danger in what we're going to do, I think it best that we have an escape plan should things go wrong. Do you think a private ride service like Uber might be our best bet? We could call once Ms. Washburn drops us at the house."

Mike shook his head. "I've seen Ubers, and they're hit-or-miss," he said. "Personally I'm inclined to go with a licensed cabbie like myself, and remember that you are somewhat particular about the kind of car you're willing to sit in, Samuel."

It was true; part of my fondness for Mike's driving is grounded in the fact that I know he keeps the interior of his vehicle immaculate. I was the first passenger Mike drove in his taxicab and I had let a number of passengers in line take rides ahead of me because the cars that drove up were not at all clean. I am not a germophobe but I do not understand how people can sit comfortably and chat in cars that appear unsanitary.

I nodded. "Perhaps we should make sure we have the phone numbers of taxicab services programmed into our phones to save time," I said.

"I have a better idea," said Ms. Washburn. "I'll park by the Jamieson Avenue house. I'll stay in the car. If I have to leave to catch the tour, I'll call a cab myself and leave the rental with you. Then if you're in a bad situation, you can drive the car to pick me up at the studio, Samuel."

"That is not a funny joke, Ms. Washburn," I said.

"I'm not joking."

"I have not driven a vehicle in years," I reminded her. "I have no intention of resuming my driving in a vehicle that belongs to someone else in a city I don't know."

"We'll play it by ear," Ms. Washburn said. It is an expression that means something about playing a piece on the piano without written sheet music. I did not see the relevance.

"I will not drive the Kia Soul," I told her. "I would not drive any vehicle in such unfamiliar areas and I will not take responsibility for a rental vehicle."

"I took the insurance."

Mike saw the dynamic between Ms. Washburn and me, possibly the first time he had seen us disagree completely. He cleared his throat after taking a bite and said, "What are we going to do when we get there, Samuel?"

I had considered the logistics and the goals of our visit. "I think we will begin with a scan of the perimeter, as you would say, Mike. And depending on what we find, perhaps we will knock on the door and talk to the young lady who works there again."

"Remember, the woman at the Neighborhood Council said people have seen gun barrels pointed out of the walls of that house," Ms. Washburn reminded me. "You can't just be snooping around on the outside."

"That's what I'm for," Mike assured her. "If there's something dangerous there, I'll see it. Besides, I'm hoping we get to knock on the door."

It hadn't occurred to me that Mike would have a preference in the outcome of the visit. "Why?" I asked.

"See if she gives us another forty grand."

TWENTY-TWO

"I don't see any guns."

That was encouraging news, but it was not definitive. Mike the taxicab driver was sitting in the rear seat of the Kia Soul behind Ms. Washburn and looking at the Jamieson Avenue house listed as the headquarters of Kaplan Enterprises. We had been very careful to circle the block twice and satisfy ourselves that Kaplan's black car was not in the area. Mike could see the house, but we did not have a pair of binoculars. He was using a telescope application he had found for his cellular phone.

"It is probably safe for us to walk the perimeter of the house," I said. I checked the time on my iPhone. "Ms. Washburn, you have fifty minutes to get to your tour. You should leave as soon as Mike and I exit the Kia Soul."

"I'll stay a couple of minutes," she said. "They pad the time you have to wait because they don't want people showing up late."

That thinking sounded reasonable, but I knew Ms. Washburn was concerned about leaving Mike and me without a ride and wanted to

197

take a taxicab to the studio tour. "Please remember that I will not, under any circumstances, drive this vehicle," I said to her.

"I know." Her tone, if I was reading it properly, indicated otherwise. It was hard to know.

"What do you say?" Mike asked. "Are we going?"

I answered in the affirmative and opened the passenger side door as Mike exited the vehicle from his side. We walked into the heat, always a mild shock when one has been in conditioned air.

The house was exactly the same as the day before, but this time I noticed two cars in the driveway, one a Honda Civic coupe in gray that was four years old. The other was a Scion iA from the previous model year.

"There is more than one person inside," I noted to myself.

"What?" Mike said.

"If we go inside we can assume there are at least two people in the house," I told him.

Mike nodded. "What am I looking for?" he said as we approached the house.

I was watching over my right shoulder at the Kia Soul, which had not moved. I frowned. "You should be looking for extended gun barrels or anything you consider dangerous," I told Mike. "I will be looking, or rather listening, for something else. Please follow me." It is important to say the word *please* when instructing another person in the course of action because otherwise they will believe you are taking a superior position and ordering them to act upon your will.

Mike nodded. I saw his hand rest on his hip pocket, where I believed the small pistol he had brought with him from New Jersey was being concealed. We walked slowly toward the house and I led Mike to the left side facing the street. Mike was very carefully scanning the windows and the outside walls of the house.

I looked back at the Kia Soul again. It was still parked across the street. That was not what I had hoped to see. Ms. Washburn must have been waiting for us until the last possible moment to reach her studio tour in time.

"Nothing suspicious," Mike said softly. I did not know if he was referring to the house or Ms. Washburn's insistence on waiting for us.

I turned my attention to the task at hand. The house was one story, but there was a foundation and a basement. The basement windows were the focus of my interest. Mindful of the windows on the main floor and the possibility that someone inside could see Mike and me, I kept my head low as I approached, then dropped to my knees next to the basement window closest to the back of the house.

"Would it be better if I turned the corner and checked the backyard?" I asked Mike. I relied on his military experience and strategic thinking process.

He shook his head negatively. "They can do anything they want to us back there and nobody will see it," he said. "Here there's still the danger someone can see from the street."

That unpleasant suggestion led me to check the street for the Kia Soul again. It was still there. I checked the time on my iPhone and calculated that Ms. Washburn was in danger of being late for her tour.

"Damn," I said to myself.

Mike, who had been scanning the upper floor windows, looked down at me. "What?"

"Nothing," I said. I leaned over and put my ear to the casement window in the house's basement.

I did not see Mike's expression because my head was turned toward the driveway, but I could hear some consternation in his voice. "Samuel, what are you doing?"

There *was* a humming noise, punctuated by clicking. Some kind of machinery was present in the basement. Mike stood by, not distracting me or interfering with my ability to hear inside the house. But the windows were boarded up on the inside, so the hum of the machinery was muffled and there was no way to see inside the basement.

I started to stand and found Mike's hand extended at my eye level. Normally I am not fond of touching other people, but the help in regaining my stance was welcome; I took Mike's hand and he helped me up.

"What'd you hear?" he asked.

"Enough to think we should go inside," I told him. "But before we do, let's go around the back and make sure there isn't anything we need to know."

Mike nodded. "Me first." He led the way as we reached the backyard, which was fenced only across the rear of the property, a chain link fence that likely belonged to the homeowner behind the Kaplan house. I found that surprising.

No one was in the yard, which was helpful and not terribly unexpected. Even back here the windows were boarded from the inside or covered with black sheet plastic. I walked toward the back door, which was similarly shielded.

"I wouldn't get too close," Mike said. "Those people at the council weren't kidding. There are holes drilled into the walls that would let somebody push a gun barrel through."

I stopped in the spot I was standing. "Are there any gun barrels now?"

Mike chuckled lightly. "I wouldn't sound so calm if there were."

That meant there were none. I had never intended to enter through the back anyway; I wanted only to examine the door to see if it was frequently used. Worn concrete in a pattern of a door swinging open and closed indicated it was.

"Other side?" Mike asked, pointing to the side of the house we had not yet examined. I nodded and he began toward that path.

There was no driveway here, although the houses on the block were fairly close together. Instead the space was fairly untouched except for the concrete that had been poured to create a path. There were not the same signs of wear as just outside the back door, but there were occasional scratches. My guess was they were from the wheels of a hand truck being badly misused. Most of the indications of traffic had been in the driveway on the opposite side.

This pathway had no significant features to note, although the windows here were in the same condition as elsewhere on the property and the holes drilled in the walls were visible, if currently unoccupied.

"Why haven't we set off an alarm?" I wondered aloud.

"It's possible we have but it's silent," Mike said, which was not very reassuring. "But I didn't see any video surveillance cameras anywhere on this property. Maybe these guys aren't as smart as they think they are."

Recalling the young woman who had given the bundle of cash to Ms. Washburn and me when we were asking only to see George Kaplan, I had to agree.

When we returned to the Jamieson Avenue side of the house, I noted the Kia Soul was still where it had been parked. The sunlight glinted off the windows and made any visual communication with Ms. Washburn impossible.

We reached the front steps and I walked to the door without hesitation. Mike, now following, touched the pocket of his jeans but left his gun where it was. I waited.

"What's the matter?" Mike asked after two seconds.

"Would you ring the doorbell, please?" I asked.

He hesitated only briefly and reached over to touch the button. We could barely hear the sound of the electronic bell ringing inside but it was enough. The front door opened almost immediately.

Standing inside was not the young woman I had encountered here before. Instead there was a man in his early twenties, thin and pale, a forelock of hair falling in his face. "Who are you?" he said.

That hardly seemed an appropriate greeting. Everything I'd learned in social skills training indicated that the young man was being rude. I wondered if it would be to our advantage for me to make that point clear.

I decided it would not. Against my instincts, I extended my right hand and said, "Allow me to introduce myself. I am Samuel Hoenig, proprietor of Questions Answered, and this is my associate Mike."

The young man looked at my hand as he might a dangerous weapon. "What do you want?" he asked. I find that an interesting question whenever I hear it: Suppose the other person does not want anything in particular? Why is the assumption made?

Perhaps that was not relevant at the moment.

I withdrew my hand, which actually made me more comfortable. "We are here to ask a question. I have been here once before, with my associate Ms. Washburn."

The young man stared blankly at me.

"We were looking for George Kaplan," I continued.

"He's not here." The young man had been well schooled in the response to that suggestion.

"I'm aware. I have found Mr. Kaplan elsewhere. May we come in? It's very hot out here."

The young man, who was wearing a bowling shirt and cargo shorts, took a half-step forward to further establish his position blocking Mike and me in the doorway. "It's not that cool in here," he said.

"Even so," I countered, "it is much easier to speak indoors, don't you agree?"

The young man did not move. "What do you want?" he repeated.

I usually plan every encounter as meticulously as I can ahead of time. I am not fond of surprises, and since dealing with other people makes me anxious as a rule, I see no advantage in entering a situation without a clearly defined strategy. But in that moment an idea presented itself to me that seemed to offer the fastest and most direct route to success.

"We are here to pick up a large sum of money and don't wish to do so in the street," I said. "Please let us in. I'm sure Mr. Kaplan would agree with me."

I did not look at Mike but I would guess his expression was one of astonishment. He had probably never heard me act in so assertive a manner before. I did not have time to think if I could remember a time when I had done so.

The young man in the bowling shirt, with the name Nate stitched on the left chest, looked at me blankly for a moment and then stepped back. "Yeah, okay," he said.

Mike waited until I walked inside and then followed me, his hand in his pocket.

The room had not been changed in any way since the day before, which was not unexpected. The same overall emptiness was enhanced by the dark window coverings. The same sole pole lamp shone dimly in the corner.

The same humming sound, louder now, was audible in the room and I felt a slight rumble in the floorboards. There was definitely some heavy machinery active in the basement, probably because it was the only place a large mechanism could be safely housed and operated.

I had envisioned this moment and had devised a plan, but I was hesitant to put it into action. This is often the case: When one is in the midst of a situation it is more difficult to act than when one is planning it hypothetically. Nonetheless, I had no other clear option.

"May I have a glass of water?" I asked the young man, whose name might or might not have been Nate. The house did not seem to have air conditioning working at the moment but it was considerably cooler inside due to the lack of direct sunlight.

The man in the bowling shirt wrinkled his nose. "What?"

"Water. It's very hot outside. Even better, do you have a bottle of spring water in your refrigerator?" I glanced at Mike, with whom I had discussed this plan during the ride to Jamieson Avenue. He did not acknowledge my look but I knew he had received it.

Before Nate could respond I began walking briskly toward the kitchen, which I had observed the day before. Most often basement access is found in the kitchen in such houses, and while I had not gotten a clear view of the room from every angle the day before, I had an idea where such a door might be located.

"Hey!" Nate said as Mike followed me, still facing the young man, into the kitchen. "You can't go in there!"

I had no intention of drawing a glass of water from the faucet in the kitchen. For one thing, I would never have drunk from any such tap in a home I did not know well. I drink spring water from a bottle in my own house. For another, I knew the Southern California area was in the midst of a serious drought and would not have wasted precious water on an empty pretense.

Still, I felt it necessary to keep up the charade and opened the refrigerator door. Inside I saw four bottles of beer and two slices of pizza, unwrapped. But my glance was actually aimed at the door just to the right of the refrigerator, which I assumed would lead to basement access.

I hoped it was not locked.

"No water," I said, as if it were a surprise. "Maybe here. Is this a closet?"

Mike was creating an obstacle for young Nate, who was protesting, "Hey! No!" but could not get past the taxicab driver. I reached for the knob on the door after taking a handkerchief from my back pocket and placing it over the metal knob. It was the only way I would have been able to gain access.

To my relief and slight surprise the door was unlocked and the knob turned. I acted quickly now, flung it open, and headed inside.

Nate protested more loudly and I heard the sounds of a light scuffle behind me. That meant two things: There was a reason Nate did not want me downstairs, and I could not definitely rely upon Mike for help. I assumed there was at least one additional person in the basement who might object to my presence there. If he or she offered resistance before I could confirm my suspicions, I would be on my own. It would be best if the person or people had no weapons. I had now legitimately gone too far to turn back.

The stairs, as in most such structures, were fairly dark and not well lit. It made me wonder how machinery such as I was expecting could have been brought into the basement. I decided that it must have been delivered in sections and assembled once inside. I used the handkerchief on the banister as I descended.

It took six seconds to walk carefully down the stairs. I did not wish to rush no matter what the situation behind me might have been, although the scuffle was fading. My concern now was more what was before me than on the level I had just vacated.

There was only one other man in the basement, and due to the significant noise being made by the machine he was operating, he appeared not to have heard the scene upstairs or my footsteps on the basement stairs. He did not look up.

He was wearing a heavy apron, goggles, and a visor as he tended to a large machine. It had a number of gears, which were spinning and a belt turning toward the rear. I could not see the back end of the machine, where the man seemed to paying most of his attention. I walked slowly, attempting to obtain a better vantage point.

I could hear nothing behind me because all sound was being drowned out by the workings of the machine. I noticed the man operating it, who had not looked up from a clipboard he carried, was wearing earplugs. That was probably an intelligent choice given the decibel level in the basement. I resolved to be done with my observation quickly.

The man was standing to my left, partially obscured by the upper sections of the machine. I walked to the right, hoping to reach a spot where I could view the operation without being noticed myself. I crouched down a bit to better obscure my head and my movement. The longer I could keep the machine operator from seeing me the safer I would be. But I felt my left hand begin to flutter just a bit as I became a bit more nervous. I forced myself to stop the movement and kept walking slowly toward the machine.

As my line of sight cleared the more cumbersome part of the apparatus I was focusing more on the operator than the operation. His seeing me would be more dangerous than confirming what I was fairly sure I had already surmised.

But he continued to consult first his clipboard and then the open end of the machine he tended, one then the other in a series of repetitive movements that seemed to have no variation and no surprises. I thought that under different circumstances this would actually be a fitting occupation for me.

After some slow progress I could see around to the front of the machine and found I had been correct in my assumption. The machine was spitting out, after the spinning of a large gear and onto a belt that emptied into a large tray at the end, sheets of paper treated with at least two and probably three shades of ink. The man was counting the sheets, examining them as they fell off the belt and noting their quality and quantity on a form he carried on the clipboard.

I was surprised at the low level of technology involved. The printing press was not a laser printer and the clipboard was not a tablet computer. This scene could easily have been thirty years old but it was playing out before my eyes in the present day.

Having satisfied my curiosity and my need for confirmation I turned to head back to the basement steps but my movement must have been too sudden. The man looked up from his clipboard and directly into my face. We stared at each other for two seconds.

He spoke, probably loudly, but the noise of the printing press drowned out his words. I have a developing talent for lip-reading but probably needed none of my training to understand him saying, "What the—"

I did not wait for the next word.

I turned and ran, no longer concerned with being unseen, for the stairs. I reached them as the man, apparently stunned, stood and then walked toward me with a questioning look on his face. I did not see him again as I reached the staircase and took the steps two at a time until I was on the upper level.

The first thing I noticed was the considerable drop in ambient noise. The second was Mike the taxicab driver holding his pistol on the young man in the bowling shirt, who was seated on a barstool in the kitchen. The young man looked worried.

"Did you see what you had to see?" Mike asked.

"Yes. Let's go." I turned toward the front door and took two steps.

"You can't barge in here. This is trespassing," the young man who might have been named Nate said.

"I'm not sure we should leave him like this," Mike said. "How many more are there in the basement?"

"Just one," I told him, "and I don't know if he was interested in following me."

Mike pivoted to hold the gun aimed at Nate and still have a clear view of the door to the basement stairs. "They're going to get in touch with Kaplan as soon as we leave here," he warned me.

"That's fine," I told him. "It is what I expect them to do and it will help us achieve our goal. Our best strategy is to leave now. Is this young man armed?"

Suddenly my ears were not ringing. The printing press had been turned off. In seconds I guessed we would hear footsteps on the basement stairs.

"No," Mike answered. "I made very, very sure."

"I can have you arrested," said the possible Nate.

Mike ignored his remark. "What about the guy in the basement?" he asked. "Did he have any weapons on him?"

"I did not see any." The footsteps were now audible.

"We're about to find out," Mike said.

"Jerry!" Nate shouted. "He's got a gun!"

The man from the basement appeared in the doorway and stopped. He stared at Mike, then at me.

He was holding a tennis racket. "Holy shit," he said.

"Look, guys." Mike used his most ingratiating, calming tone. "Nobody wants to hurt anybody here. All my friend and I are going to do is leave. That's it. We're going to walk to the front door and go. As long as you guys don't do anything stupid, there will be no reason to be the least bit scared. Are we all okay with that?"

The man from the basement looked at me directly. "You weren't supposed to go down there," he said.

"I know," I told him. That actually had been the point of our visit.

"We're going now," Mike said. Still aiming the pistol at the two young men, who looked absolutely determined not to move at all, he

208

began to walk backward toward the front of the house. "Open the door, Samuel."

I made sure to arrive at the exit before Mike and opened the steel exterior door. A hot blast of humidity immediately entered through the opening.

Knowing Mike would need room without turning his head I stepped outside and down the two front stairs. "You are at the threshold," I told Mike.

He did not turn but nodded. "Okay, fellas, that was good," he told the two young men. "Just don't do anything for about a minute and everything will be fine." Transferring the gun to his left hand he used his right to close the door. He rushed to my side on the pavement outside the house.

"Okay, let's go," Mike said. He looked at me pressing on the touchscreen of my iPhone. "What are you doing?"

"I am summoning a taxicab," I said.

Mike pointed. "But there's the rental."

"Ms. Washburn is not inside," I informed him. "There is no one to drive."

"Samuel, people are going to come looking for us." Mike began walking toward the Kia Soul. "We need to be invisible right now."

He was right. "Very well. Follow me." I walked briskly, as I do when exercising, in the opposite direction, toward the corner. I considered raising my arms above my head and getting the desired aerobic effect but felt the motion would attract attention. Mike fell in behind me.

"Where are we going?" he asked.

"We are going to a corner two blocks away to wait for the taxicab," I said.

Mike was silent for four seconds. I did not look at his face because I was certain I would not be able to interpret the expression.

"Okay, fine," he said. "What did you find out in there that was worth our running away and being chased by guys bigger than me? And how come we didn't take another package of money? Could have used that."

"It would not have done us any more good than the first package. George Kaplan is a counterfeiter."

TWENTY-THREE

IT WAS ON THE taxicab ride to the hotel in Burbank that I received another text message from George Kaplan.

I had spent my time before this trying again to reach my mother and was equally as unsuccessful as in my previous attempts. I was more resolute than ever that this would be our final day in the Los Angeles area. When the text message signal was sounded by my iPhone I hoped it was Mother and found Kaplan's name listed instead.

The message read: BAD MOVE.

There was no further explanation.

I had observed that aggressive behavior had been the most productive in dealing with Kaplan. The lesson I'd been taught in early social skills training, that a bully respects those who oppose him, had been difficult to learn but was becoming useful here. The question now was whether a passive-aggressive approach—no response at all—would be more or less effective than a direct assault. I asked Mike for his opinion.

He was carefully evaluating the car in which we were riding and clearly finding it acceptable if not excellent. I had been adamant in speaking to the person at the dispatch station of the taxicab company that the unit driving us must be absolutely impeccable in its cleanliness. This was the manifestation of that request and it was not noticeably dirty. That was as far as one could go in praising the vehicle.

"I think you're better off not answering," Mike suggested. "He's trying to threaten you. You still want something from him. Let him come back with an answer for you about a place and time to exchange your dad for the money and then he can expect a message from you."

I would have asked Ms. Washburn for her opinion as well but she was not answering my text messages any more than Mother this afternoon. We would be on an airplane heading for New Jersey the next day. Time to answer Mother's question and successfully complete our excursion was running out.

"I believe you are correct," I told Mike, trying not to notice the somewhat reckless manner in which the driver was maneuvering his car through the inevitable traffic. He switched lanes without first exhibiting a turn signal. I found myself having to remember to exhale. "We must bargain from a position of strength. We have Kaplan's packet of counterfeit cash. If he wants it back he will have to give us what we want, which is Reuben Hoenig."

"You were the one who wanted to go back to that house," Mike reminded me. "What made you think there was a fake money operation going on in there? Most people would look at the place and assume it was a drug house of some kind."

"I had noticed the sound of the machinery when Ms. Washburn and I visited the house the first time," I said. "That itself was not enough to do more than pique my curiosity. I had to think about what would cause that kind of noise and why someone like George Kaplan would have it in the house he owns for business purposes. I had mused about it but come up with very little until I realized Kaplan was too concerned about the forty thousand dollars Ms. Washburn and I had been given."

The taxicab driver pressed hard on the brake pedal of the vehicle and barely avoiding a rear-end collision with the Sport Utility Vehicle in front of us. I gasped and was about to ask the driver to be more safety conscious when Mike cleared his throat and drew my attention. In retrospect I believe that was an intentional action on Mike's part to distract me from the tension of the ride.

"Why shouldn't he be concerned?" Mike asked. "Forty grand is a lot of money. You had it and he wanted it back. I don't see anything strange about that."

I had refocused my attention but the fingers on my left hand were wiggling and I was not doing that by design. "Consider the amount," I said. "George Kaplan probably owns at least three businesses. There is the advertising time scheme, selling the spaces from television and radio stations to private buyers for resale. There is the practice of sending multiple George Kaplans into competing firms to uncover unsavory employment practices or other infractions that can hurt the competitor. I imagine he has monetized that in some way. And now we know he has been using the Jamieson Avenue property, which might be one of many he owns, to manufacture counterfeit cash. My best guess is that he sells it at a fraction of the face value to unscrupulous businesses like drug dealers. There were rumors that such people frequented the house, and when Ms. Washburn and I arrived we were summarily handed a packet without asking for it."

"What's that got to do with the amount?" Mike asked.

"Those three enterprises and possible others we have not yet discovered would bring in a great deal of money," I explained. "They probably earn him millions of dollars a year, and that is a fairly conservative estimate."

Mike sat back with his hand on his chin. "So the forty grand isn't that big a deal to him."

"Exactly. And yet he has been adamant about its return to the point that he has threatened violence to us or to Reuben Hoenig if it is not back in his hands, and under his terms." The driver changed lanes abruptly again, making me lean to my left sharply, then back to the right. I gasped.

Mike intervened on my behalf, knowing he was probably more adept at handling such situations. "Hey, pal," he said, "maybe you could take it a little easier. My friend and I don't need to be there in the next ten seconds, okay?" His tone was friendly and not oppositional as far as I could tell.

The taxicab driver appeared to disagree, however. "I drive how I drive, okay? I don't tell you how to do your job."

"Actually, I'm a cab driver in New Jersey," Mike informed him. "And I'm not telling you how to do your job. I'm asking that you drive a little calmer because you're worrying my friend."

"Oh, boo-hoo," said the man behind the steering wheel.

"Look, buddy," Mike attempted, "I don't want to get into an argument. There's an extra ten in it if you slow down and get us there in one piece without a heart attack, okay?"

The taxicab driver made a rude noise and increased the speed of the vehicle.

Mike smiled, which confused me. "How about a twenty?" he asked the man. I thought that was a poor negotiating tactic, rewarding the taxicab driver for being insubordinate and reckless. But it seemed to work because the man slowed the car down although he did not acknowledge the remark.

Mike leaned over to whisper into my ear, which I barely tolerate when not absolutely necessary. The thought of someone else's mouth so close to my ear is, to say the least, unsettling. But I trusted Mike and understood he had something to say that he felt was crucial.

"You got one of those fake fifties?" he asked.

———————

Ms. Washburn would not be available for another two hours, so once we arrived at the Burbank hotel, Mike and I retired to our respective rooms and I opened my laptop computer to continue some research into the George Kaplan we knew in an attempt to find out more about his background. I believed we would be hearing from him again very soon and thought any information recovered would be useful as a tool against him. I was now thinking of this George Kaplan as my opposition in the attempt to answer Mother's question.

I knew Ms. Washburn had traced Reuben Hoenig's path to Reseda, California, through his employment records starting at the Seattle branch of the Rayborn Corporation. She had correctly surmised his transformation into George Kaplan through the payroll records. Mother, I remembered, had noted the name was to be found in *North by Northwest*, Reuben's favorite film. (It was probably of note that now he was continually quoting *The Maltese Falcon* and not the Hitchcock classic, but there was little question Reuben was the man we had come to locate. The change from Hitchcock to John Huston or Dashiell Hammett was not yet explained.)

Since Ms. Washburn had not located any other George Kaplans coming directly from Rayborn in Seattle, it was logical to assume that the scheme to send emissaries to competing companies and repeatedly using that alias had germinated in Southern California after Reuben had arrived and become George.

There was, therefore, no utility in repeating Ms. Washburn's search of the payroll records. Instead, I traced back the George Kaplans we knew about to the dates of their first using that name and searched for records of men who had been reported as missing around those times in the same geographic areas as the George Kaplans who had perpetrated the scheme.

After thirty-three minutes I had abandoned that approach due to lack of relevant results. There was one man who was reported missing three days before a George Kaplan arrived in Boca Raton, Florida, but he was located a week later in a motel in Tallahassee, Florida, which resulted in no criminal charges but did instigate divorce proceedings filed by the man's wife. The idea that he was the local George Kaplan was not plausible.

I was about to begin an attempt to hack Social Security records on the current Southern California George Kaplan, something I thought would not be terribly likely to reap useful results, when my iPhone began to ring. I checked the Caller ID and noted the screen read, HOME.

Mother.

I picked up the phone and touched the screen to accept the call. "Mother?" I said as soon as the line was clearly open.

"Samuel." Her voice was not as strong as usual and sounded tired, but it was definitely Mother's. I looked at the clock on the bedside radio in the hotel room. In New Jersey it was currently 6:07 p.m. Not nearly time for Mother to sound this weary. "How are you?"

"I am fine, Mother." It seemed odd that she would ask about my health when she was the one who had been mysteriously unavailable for two days. "I have been concerned about you because I could not contact you since I arrived in Los Angeles."

"Oh, you didn't have to worry. It was just this problem with my phone, but it's fixed now." Somehow her assurances were not soothing my concern. Her voice still sounded distressed in some way. "I just wanted to make sure you had found your father."

Her agenda was still not the same as my own. "I have met with Reuben Hoenig, or at the very least a man who is going by that name," I said. "It was a brief conversation but I am intending to meet with him again this afternoon or this evening."

In fact, I expected to get a location and a time from George Kaplan shortly. He would not have taken kindly to my silence following his last text message.

"A man going by that name?" Mother's focus appeared to be very narrow. "What do you mean by that?"

"Simply that I have no way of knowing if this man is your husband," I said. "There are no facts, merely what I have been told."

"I'll send you a photograph of him in an email," Mother offered. "You can look at his face and see if it's him."

"Your picture would be at least twenty-seven years old," I pointed out. "It would hardly be definitive proof." I had considered taking one of the photographs Mother had in our house before I left but decided against it. I would essentially have to hold it up next to the man's face and make a determination, and I do not read faces especially well.

"I'm sending it." This time Mother's voice sounded sharper and a touch livelier. There was no point in arguing, although her determination did not change the facts of the situation.

"Mother, are you all right?" I asked. She was acting in a way that I did not recognize; her tone was somewhat less forgiving than usual and her attention seemed to limit itself to just one subject.

"Of course I am. Just a little tired. How was he, Samuel?"

I hesitated a moment. Mother did not refer to me in the second person. But when one asks how another person is physically, it is common practice to reciprocate the question. I realized she was asking not about me, but about Reuben Hoenig.

"He appears to be physically sound, but his responses are unusual."

217

Mother did not speak for three seconds. "Unusual?"

"Mother, when you knew him did Reuben Hoenig exhibit behaviors that would place him on the autism spectrum?" It had occurred to me but I'd had access to no medical records. I assumed his wife would know.

"Not really," she answered. "He had his eccentricities like everybody else, but I don't think your father is on the spectrum. Why? What does 'unusual responses' mean?"

I looked around the hotel room, an environment I still found sterile and unfamiliar. I would have gladly paid a great deal of money to sleep in my own bed tonight, but I knew that was not possible. Tomorrow, I promised myself. Definitely tomorrow. Just one more night.

"Samuel?" Mother said.

Her question made me focus my thoughts. "When I spoke to Reuben Hoenig he looked slightly dazed and was quoting heavily from *The Maltese Falcon*," I told her.

Mother's breath came in a light wheeze. It sounded like she was in some pain, but not a debilitating amount, as far as I could tell. "*The Maltese Falcon*?" she asked. I knew she had heard and understood the reference, so I waited for her to elaborate. "Why was he doing that?"

"I assure you I have no idea," I said. "Reuben has taken up with the man we know as George Kaplan, who is an unsavory character. It is my guess, based strictly on anecdotal evidence, that Reuben is taking some medication that is affecting his demeanor. Why he has chosen to communicate through that particular work of fiction is a complete mystery to me."

I had not intended the word *mystery* to be a pun in the previous sentence. I realize *The Maltese Falcon* falls into that category at least in terms that bookshops use to shelve their merchandise, but the fact was Reuben's behavior was puzzling me very severely. I had no explanation for it and that frustrated me.

At that moment I received a text message from the phone of the man we knew as George Kaplan. Even as Mother was preparing to speak I was reading the message: BE AT THE JAMIESON AVENUE HOUSE IN AN HOUR. There was no further explanation.

"Samuel, you have to help your father," Mother said.

I sighed. I supposed she was right, but it was not my preference.

I told Mother I would call her later, but she suggested she might go to sleep early that night. Given that it was barely evening at home I thought her suggestion was odd. But I disconnected the call and pressed the screen to call Mike.

"We need to find a clean taxicab," I said.

TWENTY-FOUR

"I don't like the setup," Mike the taxicab driver said.

We had asked the driver of the vehicle we'd hired to let us out of the car at the same corner where Mike and I had left this neighborhood not two hours earlier. Given the geography of the Los Angeles area and the way the two drivers who were not Mike had operated their vehicles, it felt as if staying here with hostile employees of George Kaplan on our heels might have been the safer option. But it was too late to consider that now. We walked back toward the headquarters of Kaplan Enterprises.

"I could not argue with Kaplan over the location now," I said. "There was barely enough time to get here."

"That's not the thing. I'm worried about those rifle barrels people said are aimed out of the house. We saw the drill holes. Nobody goes to all that trouble *not* to shoot somebody."

The thought had occurred to me. "There were not rifles or any guns when we were there last time," I pointed out.

"You think that'll still be true this time?"

"Honestly, I have no idea what to expect," I answered.

Mike did not respond.

We were approximately two hundred yards from the house in question when I stopped walking. "Do you see any black Sport Utility Vehicles?" I asked.

Mike squinted as he looked ahead in the bright sunlight. "I think there's one in the driveway."

"Like the one at the Chinese Theatre?" I asked.

"I can't tell. Why?"

"I'm not sure," I said. "I think we should approach slowly and from a direction someone inside the house would not expect."

Mike stood. His jawbone moved from side to side as he thought. "Our best bet is around the back," he said. "We'll have to go through the house directly behind." He turned and walked in the direction we had come. I had not expected the change so it took a moment before I followed and caught up with him.

"I'm concerned about the way this meeting was initiated," I told Mike, "but I'm not sure my level of anxiety merits walking through a stranger's home."

"We're not going through the home. We're going through the backyard."

We turned the corner and headed west toward the center of the block. Mike watched carefully to his left, making sure we were approaching the correct building. I had counted the homes and knew the fourth one on this side would be directly behind the Kaplan property. It was a house with beige siding and a slate roof. The lawn was patchy and brown as a result of the drought. Watering one's lawn had been outlawed.

"This is the one," Mike said. He was pointing to the correct house so I saw no reason to explain that I'd already come to that conclusion. "Follow me."

He started up the empty driveway of the house and I walked behind him as directed. The gravel driveway caused our steps to make some noise but there was enough distance between us and the Kaplan property that the sound was inconsequential. I was uneasy being on a stranger's property, even if the owner was not present. Visions of arrest for trespassing flashing through my mind.

We proceeded to the backyard and surveyed the area. The yard was dominated by the same brown, sparse grass as the lawn, although there was a small swing set in the northwest corner and a shed opposite it with a heavy steel chain hanging from the door latch.

There was also a seven-foot wire mesh fence at the back of the yard separating it from the opposite area at the headquarters of Kaplan Enterprises.

"Can you climb a fence?" Mike asked me quietly.

"I have never tried." I wondered how I could do so without touching the fence. It seemed impossible. I had only one cloth handkerchief in my pocket. The one I'd used earlier was in a plastic bag in my suitcase at the hotel room. I would launder it when I returned home the next day.

"Well, here's your chance," Mike said. "Hang on a second. I want to get a better look at the house." He meant I should wait longer than one second, but I did not comment.

He stepped forward to the fence and held up his cellular telephone. Undoubtedly he was using the camera application or a telescope application to see the Kaplan property more clearly. "I don't see anything we don't want to see," he said. I interpreted that to mean there were no gun barrels protruding from the walls. "The windows are still covered. That does appear to be a black SUV in the driveway, a Cadillac."

"Will we be able to approach without being seen or heard?" I asked. Still, my mind was concentrating on the necessity of touching the metal fence, whose owner I had never met. I was not certain I could make myself walk to the spot where Mike was standing.

"We can get to the back door but I bet it's locked," he answered. "Our best bet is to go around the side without the driveway. There's just another house on that side and they're probably not watching it as closely."

"Do you have a cloth handkerchief?" I asked Mike. Although I certainly would have preferred not to use such a personal item from another person, it was preferable to placing my bare hands on the fence.

Mike looked at me. "Why? Are you gonna sneeze?"

"No. It's for the fence." I pointed at the fence, which was redundant. Surely Mike knew which one I was referencing.

"What about the fence?" he asked.

"I have to touch it to climb it and I only have a handkerchief to cover one hand," I explained.

"Oh." He searched through his pockets. "Sorry, Samuel. I don't think I have one."

"Perhaps we could go to a store and purchase one," I suggested.

"There's no time," he said. "You'll just have to cope."

Cope? What did he mean by that? This was not a negotiable circumstance.

But then I could no longer delay the move. Behind me I heard the sound of car tires on gravel. Someone from the house in whose driveway we stood was coming home. And very shortly after parking his or her vehicle, the person would see Mike and me trespassing on the property.

"Come on, Samuel!" Mike hissed and beckoned toward me.

I had no choice. I forced my legs to move and ran toward the fence. "I'll give you a boost," Mike said, interlocking his fingers and holding his hands down for me to step upon them.

"No." I was figuring the placement of my feet and used the handkerchief from my pocket to cover my right hand, which was reaching for the wire fence. "I will ... cope."

With the cloth wrapped under my fingers I grasped the fence with my right hand and pulled. Stepping up as I did, I could place the toe of my left shoe in the fence to use for a foothold. My left hand dangled at my side.

Mike, who had already elevated himself halfway up the fence, looked down at my hand. "What are you doing?" he asked.

I did not answer. As rapidly as possible I identified the correct second position for my right hand and lunged with my legs, releasing the fence and then grabbing it again with the cloth wrapped around my fingers.

The maneuver almost proved to be disastrous when my right foot slipped slightly on the fence, but I was able to recover and reposition it quickly enough. Using one arm to lift myself up, however, was tiring me. I would have to be certain to ensure I would be over the fence and on the Kaplan side with my next lunge.

Mike was already on the ground of the opposite backyard looking up at me. "Use your shirt," he suggested. He pointed to his own t-shirt, pulling on his short sleeve, to illustrate.

I considered his suggestion, but pulling on the sleeve of my left arm would require letting go with my right and I would fall to the ground. Instead I prepared myself to propel upward and lunged with both feet, releasing the fence and reaching for the top at the same moment.

There was a very tense moment when I felt myself lean backwards, but the hand with the cloth on it grabbed unsteadily at first on the top of the fence and then managed to secure itself. My feet found their places in the links and in a moment I was able to position myself with one leg on the Kaplan side, and then the other.

I continued to hold on with the cloth on the hot metal tube at the top of the fence. I let my weight down carefully until I was almost standing straight and then let go of the fence. A short drop followed and I landed on my feet.

Mike smiled at me. "You never do anything the easy way, do you?" he asked.

I was sure there were some things I did in the least difficult fashion possible but none came to mind at the moment. I did not answer, but looked at the handkerchief as I unwrapped it from my fingers. It was almost black with dirt and damp with perspiration. I looked around the yard.

"What do you need?" Mike asked.

"A trash can." I could not put that cloth back into my pocket.

Mike shook his head a little and put out his hand. "Just give it to me," he said. "I'll take care of it later."

I couldn't bear the thought of Mike having to handle the grimy cloth. "I wouldn't impose," I said. "I'll just find a trash can."

Mike reached over and pulled the cloth out of my hand, then jammed it into his back pocket. I shuddered a bit at the thought but appreciated the gesture. "There's no time for that," Mike said. "We need to scope out this house and figure what their play is going to be." He looked carefully at the house. "No gun barrels back here," he said. "Anything you need to see in the yard?"

I scanned the area. Nothing had changed since the last time Mike and I had been here but I was certain the same two inexperienced young men would not be the only people inside the house if we entered this time. The black Sport Utility Vehicle in the driveway indicated Kaplan or one of his associates was inside the house. Perhaps they had brought Reuben Hoenig for an exchange; perhaps not. Either way, it was fairly certain Kaplan was not pleased with me. He seemed to have some strange competitive drive that would not allow him to concede even when it got him what he wanted. If he was present, he might be angry. If he wasn't, he had left instructions.

In short, Mike and I could anticipate an unfriendly welcome.

"There is nothing of note here," I told Mike. "We should confirm that there is no immediate danger elsewhere."

"Exactly what I had in mind," he answered. He gestured with his left hand to follow me. I noticed a glint of metal in his right. He was carrying his pistol but concealing it as well as he could.

We followed our previous pattern, heading to our left and the side of the property that was not paved or landscaped, other than the small palm tree at the front. Without the gravel our feet did not make an unusual amount of noise. But approximately twenty feet after we entered the narrow lane between the house and the property to its east, Mike held up his left hand behind him, indicating I should stop.

"I see movement," he whispered as I leaned toward him to hear. He pointed toward the nearest window.

The heavy dark drape covering it and blocking the light from within was fluttering slightly.

"Did they see us?" I asked in a tone I believed to be matching Mike's.

I must have been mistaken because he winced when I spoke. "Keep it *down*, Samuel!" I put my hand to my mouth. Mike held both his hands up, palms out, to indicate no serious harm had been done. "I don't know. Watch the drilled holes near the window."

There were indeed the covered spaces we had observed before, which Carmen Sanchez at the Reseda Neighborhood Council had suggested were installed to provide stations for firearms, although she had said no one ever reported any shots being fired.

I watched the one closest to the window with the fluttering drape. There was no metal barrel being extended through the opening. I made certain to whisper very quietly this time. "I don't believe there is a firearm there," I said to Mike.

He leaned over toward me. "What?"

I repeated my observation just as quietly and this time Mike nodded. "Keep following me but be very careful about the areas near those holes," he said.

Mike proceeded ahead slowly and I followed in suit. When we reached the second window, the one closest to the front of the house, I heard a slight squeak behind me. I stood still and turned my head to see what had caused it.

There was a metal tube extending through the hole into the open space next to the house where Mike and I were standing.

"Mike," I said.

"I see it. We have two choices."

The tube began to move in my direction. "Please tell me quickly what they are," I said.

"We can stand directly under the gun barrel where it's hardest to get an angle or we can run very fast," he said. "Which one?"

There was very little time to deliberate but the thought of the gun barrel, perhaps that of a rifle, directly over my head was enough to make both hands start to flap at my sides. "Run!" I said. And I began to do exactly that toward the street.

Mike, having waited for my response, began running one second after I did but he was in front of me to begin and spent a good deal of time exercising, whereas I walked laps in the Questions Answered office while raising my arms over my head. He was ahead of me quickly.

We reached the sidewalk and searched for a place to shield ourselves, although there had been no shots fired as yet. The street did have some trees but they were not wide enough to conceal two adult men. We could conceal ourselves behind the walls of an adjacent house but that would limit our view of the Kaplan property.

Mike pointed. "The rental car is still there."

Of course the Kia Soul was still where Ms. Washburn had parked it. I reached frantically into the hip pocket on the right side of my trousers. I had not been checking it as often as the opposite side, where my iPhone is kept.

But the second key fob to the Kia Soul was still there. I retrieved it and ran toward the vehicle, looking at the buttons on the fob to determine exactly how to open all four doors and the hatchback. A shot did ring out as we ran across the street. I did not see any evidence of a bullet landing anywhere near us but as I was running and desperately staring at the apparatus in my hand my viewpoint was somewhat limited.

"It's the one without the raised dots!" Mike shouted as he ran around the vehicle to the passenger side. "The one with the picture of an open lock!"

As he instructed I pressed on the button with the appropriate diagram and the turn signals on the Kia Soul flashed twice. I reached for the driver side door and it opened. But Mike was still standing on the opposite side looking at me through the window.

"Push the button again!"

I did so and the other three doors unlocked. Mike opened the passenger door and sat in the seat next to me as I closed the door on my side. I found the locking mechanism on the panel next to me, on the vehicle's door handle, and pushed it.

We sat there for seven seconds.

"Let's go," Mike said.

I didn't understand. Go? When we'd just achieved some measure of safety? Go where? Leaving the vehicle seemed especially reckless. While no further shots had been fired, there were now metal tubes extending out of the drilled holes in the front facing of the Kaplan house. The possibility of being shot increased exponentially if we were to leave the relative safety of the Kia Soul.

I must have stared at Mike with an especially uncomprehending expression on my face, because he pointed at the ignition mechanism and said, "Start her up. Let's get out of here."

That was not an option. "I am not going to drive this vehicle, Mike."

"Well, I know you're not going to let *me* drive it because you're worried about the rental insurance, and you're listed on the agreement, so you're the only other choice. Janet's not coming back here to pick up the car."

"There has to be another way," I said.

"For the time being we're relatively safe," Mike suggested. "They're probably not going to try and hit us from there unless they have scopes, and I don't think those holes would accommodate scopes. But if you won't drive us away we don't have a lot of options."

"I can think of one," I said. I picked up my iPhone and pressed the screen to call the man we knew as George Kaplan.

"Yeah," he said after the third ring.

"This is Samuel Hoenig," I said.

"No kidding." I believed that was said sarcastically.

"I do not understand why you have asked people to shoot at us," I said. "We have brought your counterfeit currency."

Mike winced.

There was a long pause of four seconds. "Counterfeit?" Kaplan did not sound surprised, but it might have been an error to let him know I was aware of his money-printing operation.

Still, there was no point in denying my discovery. "Yes. I have no interest in the fact that you are creating the bills, Mr. Kaplan. I am concerned only with the welfare of Reuben Hoenig and my offer remains.

Let me talk to him with no restrictions and no medication and I will return your property."

"Of course." Kaplan sounded oddly conciliatory much too quickly. "Just come walk to the house and we'll make the exchange."

Mike could no doubt hear the conversation because I was not holding the phone very close to my ear. He immediately shook his head in a negative gesture, but it had not been necessary. I would not have agreed to those terms.

"You are not on the premises at Jamieson Avenue, Mr. Kaplan," I asserted. "The vehicles in the driveway confirm that. Your own Sport Utility Vehicle is not here and there are not enough vehicles for you, your associates, and the three people clearly aiming guns at us right now. If my associate and I approach the hous,e we will undoubtedly be shot. But I am telling you violence is not a necessary tactic. Simply let me see Reuben Hoenig and our business will be concluded."

There was on the other end of the conversation the kind of complete, sterile silence that ensues when one engages the mute feature. Then the background noise reasserted itself and I heard Kaplan say, "That's not going to happen."

Mike frowned. I engaged my own mute feature and he said, "I don't like the way he sounds so final about it. Is there any way for us to get out of here without getting shot?"

"I am fairly certain we could exit through the passenger side of the vehicle and escape without serious harm by moving in the direction away from the house," I told him. "But it is not a certainty. You have the experience in this kind of circumstance. What would be your plan?"

Over the iPhone I heard Kaplan say, "Hoenig? You need to give me back my money. It's not yours."

"I'm not crazy about your idea because we don't know what kind of weapons the enemy has," Mike told me. "If they're pistols or revolvers, we probably don't have a problem. I don't think they can see through scopes but I'm not definite on that, assuming those are rifle barrels, which I think they are. Yes, we can get out on the other side of the car, but if they don't care about shattering glass—and they don't— there are any number of ways this can go south."

I understood approximately seventy percent of what he had told me and was not encouraged. "What would you suggest?" I asked.

"They're in the house and we can be pretty sure that's all of them," Mike answered. "They can deal with distance if they want to but they can't deal well with movement. Our best bet is still driving this car away as fast as it can go."

I did not see that scenario as possible. Mike was not listed as a driver on the rental vehicle and without Ms. Washburn, who had engaged the Kia Soul, it would be impossible to call the company and add him to the list now. I was not equipped, either in terms of practice or temperament, to drive a vehicle in Southern California.

"We need an alternative," I said.

"Hoenig!" Kaplan insisted.

I decided the least I could do was stall for more time. The longer I kept Kaplan on the line the less likely his associates in the building would fire on us. I disengaged the mute function.

"There must be some compromise we can reach," I said. "Surely both of us can come away with something we want. Suppose I give you half the money for a short conversation with Reuben Hoenig."

"Let me think about it," Kaplan said, and the mute function was engaged again. Aware that we could be heard if we spoke, I did the same on my iPhone.

"He's not going to go for that," Mike said.

"I understand that. I am attempting to, as you would say, buy us time to think of another solution to our dilemma." The idea of buying time is a misnomer. If it were possible to do so, very wealthy people would live much longer than others. That is not statistically the case in a proportional study. It is a metaphor.

"I could try to fire at them, but all I have is a handgun and there are three of them and one of me," Mike said. "I don't like our chances."

"Neither do I. In addition, I am not an advocate of proactive violence. I believe it is a tactic that should be used only defensively."

The gun barrel to our right as we faced the house moved to better aim at the driver's side window, which was my sector of the vehicle.

"If you mean only when the other guy fires first, that's already the case and it looks like it might happen again soon," Mike said. "At least start the car, Samuel. Get the air going."

The heat was becoming intense inside the Kia Soul so engaging the engine was a viable option even if only to operate the air conditioning. I inserted the key into the ignition slot and started the vehicle's motor. Cool air began to blow through the vents.

Again a squawk of noise indicated Kaplan had removed the mute function on his phone. "Not a chance, Hoenig," he said. "You're gonna give me my money and I'm not going to let you talk to your dad."

The way he said, "your dad" caused a flutter of anger in me. I felt my neck spasm and my expression must have changed because Mike said, "Are you okay?"

I nodded. Then I turned off my mute feature and addressed George Kaplan. "That is not a viable business arrangement. In order to get something, a party must give something." I had heard that on a television program. I believe I used the axiom correctly.

"Oh, I'm going to give you something," Kaplan said. I tried to analyze how one can tell a person is smiling when hearing his voice but could not make the calculation quickly enough. "I'm gonna give you something you really want, and you're gonna give me all of my money."

"The only payment I require from you is access to Reuben Hoenig," I told Kaplan.

"That's what you think," he answered. There was a rustle on his end of the conversation that indicated something in the space he was occupying was being moved. "You have to come to my office on Magnolia in Burbank and bring every dollar you took from me. Be there in an hour."

I looked at Mike, whose eyebrows were down and close together. He was concerned.

"What do I get in exchange for the package of counterfeit cash?" I asked.

"This," Kaplan said. The scuffling sounds became louder. I felt a flutter of anxiety in my stomach but could not identify what was making me feel uneasy. Then I understood as soon as I heard the next voice to come through the phone.

"Samuel, don't you do anything," Ms. Washburn said. "I've got—"

Then her voice was cut off and Kaplan's returned.

"Get here in an hour or less. Are we clear?" he asked.

But I had already engaged the transmission of the Kia Soul and begun driving toward Burbank.

TWENTY-FIVE

"Speed up, Samuel," Mike the taxicab driver suggested.

I had thought I was driving the Kia Soul at the posted speed limit for the area, and checked very briefly the dashboard display. "I am driving at the limit," I informed Mike.

I did notice that other vehicles were passing the rental as I drove, which was not surprising but difficult to understand. This was the absolute fastest a motor vehicle could legally travel, but so many were choosing to break the law and exceed the limit.

Mike had programmed into the Global Positioning System device the address George Kaplan gave me for his office on Magnolia Avenue in Burbank near where Ms. Washburn had been touring the Warner Brothers studios. Mike held the device with both his hands and secured it in his lap. I could not see the screen and Mike had deactivated the vocal instructions to direct me himself. He had, as soon as I had engaged the drive gear, fastened his safety harness. I had done so immediately upon occupying the vehicle.

We were now on White Oak Avenue and Mike had instructed me to stay on this road for two miles. I was perspiring at my hairline and upper lip despite the strong flow from the Kia Soul's air conditioner.

"The police don't expect you to strictly stick with the limit," Mike informed me. "They know you are going to go above it. Just don't go too fast. Stay at the same speed as other drivers and you'll be fine."

My desire to reach Ms. Washburn and extract her from the situation in which she had found herself had temporarily overcome my serious misgivings about driving, particularly in unfamiliar territory. But now that we were en route I found the process of getting to Magnolia Boulevard was making me perspire with anxiety. My hands on the steering wheel at the designated positions of ten and two in correspondence to a clock's face were damp. My eyes were not diverting from the road. I felt like I could not move my head from that position. I could not see Mike except in the limits of my peripheral vision.

"In about a half a mile you're going to make a left," he told me. "Go ahead. Speed up."

Left turns were not comforting. I felt my jaw clench. If my hands had not been gripping the steering wheel tightly they might have been flapping at my sides. I found it difficult not to vocalize with sounds Mike no doubt would have considered incomprehensible.

Against my instincts I pressed on the accelerator and felt the engine respond. The number on the display exceeded the posted limit and I was not pleased with that reminder. I focused my mind on Ms. Washburn and thought of her being detained by George Kaplan.

"Watch it, Samuel!" Mike said emphatically.

My eyes immediately refocused on the vehicle in front of me, a Toyota Prius like Mike's taxicab, but not painted yellow. This one was blue. And if Mike had not engaged my attention, I probably would have struck it in the rear with the Kia Soul. Traffic had stopped at a red traffic signal.

"Easy," Mike said, exhaling. "I'm worried about Janet, too. But Kaplan isn't going to do anything to her because he wants his money. As long as he doesn't have it, Janet is safe."

"Yes." I let my head drop forward, keeping my foot firmly on the brake. "You are right. Perhaps I should have let you drive, Mike. I am useless at the task."

"You're doing fine. Just keep your focus and get into the left lane when you can. I'll watch for the right time to make the change." I do not trust a vehicle's side mirrors because objects one sees in them might be larger than they appear. They are not accurate reflectors. "Look up, Samuel. The light turned green."

Indeed, when I adjusted my view I saw the open space before me and moved my foot to the accelerator. "How do you think Kaplan got to Janet?" Mike asked me. He knew I preferred not to converse while anyone is driving, but this was a new experience for both of us. Perhaps he was attempting to keep me engaged and lower my level of tension. If so, it was not helping a great deal.

"My best guess is that somehow Kaplan or one of his associates discovered Ms. Washburn was taking the studio tour," I said. "They would know, therefore, when the tour was completed and wait by the gate to intercept her. It is much more important now to determine what they intend to do with her and, when we arrive, with us. It is clear that Reuben Hoenig is important enough to his interests that Kaplan is absolutely unwilling to release him to our custody."

"Why?" Mike asked. "What could he be doing that's so important to a guy making fake money?"

"That is an excellent question."

"Here's the left turn," Mike pointed out. "There's a left turn only lane so you don't have to worry about waiting for an opening in traffic."

I looked up toward the intersection and my stomach clenched more tightly. "This is a freeway entrance," I told Mike, who undoubtedly had that information already.

"Yes. You're getting on the One-Oh-One."

"I don't think I am," I said even as I made the left turn in accordance with the arrow shining green on the traffic signal.

"We don't have time to think about that," Mike said. "We have to be thinking about Janet and your dad."

"I need to be thinking about the drive." A glance at the freeway before me was disheartening. There was a traffic signal indicating when a vehicle on the ramp should accelerate. I stopped before it and watched the oncoming traffic.

It was virtually at a standstill.

"We are not going to get there quickly," I told Mike.

"The light's green, Samuel," he said. "You have to go onto the freeway." He pointed at the signal, perhaps not understanding I could see it was showing my lane was clear to proceed.

"I know," I said. But I did not move my foot to the accelerator. The vehicle behind the Kia Soul, which was a Nissan Sentra, sounded its horn.

My mind raced; there had to be a faster way to reach Ms. Washburn, who was undoubtedly in some kind of distress even if she was not in immediate danger. I became angry at myself for placing her in this position. I should have argued more vehemently against her touring the studio when we were dealing with unsavory characters.

The Nissan Sentra's horn sounded again. Mike looked at me. "Samuel," he said.

"Program the Global Positioning System to find an alternate route," I told him. "I am not willing to enter this freeway. I am not confident in my skill as a driver and I cannot allow this traffic to slow us down. Find another way."

In my side mirror I saw the driver of the Nissan shake her fist at me.

"You're on the onramp, Samuel," Mike reminded me. "You can't back up. You have to get on the freeway."

"I will not. There must be a faster route."

The Nissan's horn was joined by those of three other vehicles. I felt my neck begin to dampen with perspiration.

"I'll look for it, but you have to get on the highway now," Mike said. "Even sitting in traffic is faster than not moving at all."

His point was reasonable and was amplified by the view in my side mirror, where one of the drivers behind the Kia Soul was exiting his car and walking toward me purposefully. I took my foot off the brake and placed it lightly on the acceleration pedal.

We moved forward to the point that other vehicles had filled the lanes and then I stopped the Kia Soul. "Just merge into the right lane," Mike said. "I'm finding us another route."

"I need you to look to my left," I told him.

Mike looked up, remembering his navigation role. "Okay. Wait. Now, go!" I moved the vehicle into the lane and was almost immediately forced to brake to a stop. We were hopelessly caught in mid-afternoon Los Angeles traffic.

"Okay. Now just move when you can and don't change lanes," Mike said. "I'm working with the GPS."

Progress was painfully slow. I had to consciously focus my mind on the traffic and not the plight of Ms. Washburn, who had not answered her cellular phone when Mike had tried to reach her. There had been no further communication from George Kaplan.

"This is the fastest route," Mike said after my seventh instance of stopping behind a Honda Civic after having inched forward a few yards. "There is no better way that wouldn't be bumper-to-bumper this time of day, Samuel. I'm sorry."

"We can't just do this, Mike," I managed to squeeze out between clenched jaws. "I don't think I can stay calm that long." Already my neck was in spasm. It was a struggle to maintain focus and control over my head.

"I don't have an answer for you." Mike sounded as frustrated as I was.

"You are a taxicab driver. Under these circumstances, what would you do?"

Mike was silent for eleven seconds, which is a very long lull in a conversation. He did make a sound deep in his throat that seemed to indicate he was thinking very deeply. Finally he said, "I'd do something you would never do."

He did not appear to understand that was why I had asked for his perspective. If the solution was to do something that would occur to me, I would have put that plan into action by now. "What would that be?" I asked.

"I'd drive on the shoulder of the road past everybody until I got stopped by a cop," Mike said. "But I know you'd never—"

I had already moved onto the right shoulder of the freeway and was accelerating past the dormant traffic. "Samuel!" Mike shouted. I could not tell if his tone betrayed alarm or admiration.

Horns on other vehicles sounded and there were a number of obscene gestures from drivers in the lane I had vacated. But no other vehicles followed my lead. I was torn between staring straight ahead and watching carefully in the rearview mirror for the first sign of a Los Angeles Police Department cruiser or a California Highway Patrol vehicle. None appeared immediately.

I maintained the speed posted on traffic signs as we proceeded so I would not be cited for speeding if a police officer were to stop our progress. We had gone 3.2 miles on the shoulder when Mike emitted an ominous, "Uh-oh..."

There was no law enforcement vehicle visible in the rearview mirror, so it took a moment before I understood the cause of Mike's dismay. Looking farther ahead than before, I saw what had made him groan.

"There's no shoulder ahead, Samuel," Mike said.

TWENTY-SIX

LESS THAN ONE THOUSAND yards ahead of the Kia Soul a temporary concrete barrier had been constructed in the lane I was currently using to get Mike and myself to Ms. Washburn within George Kaplan's time limit. It took up the entire width of the shoulder. There would be no driving around it except to reenter the freeway's right lane.

That was currently crammed with motor vehicles that were barely moving. I drove as far as I could on the shoulder and then engaged the left turn signal on the Kia Soul.

No vehicle left room for the one I was driving to enter. I was deadlocked on the shoulder of US 101 in Southern California, unable to drive to Ms. Washburn's rescue. I did not possess the proper skill set to cope with the present situation.

With my emotions raging I slammed my fists on the steering wheel four times. I'm sure the sound coming from my mouth was disturbing to Mike, but he did not react strongly. I raised my hands to hit the steering wheel again but they stayed next to my ears, fingers bent like talons, shaking as my frustration and concern overwhelmed my decision-making faculties. This was a nightmare—Ms. Washburn was in imminent danger and I could not rely on my mother for advice. Mike was a friend but he did not provide the kind of support I needed right now, I thought.

"Samuel," he said. "We'll get to Janet. Trust me."

His words sounded hollow. I realized he was trying to reassure me but I could find seven different ways his sentiment was incorrect and could be proven so. But I could not form coherent thoughts at the moment. I simply sat there making incoherent noises while my hands vibrated on opposite sides of my head.

"We'll do it," Mike reiterated. "But you have to let me drive. Put the car in Park and put the emergency brake on. Then we'll change seats and I will get us there, okay?"

"No!" I could force out only the one syllable. Mike was aware of the insurance ramifications of his suggestion. He knew I could not let him take control of the vehicle without a written authorization from the rental firm. I could not understand why he would put such a plan forward.

"Samuel," Mike said, his tone attempting to soothe. "We don't have a—"

He stopped as we both noted the sound coming from behind the Kia Soul, accompanied by flashing lights of various colors. The sound was clearly mechanical and amplified, a series of bleats meant to attract attention. The lights flashed consistently and constantly.

The vehicle now stopping behind us came from the California Highway Patrol. Its driver was now speaking through the amplification system, his words hitting my ears harshly and not in any way decreasing my anxiety.

"Please do *not* step out of the vehicle," he said. "Stay in the car."

I had never had any intention of leaving the Kia Soul, so it was not difficult to comply with the officer at all.

"Leave your hands on the steering wheel," he continued. I placed my hands in the driving position again and gripped the steering wheel very tightly. "On the passenger side, put your hands on the dash-board." Mike complied with that command as well.

In the side mirror I saw the officer, in full uniform, step out of the cruiser he had been driving and walked carefully toward the Kia Soul. His demeanor was not arrogant, but certainly was cautious if I was reading it right. It is not easy to discern the emotions of a person on your first meeting. Perhaps I was relying too much on fictionalized depictions of law enforcement officers I had seen in motion pictures and on television.

"Quick, figure out what we're going to say," Mike said quietly. "What do we tell this guy?"

His question puzzled me. "The truth."

"No. I mean—" Then the officer was at the driver's window standing next to me and gesturing, with a rolling motion of his hand, that I should lower the window. I wondered how to do that without removing my hands from the steering wheel. I did not move.

Through the pane of glass I heard the officer say, "Go ahead. Put the window down."

I realized I would have to modulate my voice to be louder so it could be heard through the tempered glass. "I have to move my hand off the steering wheel!" I shouted. Perhaps I spoke a bit too loud, because I saw the officer take an involuntary step back and when I glanced at Mike his eyes were wide.

"It's okay," the officer said. "Just do it."

I removed my left hand from its grip of the steering wheel and touched the control to lower the window. The officer looked at me as the power window lowered. His nametag read CRAWFORD. "Put your hand back on the wheel," he said. His voice was, I think, impassive.

"Yes, Officer," I said.

"Get your license, registration, and insurance card," he said. "It's okay to move your hands."

"It's a rental," Mike said from the passenger seat. "The registration and agreement are in the glove."

"Get it," the officer told him as I reached for my wallet and retrieved my license to drive.

The officer took the documents from me after Mike had handed over the packet issued by the rental company. "Stay here," he said. "Hands on the wheel." He walked back toward his cruiser.

The oppressive heat and humidity were streaming in through the open window but I did not dare raise it. I felt my head shaking. My hands were attached to the steering wheel so tightly it was difficult to believe they could ever be removed. I turned my head toward Mike with considerable effort.

"What do you mean, tell him the truth?" Mike said. "We have only twenty five minutes to get to Janet. You want some member of CHiPs to lock us up for questioning and miss the deadline? Take the ticket for driving on the shoulder and get him to help us into traffic so we can keep going."

I heard what Mike said but shook my head. "Lying to a law officer can only create more trouble than we already have," I said. My voice sounded hoarse and unsteady. "The officer will understand."

"Samuel, you don't drive very much. I'm telling you, he's going to hear what you say and think we're both crazy and Janet will suffer for it."

I shuddered. That was not a thought I cared to pursue. But there was very little time left to ponder the question; the officer was returning to the driver side of the Kia Soul.

"Think hard, Samuel," Mike said quietly.

The window remained open so there was no need to move my left hand from the steering wheel this time. The officer stopped at the door and looked into the vehicle. He handed me my license and the rental company packet.

"You know it's illegal to drive on the shoulder, right?" he asked.

"Yes, Officer, I do."

I could try to comply with the officer without lying, as Mike had advised me to do. If I was asked no more questions I would be given a summons—which was terrifying enough for me—and that would be the end of the episode. Mike would somehow navigate us to Burbank in time to comply with George Kaplan's arbitrary deadline. Perhaps it would be best for me to allow Mike, a professional driver, to take over from here. I kept my hands at the ten and two positions on the steering wheel and looked straight ahead, not making eye contact with the officer. Defying the stereotype, he was not wearing reflective sunglasses.

"So was there a reason you were doing that?" the officer said.

That was a slightly more difficult question to navigate, but I decided to try. "Yes." That was true. I did have a reason to drive on the highway shoulder.

"What was it?"

"Excuse me?"

"What was the reason you had for driving on the shoulder? Just to get around everybody else?" The officer, I could see peripherally, had his hands on his hips in a posture that is generally considered oppositional.

"I did want to get past the other drivers, yes," I said. That was still true. I understood that it did not improve my standing with the officer or reduce my probability of punishment, but it was accurate.

The officer took a moment and exhaled. I made the mistake of looking at him and saw eyes that were slits and a mouth that was a horizontal line. I'd seen that expression on social skills tools. He was angry.

"Do you think you're more important than everyone else?" he asked.

That was a difficult question. In general terms I do not consider myself more or less important than any other person. That would be to assign rankings of merit to each other living human, something I do not feel qualified to do. However, in this case I felt that my role in trying to rescue Ms. Washburn did have a higher urgency than most of the reasons the other drivers were traveling on the highway. So one could say that my purpose was more important but that I personally was not, and that was the question I had been asked.

"No, I do not," I said.

Another long exhalation of air came from the officer and his word had the tone of a last resort. "Then why?" he asked.

Finally, that was the question I could not sidestep. "Because an associate of mine is being held against her will by a counterfeiter in an office on Magnolia Boulevard in Burbank and we have only twenty-two minutes left to meet his deadline or we cannot be held responsible for her safety."

Mike put his forehead down on the edge of the dashboard. "Samuel," he said.

The officer turned his head forty-three degrees to his left and looked at me with a skeptical expression. "Your friend is being held by a kidnapper in Burbank and you have twenty-two minutes to get there?" he asked.

"Yes."

"And you're taking the One-Oh-One? You'll never get there in time. You need an escort. Turn the car around and just follow me." Without another word the officer walked purposefully back to his unit. I looked at Mike, who had raised his head and stared when the officer had spoken.

"What should I do?" I asked.

"You heard the man. Turn your car around and follow him."

TWENTY-SEVEN

TURNING A KIA SOUL 180 degrees on the shoulder of a crowded highway with concrete barriers to my right was not easy. Mike had offered to perform the maneuver but we decided he would get out of the vehicle and direct my efforts. Within a minute the Kia Soul was pointed in the other direction and I was following quickly behind the California Highway Patrol cruiser, which the officer was driving back toward the ramp that led to the nearest freeway entrance.

Mimicking his every move we were bypassing traffic in the oncoming direction, but driving against the traffic was fraying my nerves. I heard myself breathing more heavily than usual. I felt perspiration streaming down my cheeks. That was partially due to my inability to move my left hand off the steering wheel to raise the window and fully utilize the vehicle's air conditioning.

"Take it easy, Samuel." Mike could no doubt sense my tension. "The cop isn't going to let you get into an accident. Just do whatever he does."

I did not speak. I do not speak when driving unless it is unavoidable.

The officer in the California Highway Patrol vehicle must have communicated with his base. Two other cars from the same agency met him at the top of the ramp when he had cleared away oncoming cars and ushered the Kia Soul back onto the city streets. One fell into formation behind me and the other took a position to my left.

"They're protecting us the whole way," Mike said. "We'll get there for sure now."

But I was aware of the sixteen minutes that had passed since the last time I had checked our progress. "How much time does the Global Positioning System device indicate we will need to arrive at the address in Burbank?" I asked Mike.

I barely saw his head movement because I was attending to the road but he looked down at the instrument in his hand. "Fourteen minutes," Mike said.

He was lying. I was certain of it but had no doubt Mike knew he was underestimating the remaining time because it would upset me to know we would not hit George Kaplan's deadline for no harm to come to Ms. Washburn. I asked Mike to call Kaplan on my phone and put the call on the speaker feature because it was not connected to the Bluetooth system in the Kia Soul.

"You have eleven minutes." Kaplan wasted no time with niceties.

"We are in heavy traffic," I said. "We will be there but we will not be there in time."

"That's too bad for you. It's too bad for your friend, too."

I felt bile rise in my throat. "Mr. Kaplan, you must understand the kind of obstacles that Los Angeles traffic represents. I should not be talking to you at all now but I am because I want you to understand that we are on our way and will be only a few minutes late."

"Get here on time," he said. "That's the deal. Now—"

There was a commotion I could not decipher and then the call was disconnected. That was the last thing I had hoped to hear.

Shaking with frustration and fear I pressed harder on the accelerator. The California Highway Patrol vehicles had already been moving at a speed higher than the posted limit and I had reluctantly kept pace because they were officers of the law and had no doubt sanctioned my violation. But now we needed to go faster and I was going to take control of our speed.

The police officers did not hesitate; they matched my pace but continued to lead the vehicles. Within seven minutes we had passed the posted Burbank city limit. My mind racing, I noted the sirens and flashing lights of the California Highway Patrol vehicles. If George Kaplan knew I had brought the authorities with me, Ms. Washburn would undoubtedly be in considerably more danger.

But I did not have a telephone number for any of the officers in the other vehicles so I could not discuss the situation with them. I bit my lips as I considered options.

"You have to pull over, Samuel." Mike clearly knew what I was thinking about. "Stop on the side of the street and they'll stop and you can talk to them then. Hurry."

His analysis was perceptive; there was no other efficient way to complete the task. I very carefully moved the Kia Soul to the curb and slowed it to a stop. The first California Highway Patrol officer, the one who had approached us on Highway 101, immediately drove far ahead of the Kia Soul, not anticipating my maneuver. Once I had stopped, however, he had realized what I was doing and both escort vehicles came to a halt near me, lights still flashing.

The officer walked to my side of the vehicle. "What are you doing?" he asked. "We only have a couple of minutes to get there."

"Your sirens, your flashing lights," I noted. "If the man in the office building hears or sees you, my associate will be in greater danger."

He half smiled. "We're aware of that," he said. "We were going to cut the sirens and lights when we were close. Come on. We'll turn them off now unless we hit traffic. Let's get you there." He turned and ran back to his vehicle.

"California police officers are very polite," I noted as we started moving, even more swiftly than before.

"Most of the time," Mike said. I did not ask him what that observation meant.

We arrived at the building on Magnolia Boulevard with one minute to spare. Three other cars, not marked with insignia but clearly belonging to law enforcement agencies, were parked in front of the building. Three men and a woman in business clothing, but with visible weapons inside their jackets, approached the lead officer as we exited our vehicles.

I headed directly for the building entrance, knowing I would have to climb stairs to the second floor and had only seconds left. But one of the men in business clothing stopped me at the door.

"You're not authorized to go in there," he said.

My iPhone rang. George Kaplan's number was showing in the Caller ID display. I needed to be in his office right now.

"I don't care," I said and pushed my way through the door.

Behind me I heard Mike protesting but the door did not open again and I did not wait. I found the staircase and ran up, three stairs at a time, until I reached the second floor. Once there I searched for the proper suite number and found a door marked KAPLAN ENTERPRISES LLC.

I stood momentarily at the door and considered my options. The counterfeit money was in a pocket of my cargo shorts. I could easily hand it over to Kaplan, but I had severe reservations that he would honor our agreement, largely because he had been given many opportunities to do so and had refused each time. I still needed to talk to Reuben Hoenig in order to complete my business in Southern

California, and had no assurance he would even be present in the room once I opened that door.

None of that seemed important, even as the iPhone in my pocket continued to vibrate with Kaplan's call. At least his attempt to contact me could be seen as a sign that he was not in some way mistreating Ms. Washburn yet.

That was the only thing that mattered. I needed to envision myself bursting through the door and readying myself for any possibility that would protect Ms. Washburn, even if it meant placing myself in some peril. Ms. Washburn's welfare was obviously more important than my own now.

It was the first time I had ever truly believed that about anyone.

There was no time to consider any implications of that thought. Kaplan had set the deadline and it was passing at exactly this second.

Visualizing myself as confident and triumphant I banished any thoughts of Ms. Washburn in peril. The iPhone in my pocket buzzed once again but I could talk to Kaplan right now, I decided. I turned the knob on the office door and pushed it into the room hard to create a forceful entrance.

"I am—" was as far as I got.

I had been entirely unprepared for the scene that met my eyes as I entered the office, which was actually an empty space with one desk in the far left corner, a dropped ceiling with some water damage, exposed wires in some areas and threadbare brown carpet from wall to wall. This space clearly had not been used for an active business. Its actual purpose was impossible to discern immediately.

Part of the reason I could not adequately discuss the surroundings was my surprise at the people inside the relatively small room. In the center were George Kaplan and two other men: The one with the bushy eyebrows who had accompanied him to the Chinese Theatre and attempted to manhandle Ms. Washburn, and another who must have been the driver that day. I did not recognize him, but he had a very thick neck holding up a wide head. Their arms were held in a defensive position, showing the palms of their hands. The two associates looked embarrassed while George Kaplan appeared to be quietly fuming.

In front of them was Ms. Washburn, facing the three and wearing an expression that communicated determination and some satisfaction. But I thought there might too have been a trace of anger in her eyes.

She was holding a pistol in each hand.

Ms. Washburn turned and looked at me. "Oh good, Samuel," she said. "Here, take this." She extended her left hand to give me the gun she was holding. "Those were getting heavy. Can you call the police?"

"There is no need," I said. "They are already here. Why didn't you call me?"

She gestured toward the three men with the gun she was now holding with both hands. "These sons of bitches broke my phone," she said. "Then I got mad."

TWENTY-EIGHT

GEORGE KAPLAN AND HIS two associates did not appear to be in a mood to talk. Kaplan made only a few attempts to vent his anger at his two male companions for not subduing Ms. Washburn, who had apparently taken their guns from their holsters and used them to keep the three men at bay for a few minutes until I had arrived.

My iPhone continued to buzz, so I checked its screen again and saw the call was coming from Mike the taxicab driver. I accepted the call and heard some commotion around Mike as he asked, "Is everybody okay up there? The cops want to come up."

"Tell them everything is under control and we are quite well," I told him. "Please let them know they should not be concerned that Ms. Washburn and I are holding weapons in our hands; we will be happy to turn them over to the officers as soon as they arrive."

"The cops have nothing on me," Kaplan rasped.

The charges of abduction, counterfeiting, and assault immediately leapt to my mind but I ignored his remark and said to Mike, "Reuben Hoenig is not here."

"You might want to ask your pal George where to find him," Mike suggested.

"Tell us where he is or I'll shoot you in the knee!" Ms. Washburn said. She was springing up and down on the balls of her feet like a prizefighter.

George Kaplan looked at her with some amazement.

"The police are coming," I told Ms. Washburn even as we heard the sound of boots on the stairs beyond the still-open office door.

"I'll do it," she continued. "They kidnapped me and broke my phone. I'm mad."

"She's crazy," Kaplan suggested.

"Don't push me," Ms. Washburn said.

The footsteps reached the office door. "LAPD!" a man shouted behind me. "Put down your weapons!"

"We will be happy to, Officer," I said. "We have been waiting for you." I placed the gun I was holding on the seedy brown carpet, making a mental note to wash my hands as soon as possible.

Ms. Washburn, both hands on her gun, did not move.

"Put down the gun, ma'am," the officer repeated.

"Ma'am?" Ms. Washburn said. "I'm a ma'am now?"

"She's gone nuts," Kaplan told the policeman. "Thank god you're here."

"Ms. Washburn," I said quietly. "It's over now. Please put your gun on the floor so the officers can do their job."

Ms. Washburn looked at me and seemed to comprehend the situation for the first time since I had entered. A tear fell from her left eye. "They broke my phone," she whimpered.

"I know. Put the gun down."

She nodded and placed the handgun on the carpet. Then she held her hands up to show the police officers she no longer had any offensive weapon in her possession. "Sorry, guys," she said to the officers. "I got emotional. They ..."

"We get it, ma'am," the officer who had entered first said. "They broke your phone."

"You know what I paid for that phone?"

The policemen and women—there were five in all, three men and two women—picked up the two weapons and handcuffed Kaplan and his two accomplices. They complained as they were led out of the room that Ms. Washburn had been the aggressor, but the officers did not respond. Once the three men had been removed they escorted us downstairs and out of the office building.

There we met again with Mike and the California Highway Patrol officer who had first met us on the highway, Officer Crawford. He shook his head when he saw me. "You shouldn't have gone rushing up there by yourself."

"I was concerned for Ms. Washburn."

Crawford looked at Ms. Washburn. "From what I hear you didn't need to worry that much."

"I got mad," Ms. Washburn said. "They—"

Crawford nodded. "I heard. I'm very sorry."

"Officer," I said, noting Crawford's smile at Ms. Washburn, which I took to be a gesture of consolation, "I am concerned that the man we were attempting to find, Reuben Hoenig, was not on the premises. Mr. Kaplan had agreed that we would exchange him for the counterfeit funds we had mistakenly been given, but Reuben was not here. It is very important that we find him."

Crawford averted his gaze from Ms. Washburn and looked at me with an expression of some consternation. "You have counterfeit money on you right now?"

I reached into my pocket and retrieved the packet. "Yes. Slightly less than forty thousand dollars by its designation." I extended my hand to the officer.

But Crawford shook his head. "That's over my pay grade," he said. "Let me get a detective over here. That's their thing." He walked to a group of police officers who were engaged at the moment in getting George Kaplan and his associates into the backseats of two Los Angeles Police Department cruisers.

"What do you think?" Mike asked as I watched an officer point Crawford toward a very tall man in what the police refer to as "plainclothes," meaning they are not in uniform. The two men spoke and Crawford clearly indicated Ms. Washburn, Mike, and me as they did.

"I think the counterfeiting is what will be the point of interest for the detective," I answered. "The other things George Kaplan has done—and hopefully we will find out his real name soon—have been unethical, but probably not illegal."

"He broke my phone," Ms. Washburn pointed out.

"True. And he told men to fire guns at Mike and me. I imagine that will bring some charges as well."

"Samuel!" Ms. Washburn looked alarmed even though it was clear that neither Mike nor I was injured.

"We are fine," I assured her as the man Crawford had approached walked over toward us.

He showed us a gold shield attached to a credential and did not keep it open long enough for me to determine its authenticity. "I'm Detective LaGrange," the man said. "I understand you have some counterfeit money in your possession."

I once again extended the packet toward the detective. He took it after putting a latex glove on his right hand and dropped it into an evidence bag. "How did you come by this money?" he asked.

In the shortest time possible I explained the situation to Detective LaGrange with some interjections from Mike and Ms. Washburn. He nodded, took no notes, and removed the latex glove from his hand.

When we had completed the explanation LaGrange nodded. "So you think your father is involved with the counterfeiting?" he asked.

"I have no way of knowing if Reuben Hoenig has any involvement or not," I told him. "I am concerned only with finding him and obtaining his address so that I might pass it along to my mother."

"Samuel can be very single-minded about completing a task," Ms. Washburn said, probably in response to the facial expression LaGrange had assumed.

"Any ideas where he might be?" the detective asked Ms. Washburn, whom he seemed to think was the person most appropriate to discuss the events of the day with.

"I have no clue," she told him.

"But I do," I said. "I believe our best bet is to find Reuben Hoenig in the house on Jamieson Avenue in Reseda where the counterfeit cash press is operating. I think it is best we go there immediately."

Mike groaned. "At this time of day? The traffic will be horrendous."

LaGrange looked me directly in the eye, which I found slightly discomfiting. "We'll drive," he said.

TWENTY-NINE

TRAVELING WITH A POLICE escort had been much less difficult than without, I had discovered. Riding in vehicles being driven by police officers, with their various methods of clearing away traffic, was considerably faster and smoother. This was not so much a surprise as it was something I had not contemplated until now.

Detective LaGrange, sitting in the passenger seat in front of Ms. Washburn and me, did not turn around when he wanted to tell us something; he merely spoke in a deep, serious tone that communicated authority. "You don't get out of the car until I tell you it's okay, understand?" he was saying now.

I realized the police officers had not been pleased when I had rushed into the office building in Burbank without escort. Indeed, I understood why they were not enamored of the idea. Had I been thinking of anything other than Ms. Washburn's safety I probably would not have done so.

But in this case, we were traveling merely to see if Reuben Hoenig was in the house on Jamieson Avenue. I had already been shot at from that house once today and held no desire to repeat the experience. "Absolutely, Detective," I said.

No doubt Mike the taxicab driver, who was in one of the other vehicles now hurtling toward the home of Kaplan Enterprises, was being given the same instructions.

"Good." LaGrange did not wait for Ms. Washburn to duplicate my statement; perhaps he believed I spoke for both of us. "Now, explain to me how these gun turrets in the house work."

"I am not especially well informed on their functionality," I told him. "What I can say is that they are small holes drilled through the facing of the house at strategic points with enough latitude for the shooter to move the barrel from side to side and adjust its trajectory vertically, although the horizontal movement is probably more flexible than the vertical. Mike suggested that telescopic sights would not be possible there."

LaGrange looked blankly at me for a moment and then said, "Okay." I believe Ms. Washburn put her hand to her mouth at that point.

We approached the now-familiar house but the police vehicle in which we were riding parked well out of range of any weapon the people inside might be wielding. "You stay in the car," LaGrange reiterated. "If the man you're looking for is inside, we'll let you know." Without awaiting a response from Ms. Washburn or me, he opened his car door and simultaneously removed a handgun from a holster he wore around his left shoulder.

LaGrange walked away, gun barrel pointed toward the ground, and followed three uniformed officers, one of whom had been driving the cruiser we had ridden in and the other two from the second Los Angeles Police Department vehicle, in which we knew Mike was now sitting with similar instructions to the ones LaGrange had given us.

After a moment Ms. Washburn, who had intertwined her fingers in front of her, let out an audible breath. "Are you worried?" she asked.

"Why should I be worried?" I asked. "It is the police officers who are taking the risk, not you or me."

"About your father," Ms. Washburn said. "If he's inside and something goes the wrong way..."

"I have every confidence in the professionalism I have seen from the police officers we've met here," I said. "Reuben Hoenig is involved in something that could be seen as dangerous. I assume he knows there are risks inherent in that activity."

"Samuel," Ms. Washburn said. "He's your father."

I was aware of Reuben Hoenig's biological role in my existence. I had spoken with him only once since I was a very young child and his contribution to the conversation had been a series of quotes from a classic detective novel. The insistence of others on manufacturing an emotional bond between us was baffling to me, so I had no response to offer Ms. Washburn. But I felt I had to say something.

"I know," I told her. Because that was true. I did know Reuben Hoenig was my father.

Ms. Washburn seemed unsatisfied with that response. "What are you thinking about?" she asked.

"Going home tomorrow."

LaGrange and the uniformed officers dispersed as they approached the house. One officer climbed the stairs and stood next to the front door but not directly in front of it. The other two in uniform separated and each walked to a side of the house and toward the rear until they were no longer visible. LaGrange stood closer to the street. All four had their weapons drawn.

I saw one front door of another house, two properties to the south and on the opposite side of the street, open and a woman's head emerge. LaGrange must have noticed it too because he gestured for her to go back inside. The woman's head withdrew and the door closed.

After having checked his communications link the officer at the front door reached over and knocked without moving his body to a position directly before the door. It was difficult to know if he received a response, but he did not knock again.

The cruiser in which Mike had been brought to this house was parked directly in front of the one in which Ms. Washburn and I sat. Mike appeared to know we were behind him because he turned around in the back seat and looked out the rear window at us. Ms. Washburn waved but Mike did not respond.

"I'm not sure Mike can see us," I noted. "There is a barrier between our seat and the front, and he is looking from—"

There was the sound of a gunshot from the direction of the house.

Then another. I heard a total of four reports from firearms. Ms. Washburn's body tensed and her head turned quickly toward the house. Mike, in the car ahead of us, turned away from the rear window.

Unexpectedly, I felt a tightening in my stomach.

I had never known my father. He had not been a presence in my life to the point that I had stopped thinking about him at all by the time I became an adult. But I had realized some feelings of resentment toward Reuben Hoenig for the obvious pain and difficulty he had inflicted upon my mother. That was something I had not been able to overlook or forgive.

Mother, I had to admit, had continued to love the man she married even decades after they had been in the same room or even the same time zone. Because I respected her feelings (even when I did not understand them) and her judgment, I was forced to confront the possibility that Reuben Hoenig was a man worthy of consideration. I knew he was my father, but having dismissed the idea of a father many years earlier, I had taken to thinking of Reuben as my mother's husband, someone she had known a long time ago.

It would be very difficult now to go home and tell Mother her husband had been shot dead in a police raid on the building where he worked for a counterfeiter.

There would have been no point in attempting to leave the vehicle in an attempt to view the police action on the house. LaGrange had been very careful to note that the doors in the back seat of the cruiser were locked from the outside. It led me to wonder how Ms. Washburn and I would escape if the officers did not come back to let us out.

I felt her hand reach for mine and I took it without thinking.

Mentally I was preparing for a very unpleasant conversation with my mother. Was it more appropriate to call her and give her the news or to wait until we were back in New Jersey where I could tell her face-to-face? Once we had the details I would consult with Ms. Washburn on the proper etiquette in such matters.

It was not a pleasant exercise to project ahead to telling Mother what had happened, assuming the gunshots indicated some harm had come to Reuben Hoenig. I considered it likely that he was inside the building, that there were no more than three people in total there before the police officers arrived, and that the gunshots had not all come from the police. The arithmetic involved was not complicated; the probability was high that Reuben Hoenig was involved.

Why did I not feel anything about that? Everyone seemed to think I should, particularly the people I trusted most—my mother and Ms. Washburn. From a strictly objective viewpoint it was obvious that Reuben had never sought out my attention or attempted to make any connection, emotional or otherwise, with me since I was four years old. I barely remembered him in an incarnation other than the one I had met the day before.

261

People whose behavior indicates they fall on the autism spectrum as described by the neurotypical are thought not to have strong emotions. The uninformed believe we do not have feelings at all. These beliefs are incorrect. I have the same types of emotions as almost everyone else, but my responses to them do not fit into the norm as dictated by society. I tend to internalize because when I do act on my strongest feelings my reactions are seen as inappropriate.

I believe the saying is that one can't win for losing. I do not understand that axiom, but I have heard it used in the context I was describing.

Sitting in the back seat of the police cruiser, my thoughts were not about possibly losing my father—I had never considered myself as having a father. I concentrated, therefore, on the reaction Mother would have because she clearly felt a strong connection to her husband. She had spent twenty-seven years alone and never even entertained the thought of divorcing the man who had left her alone with a small boy to raise. I could argue the logic of that decision but I could not contest the obvious dedication behind it.

Mother loved Reuben Hoenig, and there was a very strong probability that I would now have to inform her that he was dead.

"I'm sure he's okay," Ms. Washburn said. I did not ask for her train of thought leading to that conclusion; I had learned the answer would be unsatisfying to both of us. I nodded, although I immediately wanted to explain that it was not a means of agreeing with her statement. Perhaps to distract me from watching the house—which was now quiet and, if I was observing accurately, no longer sporting gun barrels through its turrets—she asked, "What made you think your father was here?"

"He is the key to the counterfeiting operation," I said. "He had an expertise in color transfer onto paper that was apparently unique in the industry. It required equipment that would be considered somewhat archaic in printing circles now, but which makes remarkably accurate reproductions of paper money. His abilities were what George Kaplan wanted to exploit, and Reuben's drug-induced state of compliance indicates he might not always have been eager to participate. I believed he was here because when Kaplan is not otherwise occupying his time, Reuben is probably overseeing the printing of false capital."

The sound of the car door opening startled me; maybe Ms. Washburn's attempt to distract me had been successful after all. I looked up and saw Detective LaGrange holding out his hand. He appeared to be beckoning to me to exit the police vehicle.

"He wants to talk to you," he said.

Ms. Washburn's hand grasped mine more tightly, and she would not release it even as I moved out onto the street.

THIRTY

"I DID LIKE YOU said when you whispered to me by the Chinese Theatre," Reuben Hoenig told me. "I stopped taking my meds. Stuck them in my jaw and spit them out when nobody was looking."

I sat in the kitchen of the Kaplan Enterprises house while Reuben continued to crouch in the pantry closet amid empty shelves but for six packs of beer and containers of table salt. He was almost completely unharmed except for a bruise on his forehead, which Reuben said he had sustained when the gunshots rang out in the house and he had foolishly attempted to stand up, hitting his head on the shelf above him.

"Did that help clear your mind?" I asked. "I noticed you have not been quoting *The Maltese Falcon* since we arrived."

Ms. Washburn, having let go of my hand, stood to my right side and watched Reuben closely. She seemed about to weep but I could not understand why. Reuben was not dead; he was not even seriously injured.

The conversation I had been rehearsing to have with my mother would not be necessary.

"I think I always knew Manny was using the drugs as a way to control me," Reuben said, nodding. "At the beginning I thought it was just to calm me down. But when they started up the dosages, it was too late. I had pretty much lost my will at that point and I'd do whatever Manny wanted me to do."

"Who's Manny?" asked Detective La Grange, who was standing behind Ms. Washburn and holding a voice recorder. Reuben had not been advised of his Miranda rights, so I was assuming he would not be charged with a crime and did not—at least not yet—need the services of a criminal attorney.

Reuben Hoenig looked at him with an expression of disbelief. "The guy you arrested," he said. "The one who was running this whole operation." He waved his hand around in a grand gesture as if the simple house on Jamieson Avenue was the center of a vast criminal empire.

"George Kaplan?" Mike asked. He was standing behind me, leaning against the far wall.

I chuckled. I looked at Reuben Hoenig. "Do you want to say it, or shall I?" I asked him.

My father turned and regarded him with a small smile. "Mr. Thornhill, there is no such person as George Kaplan."

"My name's not Thornhill," Mike replied.

Ms. Washburn smiled back at him. "It's from *North by Northwest*, Mike. But Mr. Hoenig, I thought the whole George Kaplan thing was your idea. You were the first man to use the name, weren't you? When you moved here from Seattle?"

Before he could answer there was a commotion from the basement. A uniformed officer appeared followed by the young man we had seen before, no longer wearing a bowling shirt identifying him as Nate. He was wearing plastic zip strips on his wrists, which were held behind his back. He appeared to be uninjured. They walked through the kitchen without saying a word, although Nate did glare at me unpleasantly as he walked.

Reuben Hoenig turned his attention back to Ms. Washburn. "I never actually used that name in day-to-day life," he explained. "I had the company create a payroll account in that name so I couldn't be traced once I was transferred here. I got a bank account that I opened with ID I'd, let's say *obtained*, bearing the name George Kaplan. Then I moved in here and used my own name everywhere but in official records. I figured I was safe."

"Safe from what?" LaGrange asked. "Were the Seattle police looking for you?"

My father shook his head and held out his hands to dismiss the notion. "No. I never did anything illegal, except maybe obtaining that ID. No, I was trying to hide from Manny Hastert. He'd been bugging me about printing the whole time in Seattle. Wanted to know could I make something that looked like money. I'd talked to him in a bar one night after work and then he thought I was a mastermind or something."

"That should not warrant a false identity and a change of location," I suggested. "Wasn't it merely possible to refuse Hastert, or at worse to change your place of employment?"

An Emergency Medical Technician in full uniform walked into the kitchen, noted Reuben's head wound, and set about cleaning and bandaging it. He asked LaGrange if anyone else in the house was hurt more seriously and was told this was the only injury.

While being attended to, my father looked at me. "Manny was persistent to the point of stalking," he said. "He'd be outside my apartment at night. He'd be in the lunchroom whenever I went in for a break. He'd be standing next to my car in the parking lot after work. He'd call me twenty times a day. He told me that if I went to the police he would make a call and someone would put a bullet in my head. I had to get out."

"But he found you down here in Los Angeles," Mike said.

Reuben nodded. "I wasn't very good at hiding. I didn't want to be George Kaplan for real. He tracked me down and got himself transferred here and got after me about the funny money again. One time I said I was going to call the cops and there was a dead squirrel on my front step in the morning."

Another uniformed officer emerged from the basement, this time escorting the man I'd found operating the printing press when I'd ventured into the space. The young man was uninjured. Whatever gunfire had taken place appeared to have missed its intended targets. They too marched through the kitchen on the way to the front door, where four more Los Angeles Police Department vehicles were waiting.

"You agreed to help after you were threatened?" LaGrange said to my father when they were gone.

Reuben's eyes narrowed. "Do I need a lawyer?"

"Did you profit from the counterfeiting?" the detective asked. "Or were you coerced and forced to do what you did?"

"I never made a dime from it, unless you count Manny moving me from one dingy rented room to the next so I wouldn't be found. And after I outlined the process for him under threat of injury or death, he drugged me up so I was just coherent enough to oversee it but not enough to break away or get help."

"What about the army of George Kaplans?" Ms. Washburn asked.

"Those were a smokescreen," my father told us. "Manny figured the way to cover the profit he was making by supplying local criminals—drug dealers and others—with fake money was to launder it through his business selling ad time. But nobody was falling for that stupid scam, so he sent all these George Kaplans around to screw up other businesses that were doing roughly the same thing, only more legitimately. That made it look like he was getting all these new clients when the other businesses went belly-up. He's crazy, but he always has a plan." Then he looked at LaGrange again. "So? Do I need a lawyer, or have I already said too much?"

"I'll talk to the DA, but I don't think you're going to get charged," LaGrange said. "I'm not reading you your rights, so even if you tell me something, we can't use it in court. How's that?"

"I'm afraid it's not enough, Detective," I said. "Unless you can guarantee he will not be facing criminal charges, we will be seeking legal counsel for my father."

"Your father," Reuben echoed faintly.

"Your father." Ms. Washburn looked quite pleased.

"Then I won't ask any more right now," LaGrange said as the young Emergency Medical Technician finished his work. "I'll call you tomorrow."

"We are flying back to New Jersey tomorrow," I told him. "Flight 247, leaving at seven a.m."

Ms. Washburn rolled her eyes. "Oh yeah. Seven a.m.," she said.

———————

"You never answered my question," my mother said.

She was lying on her bed in our house, her left leg extended on an electrical device that included a brace. Her knee was heavily bandaged. The device slowly bent and then straightened the knee continuously. When it bent most severely Mother grimaced just a little.

"You didn't tell me you were having knee replacement surgery," I countered. "That was a devious thing to do, Mother."

"I know how you worry about me," she said, waving a hand. "I figured since I had to be in the hospital overnight and you needed to be in Los Angeles—"

"You *insisted* I go to California," I said, not correcting Mother for referring to my destination as Los Angeles because technically Reseda is part of the city. "You planned this ahead of time so that I would be away when you were having surgery."

She shrugged. "It worked, didn't it? You came back and you can see I'm fine."

I did not mention her wincing as she said that. Ms. Washburn would probably commend me on my display of tact when we spoke later. Right now, she was standing to the left of me, at the side of Mother's bed.

"So instead of letting me be concerned about your surgery, you decided to let me worry about your absence and your inability to communicate," I scolded her gently. This constituted a kind of humor Mother and I have cultivated. It seemed as if I was angry with her, but I was not. I was only pretending. Please do not misinterpret. "I sent Mrs. Schiff to look for you and she did not call me back even when you returned home."

"I asked Claudia not to," Mother said. "She came by as soon as the ambulance dropped me off here, but I was afraid you'd cut your trip short. It was important that you finish what you were doing out there."

It occurred to me that had we come home a day earlier we could have avoided being shot at, threatened, abducted, and almost arrested, but we had managed to liberate Reuben Hoenig from his semi-captivity under the thumb of Emmanuel Hastert, known to us previously as George Kaplan. That, I supposed, came close to balancing the scales.

Detective LaGrange had indeed consulted with an assistant district attorney for Los Angeles County and it had been determined that Reuben should face no criminal charges. While he had technically provided Hastert with the means to produce counterfeit currency, it had been done under duress and the medications he was

269

forced to take had diminished his capacity to make sound decisions. He would be more valuable as a witness than as a defendant.

We'd had dinner with Reuben the night before we left California. The more his head cleared the more interested he was in Mother and me. He asked many questions, some of which I was not able to answer. I'd told him about Mother, how she had raised me with understanding and pride when many wouldn't. Reuben looked down at his plate but did not take a bite of food.

"I wasn't there," he said. "I left, but you have to know, Samuel, it wasn't because of you."

I actually suspected the opposite was true. "I was not an easy son to have," I said.

Ms. Washburn did not take my hand because she knew it would embarrass me, but she looked at me with some sadness in her eyes. Mike the taxicab driver looked in another direction.

"It was me," Reuben continued. "I didn't know how to be a husband or a father. You were just a little kid. Yeah, there were some problems when you played with other children but I didn't have any trouble dealing with that. I just didn't know how to stay in one place."

"You could have asked Mother to bring us along with you," I countered.

"I did."

That had not been mentioned when Mother had told me about her days with Reuben. She had never said he wanted us to come with him on his journey. "That is not what I have been told," I said, assuming Reuben was trying to make himself seem more sympathetic.

"It's the truth. Did Vivian say I *didn't* want you two to come?"

I had to admit she had not. The subject had never been broached and now as an adult I wondered why I had not asked.

"It's not that she didn't want us to all be together," Reuben said. "But Vivian was rooted to our home. She liked it there and didn't want to leave. I guess she thought I was just bluffing and I'd be back in six months. But it didn't work out like that. I was always trying to find a way to support the two of you back home and maybe convince her to come out here. After a while, it just got to be the way things were."

"That is not a very precise explanation," I pointed out.

Ms. Washburn gasped a little. "Samuel," she said.

Reuben held up a hand, palm out. "He's right, Janet. I've been doing that to myself for decades, justifying what I did. The fact is I was a young idiot who thought he was going to take over the world and didn't want to be held down by a wife and child. And I acted on a stupid impulse and spent the last twenty-seven years trying to find a way back to apologize, but I didn't know how to do it."

"It is simple to come back and apologize," I told Reuben. "One simply goes to the place where the other person is located and expresses regret." That seemed easy enough, assuming the apology was sincere, and perhaps even if it was not.

But Reuben shook his head. "It's too late," he said. "We've each had these long separate lives."

That seemed illogical to me but it was outside my area of expertise. What had been important, as Mother was pointing out now, was to obtain some means of contact she could use to find my father when she wished to do so. I asked Reuben how it would be best for Mother to find him.

"Well, I haven't had an address or a real job for a while now, so it's a little sketchy," he said. "I'm going to have to start from scratch, and that's not going to be easy at my age."

"I know a place you'd be welcome," Ms. Washburn suggested.

Reuben shook his head again. "That would be asking too much. I'll manage. I know my way around a sales floor and a printing press. There isn't a lot of use for the press anymore but selling will never go out of style. I'll find something."

"What about a place to stay?" Mike asked.

"It's been my experience these things have a way of working themselves out," Reuben Hoenig had said.

I looked now at my mother, wincing a little more when the therapy device bent her newly installed artificial knee joint, and shrugged. "I bought a prepaid cellular phone and gave it to Reuben Hoenig," I told her. "I will give you the number if you wish to have it. Other than that I can offer very little in terms of contact information. He will answer if he decides to answer but he said more than once that he thought he had treated us badly and was ashamed to remain in touch. So I can guarantee nothing."

"It's all right, Samuel," Mother said. "I never really expected an answer. I just wanted you to meet your father, and you've done so much more than that. You went above and beyond with this question. But if you don't mind, that machine is making me tired and the doctor said I need to rest up." She asked that I disconnect the therapy device. I did so, reminding her that she'd need it again the next day, and then Ms. Washburn and I left the bedroom.

I closed the door very carefully and quietly, then we walked to the kitchen, where Reuben Hoenig was sitting at the table looking nervous. His heel tapped quickly on the floor and he started when he was aware of Ms. Washburn and me.

I said, "Your cellular phone will be ringing—"

It rang before I could finish the sentence. Reuben looked at it in wonderment, then activated the device. He put it to his ear.

"Hello?" he said. "Vivian." He smiled broadly.

Ms. Washburn and I left the kitchen and walked outside. Mike was waiting in his taxicab to drive Ms. Washburn back to her apartment. I walked by her side to the taxicab's front passenger door.

"Thank you for all your help on this question," I said to Ms. Washburn and Mike. "I do not believe it would have been possible without you."

Indeed, the flight home itself would have proven beyond my capabilities if Ms. Washburn had not brought two bottles of spring water she bought inside the security area of Los Angeles International Airport and distracted me with one of my favorite films, *The Seven-Per-Cent Solution* to watch on the tablet computer she had on hand. The flight was fairly smooth and I refrained from looking through the window. I had to sit in the airport restroom, fully clothed and with latex gloves on my hands, to reduce the level of volume in my ears only once.

"I'm proud of you," Ms. Washburn said. "You didn't think you could do this but you overcame what you had to face and you dealt with it. Your possibilities are endless, Samuel." She got into the taxicab before I could think of a response.

Mike grinned at me and said he'd see me the next morning. Mother had informed me it would be impossible for her to drive or cook breakfast for me until her knee was completely healed. Mike would not cook breakfast, but he would take me to the Questions Answered office.

"I think so," I told him. "I do not intend to drive a car again soon."

Mike laughed and then drove the taxicab away.

I was wary of interrupting my parents so I entered the house through the front door but I did not hear my father in the kitchen as I walked up to my attic apartment. I did hear voices coming from Mother's bedroom as I passed and that encouraged me to hasten my step.

I assumed that constituted a successfully answered question. Mother knew where my father was now.

Lying in my own bed at last, listening to the Beatles album *Revolver* (the US version), I considered the experience I'd just completed. Much of it had been unpleasant and some of it—particularly the air travel—had been frightening. But Ms. Washburn was correct in pointing out that it had been completed successfully and I had met the necessary challenges, although I was convinced I'd been correct in my assessment as well: I could not have done any of it alone. That was troubling, because people other than myself have always been something of a puzzlement and a source of tension for me. They act in such irrational and unpredictable ways.

Even in my own bed, it took a while to fall asleep that night.

Mrs. Schiff had been looking in on Mother while I was away and had agreed to drop by now that I was home but would be at my office. My father said he would see to Mother's needs if she would allow it, and I believed she would.

Mike arrived exactly on time, as he always does. We spoke very little on the way to the Questions Answered office, which was not unusual. I thanked him for the ride, he refused to accept payment, as he always does, and I opened my office door happily, glad to be back in my familiar routine.

But I was feeling nervous as the first few minutes went by. I tried to concentrate on the few questions that had been left unanswered before I left for Southern California but found my mind wandering. I was not being productive, which was very unusual.

After thirteen minutes the bell on the door to Questions Answered rang and I looked up to see Ms. Washburn enter carrying her laptop case. She walked to her desk with a welcome smile.

"Good morning, Samuel. How are your parents doing?"

I stood up and walked toward Ms. Washburn's desk. "I have not seen them since last night," I told her. When Ms. Washburn and I arrived at her workstation at the same time, she looked at me quizzically.

"What's up, Samuel?"

I consciously took in a breath. "Ms. Washburn," I said. "If it is acceptable to you, I would like to revisit the issue of kissing."

She seemed surprised by the suggestion, but after two seconds broke into a very wide smile.

"Love to," she said.

THE END